Timeswept passion...timeless love.

TEMPEST IN TIME

"I forgot to tell you last night, but you'll be staying at Clair's home for a while. She needs a secretary and I thought you would fit the bill," Thomas said, his back to her.

"Tell being the operative word," Parris stated, trying to control her reeling emotions. "And you consented to this without my permission."

"I didn't think either one of us had a choice."

"I see. We're going to pretend that I don't come from another time, that last night didn't happen, and that Clair is not a bitch."

"That's right, tootsie."

"Don't you dare patronize me, Tommy," she growled.

"Don't call me that."

"Don't ask for favors."

"I'm telling you to be civil," he corrected. "I already got your favor last night. Me and probably a hundred other guys."

He couldn't have aimed truer if he tried. And if she'd been a Victorian maiden, she would be swooning by now. Instead, she smiled. "That's right. And if I were you, I'd polish up my act."

RITA CLAY ESTRADA

INTERLUDE IN TIME

Book Margins, Inc.

A BMI Edition

Published by special arrangement with Dorchester
Publishing Co., Inc.

Printed in the United States of America.

A piece of this book belongs to so many people. For three wonderful women who are diamonds: Joan Hohl, Gail Link, and Kathi Seidick. I have such wonderful memories of our week in Cape May, where the idea for this story was born.

For Parris Afton Bonds for the use of her name as well as the talented and courageous example she's been for me as a writer and best friend. You're a sure bet....

For Bill Wilholt, thanks for your advice and help. May all your dreams come true.

INTERLUDE IN TIME

Chapter One

Thomas Elder sipped champagne from a wide crystal glass as he surveyed the yacht's elite crowd.

His daddy—damn his soul—would say Thomas was in the middle of easy pickin's.

He tapped his foot to the lively tune coming from a piano below deck. The hollow heel of his shoe sounded full. It was. Not only had he won at poker earlier, but for a hefty price, he had supplied the boat's owner with the liquor the guests were drinking.

"Toot, toot, tootsie, good-bye," someone sang, accompanied by the piano, and Thomas grinned. The song suited his circumstances. He had more money than he'd ever had in all his 33 years, and it was all in the name of his work as a journalist. As scary as his undercover work had been over the past year, at least the rewards were great. And there was more to come, he was sure, once his story was published by his newspaper and the members of the mob were exposed for being the trash they were.

It hadn't been easy infiltrating that crowd. A year of dirtying himself with their laundry, and still he'd been asked to prove himself by getting the liquor for this trip.

He'd risked his life to coerce the fishing-boat crew from Puerto Rico to turn over their stash of liquor to him instead of their regular mob contact. With limited Spanish and more derring-do than he'd ever thought he had, he'd convinced them he had been sent by the mob and talked them into a deal. When he had the liquor, he was heady with excitement. He'd done it! Considering the Prohibition laws, no mob member could turn Thomas over to the cops for stealing their booze without exposing himself at the same time.

He shot a devilish grin at Clair, the beautiful blonde gripping the brass railing. A still breeze blew her hair into enchanting disarray, and molded her lightly patterned georgette dress against her bountiful breasts and delicious hips. Clair smiled back, obviously remembering the past night's stolen kisses.

A good-size wave slapped hard against the hull, and the boat jerked. One quick look at the sky proved a storm was approaching. Thomas hoped they would make it to the dock before the rain struck.

Clair's bear of a husband stood beside her. He was a solid man, at least 25 years older than his wayward wife. Although he ran speakeasies in New York and Atlantic City, everyone knew he didn't do much of anything anymore. He played poker all morning, ate a sumptuous lunch, then drank whiskey until he was practically blind.

No wonder Clair had been such an easy mark. A year ago Thomas had crashed a party in New York, and she'd been there. His focus had been her husband Sol, but she'd made it plain she wanted Thomas's attention. She was starving for love and had fallen into his hands like warm dough. She needed a man in her bed and he'd needed an entree into her social sphere so he could expose it. He couldn't turn down a connection like that, so he hadn't. Instead, he took advantage of her associations and became a member of that elite group—such as it was. It was a fair exchange.

Thomas observed the guests. Mostly they were spoiled and rich—people who knew nothing about saving money, taking care of parents or children, or worrying about living from skimpy paycheck to skimpier paycheck, let alone no paycheck at all. For him, however, this three-day trip was the best luck he'd had in ages. His investigation was almost finished, and if his living expenses didn't eat up what cash he managed to make, he'd even walk away from that crowd with a little money. That was okeydokey with him. Just an hour ago he'd been gloating in his cabin, counting his poker winnings, and hiding the cash in the heel of his left shoe. All he needed for personal satisfaction was to win some money from Clair's husband, making his trip complete before the yacht docked in Cape May at nightfall.

The pianist drifted into a brand-new song, "I Cried For You." The tune mingled with the conversation buzzing around Thomas.

The voyage from Cape May to New York City and back was strictly for the purpose of drinking and gambling in privacy. Thomas was using it to cement a few more relationships with the mob and to learn who their rich friends were from talkative friends outside the loop. And every trip and party added one more piece of information to put the mob away for good.

Ever since Prohibition had begun nine years ago, parties like that one had become commonplace, and the crowd was usually a mixed bag. Gangsters, wealthy names from the registers of New York and Philadelphia society, and hangers-ons—all competed for space at the bashes.

Thomas drifted toward Clair and her husband. "Well, Sol," he drawled, deliberately baiting the man. "I see you're well on your way to blotting out the evening. It's a shame you're too drunk for a lively game of cards. I should have asked you before lunch, when you were sober."

Sol stared blankly at him. Then he gazed into his drink. Slowly, with careful, calculated steps, he walked away, disappearing down the stairs to the luxurious cabins below.

"You shouldn't have done that, you know." Clair brushed a wisp of hair from her carmine mouth.

Hiding his disappointment, Thomas shrugged. He had hoped to goad the drunken man into playing cards. There were two men at the card table in the lounge who might be willing to speak a little more freely if Sol was at the table. "The shape he's in, I didn't think he could tell an insult from a compliment."

"He can. He's just depressed lately."

Although Clair sounded like an understanding wife, she looked as if she didn't give a damn one way or the other. A seductive smile tinged her lips, and her eyes devoured him. Last night had been an evening of flirting and kissing, and she'd wanted him desperately.

"He's rich. He can afford to be kind," Thomas muttered. "I can't."

"No, but you want to be what he is."

Thomas smiled back. It was easy to go along with the lie. He'd been doing it for the past year. "I wanted to play a hand of cards with him. That's all."

"You wanted to win," she said softly. "But if you suddenly need money so badly, why are you here?" She glanced around at other couples

13

lounging on deck. "You could lose your shirt playing with these high rollers."

Suddenly wary, Thomas took a sip from his glass. "I was invited."

"By our esteemed host?"

"Of course."

"How nice for you," she purred. "Then why did he ask me for your name at breakfast?"

"Because he forgot." It was a good thing they were docking soon. He didn't know how much longer he could keep fielding Clair's questions. "Mr. Warren and I are business associates."

"Funny, I've never known you to do any business with him before. What kind of business?"

He nodded toward her iced drink. "You're drinking it."

Clair moved closer and her fingers trailed down his tie. "I haven't seen you in over three months, so I didn't know you were a workingman now. If it's money you're after, why not get it from me?"

"How?" he asked bluntly.

She wet her lips and he followed the movement of her tongue. "I need liquor delivered to our house for a party in two weeks. Sol is entertaining some . . . business associates from Chicago. Can you arrange it?"

"Sure. That's easy," he lied, feeling his bowtie bob against his Adam's apple and hoping she didn't notice it. He'd practically broken his neck to get this shipload, all for his story. The New Jersey mob would really be angry if he did it twice. They weren't exactly friendly people, and if he hoped to live to see his story hit the news-stands, he'd better be extremely careful.

"I'll make sure there's plenty of extras in it for you." Her eyes drifted up to his, her idea of reward apparent in her expression.

"What about Sol? Doesn't he do his own ar-ranging?"

"Not if he can help it. Sol hasn't been feeling well lately. Besides, I handle the money when it comes to things like this. He doesn't like . . . details." A feral smile lit her eyes. For the first time he noticed they were too close together.

Just as he was about to open his mouth, the floor vibrated and a roaring sound shattered the air around them. He felt the impact through the soles of his shoes and in his eardrums. The crowd on deck looked all around for the source of the noise.

Clair's face turned ashen, her eyes widened in fright. Thomas held out a hand as if to steady her. She looked as if she was about to faint. "Clair? Are you all right?"

"Dear, sweet heaven, he did it." Her voice was a whisper. "He really did it."

"Who? Sol? What did he do?"

Hands crashed discordantly against piano keys. Suddenly people poured from below deck, wailing something about sinking.

Clair gasped, then screamed.

Thomas stared at those around him, unable to understand what they were saying.

The boat rocked. With a high-pitched screech of tearing wood, it listed aft.

Screams echoed in the air. Confused, Thomas reached for the rail. He still wasn't sure what was happening, but he felt the panic of the other passengers washing over him. A loud squeal rent his ears. People began skidding, sliding, and tumbling toward him, their faces assuming various masks of stark terror.

His mind wanted to deny what his eyes saw, but it was impossible. He watched people clutching furniture, rails, or masts as they were tossed around. For Thomas, everything went into slow motion. He glanced back to where Clair had been standing. She was gone.

Then realization hit him. In shock and terror, he felt the icy Atlantic ocean swell over the brass rail. A flying table was coming straight at his head and instinct made him duck.

His last word echoed in the evening salt breeze as he slid into the cold, choppy water.

"Damn!"

Parris Harrison sat on the sand and watched a silvery jet cross the horizon while the setting sun shadowed the water of the Atlantic. Early June's full moon peeped out of a fluffy, pink-tinged cloud. The sharp, cold breeze was filled with the tang of salt and spindrift. Breakers hit the beach, curled around the sand, then frolicked with crab shells and pebbles before retreating.

She brushed a strand of hair from her eyes and continued staring at the vast ocean. A large supertanker crept south along the horizon.

In her fist was a Cape May diamond, a stone occasionally found on the beach that could sparkle as brightly as the real thing. The sharp corner of her slim wallet pinched her bottom and she shifted in the sand.

Her damp seat was the only part of her that could feel anything right now. Her thoughts were dull with fatigue. During the past two weeks she'd buried her father, mother and brother— her whole family.

They were on their way to the family summer home in Cape May when their lives were snuffed out by a drunken driver. When he had sideswiped them, their car spun out of control, careening off the road and hitting a concrete embankment head on. The drunken driver had suffered a cut on his forehead.

The bastard.

After the funeral, she'd told her father's attorney to handle everything. She'd signed over her power of attorney, then retreated to the family's Victorian home by the sea. The same home where, after seven years' absence, they'd all planned to laugh and play and eat and spend time with each other. They'd declared two weeks of fun, each carefully arranging his vacations so the family could finally be together again.

Her father owned a paint manufacturing plant in Philadelphia, so it wasn't easy for him to juggle everything. Her mother was an attorney with a heavy schedule who used her free time to work as a consultant for two women's shelters in the state. Parris's brother, Jed, had just completed a small but integral part in a movie and had been on cloud nine. The role was the break he'd been waiting for. He'd been so excited, so anxious to share every detail of his experience with his family.

They had all had something to share. Once a very close-knit family, they had all wanted— needed—to be together again for a while. They needed the contact with each other in order to continue alone in their chosen fields.

Her family was gone, but the extent of her loss was only now coming through to her. She awakened each morning thinking it was nothing but a bad dream. Her afternoons were spent in tears as she realized how much she had lost. But the worst was the evenings, which she spent with old photos and a thousand memories. Evenings were the times when she spoke to her family, saying all the things that should have been said and never were. . . .

In the house behind her, they had always joined forces and regrouped, drawing from one another. Everywhere she turned, she saw them. She needed to get away from there in order to come to terms with the terrible truth. Her memories were too strong, too real. She found it hard to believe she was all alone in the world. She was an orphan. She had no one now. She'd lost the only people she'd ever loved.

Ebb tide. Even the water was leaving.

She clenched the stone in her hand and it cut into her palm. A sob caught in her throat. She wanted to die.

Not the violent death her parents and Jed had suffered. She wanted escape. A quiet escape from all her feelings of loneliness and misery. She wanted to join her family and not be alone anymore.

The shadows lengthened.

An idea took root.

She'd been numb for the past two weeks. The numbness hadn't worn off yet, but she knew it would. Soon. And when it did, she'd fall apart like a badly made toy cracking into a thousand splintered pieces that would never fit together again.

She didn't want to be alive when it happened.

Knowing her thoughts didn't make sense, she smiled. Then, standing, she dusted the sand off the seat of her designer jeans. Still staring at the choppy sea, she began walking toward it. Water soaked her sneakers. Her socks. Her jeans.

Then she began swimming for the horizon. Salt water seeped into the cut in her hand, but she ignored it. It was nothing. Nothing compared to the pain in her soul.

When the shore was just a distant line, she rolled on her back and stared at the swiftly darkening sky. She'd done this so many times in the past, but never had she done it to escape something so awful as death. How strange, in escaping the tragic deaths of her family, she was running toward her own.

She watched the sky darken even more. Odd. She hadn't noticed that dark clouds were brewing. From the looks of the sky, the storm was going to be a beauty. She felt the first raindrops and closed her eyes.

She was ready.

The storm came up quickly. Rain pelted Thomas's head and shoulders. His fingers were numb with cold, cramping into claws around a few two-by-fours still nailed together. The small raft wasn't big enough for him to sit on. But as long as he didn't panic and drown himself, it was just large enough to keep him afloat.

He didn't know how long he'd been in the water. It had to be hours. It seemed like days. He forced his legs into another scissors kick.

Where in the hell was everybody? Somebody besides one whiskey-running impostor had to be imitating flotsam on this damn ocean!

He'd yelled every few minutes or so, but there had been no answer. He took a deep gulp of air and prayed he wouldn't drown in the rain. Come to think of it, he didn't want to drown in the sea either. He wanted to live. Damn! He wanted to live!

That thought spurred another kick. He prayed he was headed toward shore and not out to sea.

A wave swamped him, pulling him under the cold water for a long moment. Just as he surfaced and took another gulp of air, something slammed into the back of his head.

His next-to-last thought was that at least his left shoe was still on his foot. His last thought was that he was a stupid fool for thinking about his shoe at such a time.

A stupid dead fool. . . .

The storm lashed at Parris, swirling her around in the sea. As the waves swelled and crashed over her head, she realized one startling fact: She wanted to live.

Fighting to keep her nose above water, she continued swimming toward what she thought was the shore. She couldn't be sure because the sight of land was obliterated by rain and darkness. Every breath hurt, and everywhere she looked, she saw water. She was beginning to believe that all the earth was covered with water and that there was no more land. All she saw was the full moon scudding between dark clouds.

Her arms ached, her legs ached. Her throat was sore from dragging air into her tired lungs. Still, she fought the sucking water. But it wouldn't let her go. Instead, it circled her, forming a whirlpool that twirled her around and around. Frantically, she kicked her legs, trying to escape from the water's pull.

"Dear God, no! I didn't mean it! Help me! I didn't—" The whirlpool gained force, swirling even faster and forming an even deeper vortex. She prayed for her life, knowing that she was facing death.

Suddenly, thunder crashed around her, vibrating through the water. Then, just as suddenly, the noise stopped and the whirlpool dissipated. Inch by inch, she rose up to the water's surface, swirling around the broad wall of the whirlpool instead of being in the center of it. She gave a sigh of relief since she just had to contend with the storm itself. Her resolve returned. She would make it if she had to float to Europe for two weeks!

Something scraped against her back. She screamed, then grabbed for it as another wave threatened to engulf her. A splinter dug into her palm. It was wood. Wood! She almost laughed. Squinting against the rain, she stared at the crude but effective life raft. A length of dark material was wrapped around it. An arm. She held on. A male arm. It was too muscled for a female. Was he alive?

There was no time to think or reason. With the last of her strength, Parris clung to the piece of lumber. She might still have a chance of surviving.

The man groaned and his grip slipped. She covered his hand, helping to anchor it to the flimsy piece of wood. She could do nothing more. She had very little strength left.

Then everything went black.

Interlude In Time

* * *

Wearily, Parris opened her eyes and tried to focus them in the dim light. The first thing she saw was a crab scuttling sideways on the grayish-white sand. She watched it distractedly while trying to remember what she was doing there.

Had she fallen asleep on the beach? The last thing she remembered was. . . .

The ocean.

The storm.

The man!

She tried pulling herself up, but every muscle in her body protested. Finally, she made it to all fours and searched for the man she'd found clutching a piece of battered ship wood. The same piece of wood that had saved her life.

He was no more than three feet away, his head resting next to where her feet had been. The scrap of wood that had saved them served as his pillow. Lying on his side, he was still clutching the wood tightly.

His dark hair was glued to his head. His suit—what she could see of it—was a mess. And he was wearing only his left shoe.

He groaned and Parris found enough strength to crawl over to him. Then she plopped back on the sand and stared at his face. Her eyes widened. Raven dark brows were complemented by thick eyelashes, strong cheekbones and a jaw the modeling industry would kill for. He was drop dead gorgeous.

Gently, she touched his throat, sighing in relief when she felt his pulse. It was strong and regular. Then she studied the rest of him.

He was in the craziest suit and shirt she'd ever seen. It looked like something out of the movie *The Sting* or an outfit that Al Capone or Pretty Boy Floyd would have worn.

Where in heaven's name had he been? A costume party?

He groaned again.

"Wake up," she said, bending close to his sand-covered ear. She shook his shoulder. "Wake up, buddy. We made it."

His eyes fluttered, then opened. They were the most crystal-blue eyes she'd ever seen. They were also blank.

"Ohhh," he groaned again, then closed his eyes and rolled onto his back.

She took a good look at him. He had to be at least six feet tall, and he looked well built. "That's the stupidest suit I've ever seen," she muttered, unable to hide a grin. "Even Bonnie's Clyde wouldn't have worn that suit to rob a bank."

Tired or not, she still had her sense of humor.

That comment got his attention. He opened his eyes and stared down at his body. "You have no sense of style." His voice was low and hoarse. "It's the latest from London."

Her grin turned into a chuckle. "Well, who am I to say what a London tailor can do to a tourist?"

He didn't answer.

24

Parris leaned back and stared at the ocean, her gaze scanning the clouds for any sign of the terrible storm they had just weathered. Instead, there were small puffs of pink clouds skimming a dark blue sky. Dawn was just breaking.

As if there hadn't been a long silence between them, the man moved a leg, then grunted. "You're just jealous, that's all." He moved his other leg. "Tell me. Is my left shoe on?"

He sounded so concerned. She stared at him. Apparently he'd had a much rougher time of it than she had.

"Is it?" he demanded.

Parris peered at his feet. "Yes."

He lifted his head and looked down, then let his head plop back on the sand again. "Thank God." His expression was filled with relief.

"You're right one is in the sea, though. It certainly didn't come to shore with us."

"I don't care about the right one. It's the left one that counts."

She cocked her head. Was he insane? Was he hurt more than she thought? Then she remembered something she had read about Vietnam veterans. "Are you wearing a prosthesis?" she asked softly.

He frowned. His eyes opened and stared at her for a long moment. "A prosthesis?"

"Yes. You know, a plastic leg."

"A plastic leg?" His gaze searched her face, then her form. Then he locked gazes with her once more. "I beg your pardon?"

"Do you have a wooden leg?" she asked loudly, irritation edging her voice. "For heaven's sake, don't tell me that all of your good sense was knocked out of you in that storm we just rode out."

"Storm?"

"Storm. S.T.O.R.M."

"Were you on the *Mary Anna*, too?"

Relief coursed through her. He wasn't an idiot. He'd obviously been aboard a boat, maybe a cruise ship, on which they had costume parties. And the storm had either washed him overboard or had sunk the boat. That information helped Parris make sense of the way he'd been hugging that piece of wood so tightly.

"Yes," she said, unwilling to tell this stranger the real reason she'd been in the ocean during a storm. "Did you get hit on the head? Do you hurt anywhere?"

With studied precision, he tested his fingers, then flexed his legs. When they worked satisfactorily, he rolled over and sat up, arching his shoulders. "No," he finally answered. "How about you, ma'am?"

Parris smiled in relief. Somewhere in the back of her mind, she realized that she'd smiled twice in the past five minutes, something she hadn't done in two weeks. "I'm fine. Just a little sore and bruised, that's all."

She held out her hands and arms, turning them over to check for large scratches. Then she remembered that, just before she'd walked into the ocean, she had cut her hand. Looking carefully, she searched her palm. There was no cut. No remnant of a cut. Nothing.

The man brought her attention back to the present. "Where are we?" He glanced around, then searched the shoreline. "Are we alone here?"

"As far as I can tell. By the way, my name's Parris. What's yours?" she asked as she stretched her back and legs carefully. Finding that everything worked properly, she began her own survey of the land and sea. Nothing but sand and water was visible from their location. They couldn't be far from civilization. Perhaps just over that dune there was a highway.

"Um, Thomas," he answered, then muttered, "All those people. . . ." His sentence was unfinished, but Parris could imagine the rest of it.

"They might have landed somewhere else. We got caught in some kind of a whirlpool I think. Maybe we were carried farther away than they were."

He looked boyishly hopeful. "Do you think so?"

She nodded.

With deliberate movements, the man stood. He was even taller than Parris had envisioned.

"Are you fit to travel, ma'am? I've got to get back to Cape May."

She placed her gritty palm in his and felt his strength as he pulled her to her feet. Self-consciously, she dropped his hand and stared down at the sand. Although she was tingling after touching him, he'd built a wall between them just by using the word ma'am. After her own ordeal these past two weeks, she wasn't sure she wanted that wall to crumble.

"Let's go," she said. It took several steps before Parris realized her newfound companion wasn't following. She turned and stared at him, her hands on her hips. "Well?"

"You're wearing work pants."

"I'm wearing designer jeans," she corrected.

His look held a touch of disgust. "Your shoes are funny."

"No more funny than you look, standing there in a suit belonging to some dead gangster and wearing one shoe," she retorted. "Are we going to argue the merits of today's fashion and yesterday's or get to the nearest town? If we find a road, we might be able to hitch a ride. There's bound to be a highway over the rise."

"Highway?" He tilted his head as if displaying doubt concerning her sanity. "Like a high-road?"

She rested her hand on his arm, feeling the muscles clench at her touch. "It doesn't matter," Parris said soothingly. "We'll get to Cape May one way or another."

Those beautiful blue eyes stared into hers, and she could see the confusion there. She also saw the appreciation. He liked her looks—he just didn't like her choice of clothes. Tough.

She smiled. "Ready?"

He sighed, fingering the bump on the back of his head. "I think we ought to walk along the beach. It will take us to Cape May or Cape May Point."

"If that's where we are. But there might be a road just over the rise."

"I want to walk the shore," he stated stubbornly. "We've got a better chance of seeing someone."

She opened her mouth to argue, but remembered she was talking to a man in an old suit and one shoe. Obviously, walking along the shore was a matter of pride.

"Okay. I understand. After all, you really do look like you might be half a bubble off."

He acted as if he hadn't heard her, when she knew darn well he had. "What?" he asked at last.

She spoke a little louder. "That's fine! Let's go!"

Chapter Two

The storm had churned up the seabed, scattering seaweed and driftwood along the beach as far as the eye could see. Even past the dunes, the sand was gray with dampness. While Thomas looked at every piece of wood they came across, Parris searched the dunes for the shape of a body. Thomas was right. He couldn't be the only survivor of his pleasure cruise. Perhaps they would run across someone else who needed help.

It was an hour before they saw the outline of a ship on the horizon—the only sign of life they'd seen since beginning their trek.

Parris shielded her eyes. "Do you recognize it?"

"There are only a thousand or so yachts making their way between Atlantic City and Cape May. Why shouldn't I?"

"You may be cute, but you sure have a mouth

on you," Parris commented, dropping her hand and beginning to walk along the beach again.

"And you're just plain weird," he answered. "You wear men's clothes and odd shoes. And you speak in words unfamiliar to the East Coast—or the West Coast for that matter. I know. I took the train out there a few years ago."

A train? My, my. But he'd made an interesting, if incorrect, observation. "What makes you say that?"

"Because only dockworkers wear that fabric. It's too coarse for most women. And those shoes look clumsy."

"Boy, talk about being behind the times!" Parris exclaimed. "These are the best running shoes money can buy! As for my jeans, they're designer jeans. I don't know a single woman left in the world who doesn't have at least one pair in her closet. Even the Rockefellers wear them!"

"I doubt it." Thomas's derision hurt. "You're obviously demented. Someone must have opened the asylum door and let you out."

"No one had to let me out. And you're alive because of me."

"Well, if you think your clothes are the cat's pajamas, think again, miss. Are you in the picture business? Those people consider weird ways of dressing de rigueur."

Parris laughed. "Like Cher and some of the others? No, I'm afraid not. Although my brother just finished a part in a movie."

Thomas's expression was disapproving. "My

sister wants to be in the moving pictures, but she doesn't know what she'd doing. She just does whatever her boyfriend tells her to do."

The hair on the back of her neck rose. The phrase moving pictures hadn't been used for years. "Why do you call them moving pictures?"

"Because that's what they are. What do you call them?

"Movies, shows, films. I don't know anyone who calls them moving pictures."

He shrugged. "I guess it depends on what part of the country you come from."

"Where are you from?"

"I live in New York. I'm down here for a vacation."

"I'm from Philadelphia," Parris returned dryly. "In case you New Yorkers don't remember, that's only an hour away by train."

"Two," he stated absently, his eyes grazing the shoreline once more.

"More or less."

"What part did your brother play in the pictures?" he asked as an afterthought. Obviously, his mind was somewhere else.

Parris answered anyway. "He played a gangster in Al Capone's time. He was the crooked attorney for the mob."

He reached out and stopped her in midstride. "Say that again?"

Confused, she complied. "He played a crooked attorney for the mob."

"Al Capone's mob?"

"Yes." She didn't understand his sudden interest, so she guessed. "Is your sister in that movie? Is that it?"

"Parris, or whatever your name is. You must be mistaken. No one in his right mind would try to do a picture about Al Capone. They'd be dead in a minute. Sweet bejesus, haven't you ever heard of the St. Valentine's Day Massacre? Just last February they killed seven of their own. They don't give a damn whose lives they snuff out."

He was serious. Her smile slowly slipped from her face. The hair on the back of her neck stood up again. "Thomas. What year do you think this is?" she asked gently.

He gave an impatient wave of his hand, as if dismissing the question as not worthy of an response. But he answered it anyway. "It's 1929."

She froze. Her feet refused to take another step until her mind figured out how much danger she was in. Obviously the man had escaped one of the mental hospitals in the area. Good looks or no, he was insane, which made him someone to be very wary of.

"Parris?"

Her gaze focused on him. He looked so normal. He also looked concerned.

She smiled. "Yes?"

"Are you all right?"

"I'm fine. Ready?" She began trudging down

to the edge of the water with more bounce in her step. No sense letting him know she was worried. Worried, hell—she was scared!

Two minutes later, his hand grabbed her arm. "Slow down! This isn't a damn race, you know."

Her heart jumped to her throat, then settled down somewhere between her throat and her chest. "Sorry. I'm just anxious to get back home."

"Well, if you live in Philadelphia, you won't be getting home anytime soon."

For a moment, she'd forgotten that he didn't know about her little Victorian house in Cape May. Good. At least she had kept her address a mystery. "I guess you're right."

"I've got a room here, if you need it. It's behind the Grand Hotel in a boardinghouse, but it's clean and private."

"How did you arrange that?" she asked, hoping to distract him.

"Mrs. Timmers, the landlady, is an old friend of my mother's. They knew each other before they married."

Parris had to be careful. She didn't want to trigger any unwanted emotions, but she needed to keep Thomas talking. That way his mind would be occupied with other things beside her. "Where is your mother now?"

It was a long moment before he answered. "She's living with her younger sister in the Bronx. She doesn't know anyone anymore. She just sits by the window all day and stares out at people walking by. The doctor calls it brain rot."

Parris knew all about it. Her Aunt Crissie was in a nursing home with the same illness. "Alzheimer's," she murmured.

"What's that?"

"The name of the disease your mother has."

His lip curled in scorn. "And how would you know what the doctors don't?"

"I have a relative with the same disease. That's what it's called," she stated quietly. "I'm sorry. I know it has to be hard on you and your family."

"The family, as you call it, is just my aunt, me, and my sister now."

"What happened to your father?"

"None of your business," he said coldly.

For a man who thought he was in 1929, he seemed remarkably cogent. She wanted to ask more questions, but the distant look on his face silenced her.

The sun got hotter. It beat down on them with savage ferocity. It was one of those hot June days that came once or twice a summer. Shorts weather. Parris glanced sideways at Thomas. His jacket looked hot and heavy, but he didn't seem to notice. It only proved to Parris that the man had a loose screw. Anyone else would make himself as comfortable as possible for a long walk in that heat. They didn't even know where they were, for heaven's sake.

She stared straight ahead, willing her mind not to panic. Surely, they would come across someone, something soon. After all, the New Jersey coastline wasn't that sparsely inhabited. And when they did, she'd be safe from this good-looking maniac.

She stared ahead at the distant shoreline, promising God many things if He would let her find a person, a building, a town. Safety. But all she saw was a log just a little way from the shoreline, the water lapping at one end. Suddenly, the log moved.

Her eyes narrowed against the glare of the sun, she watched the long dark object. From this distance, it still looked like a log—then a branch rose up and feebly waved.

Thomas saw it move, too. "Come on!" he cried, breaking into a run toward the log, his one shoe leaving deep prints in the damp sand.

Parris ran right behind him.

The log turned into a person with wet sand covering most of his or her body. The closer Parris came, the more she saw. It was a female, and she was up to her shoulders in water.

Parris reached her side just seconds after Thomas. He knelt in the sand and pushed wet hair from the woman's face. "It's Clair! Sweet Lord, it's Clair!" he said, pulling her limp torso into his lap.

The woman wasn't breathing. Her chest wasn't moving; her face was blue tinged.

"My God, she's dead!"

"She's got water in her lungs," Parris stated. "She needs CPR." Pulling the woman from him,

Parris rolled her over onto the sand until she was flat on her back.

"What the hell do you think you're doing?" Thomas asked angrily.

Parris forgot she wasn't supposed to aggravate this man. She forgot everything except that just minutes ago the woman must have been breathing or she wouldn't have been able to raise her arm. "Trying to save her, you idiot! If you can't help, at least keep out of my way!" She began administering CPR, rhythmically pressing on the woman's heart, counting one, two, three, four, five.

"She's already dead!"

Parris ignored him. The man must have lived in a box—or a mental institution—if he hadn't heard of CPR. She tilted the woman's head and began the kiss of life, pushing air into her lungs. Then she repeated the series of movements.

Suddenly Clair coughed, then choked. Parris sat up, holding the woman's head as she spewed out salt water like a fountain. She waited a moment, holding her own breath as she watched Clair return from the dead. A feeling of exuberance flowed through her. She wanted to scream and dance at the same time. She'd taken CPR classes, but she'd never believed she'd use the technique. Now, she'd just saved a woman's life. She'd actually saved her!

Leaning over, Thomas pulled the woman back into his arms. "My God, I don't believe it," he muttered, looking at Parris strangely. "How did you know how to do that?"

"I trained at work."

Clair's eyes fluttered, then opened. It took a moment for her to focus on the man holding her. "Thomas?"

"Yes, Clair. You're alive! I didn't think anybody had made it except us. Thank God, we found you." He brushed back her hair, touching her face. One side was red from the sun, while the other was covered with sand.

"I thought I'd died," she sighed.

Thomas gazed down the beach. "I wonder how many others made it."

Clair tried feebly to sit up, then stared around her. "I did make it, didn't I?" Her voice was barely a whisper. She held her throat. "I hurt."

"Besides that, are you all right?" Thomas's voice held concern. "Can you walk?"

"I don't know," she croaked, her hand twining around Thomas's arm. "Stay with me. Don't leave. Please."

"I'm not going anywhere. I promise." He held her up while she took several deep breaths.

His tone was so soothing, so gentle that Parris stared at him in wonder. Right now the man seemed like the most sane, sensible person in the world. And apparently this woman, Clair, knew him.

Clair raised her head and stared at Thomas. Her eyes glazed with tears. "Sol did this, Thomas. He shot a hole in the boat and then turned the gun on himself."

"You don't know that, Clair."

She nodded. "Yes, I do. He threatened to do it so many times I didn't pay attention anymore. And he finally did it. I think he must have planned it. He had that big shotgun in our stateroom."

"You don't know that he blew up the boat for a fact."

She nodded again, her hand at her throat. "And you goaded him. You and I both did."

Thomas's face closed. "I don't know a damn thing about that. And neither do you. So don't say another word."

Obviously, Clair wanted to argue the point. Then, as she stared into Thomas's eyes, all the fight ebbed from her. "All right."

Silently, Thomas stood up and pulled Clair up to lean against him. For the first time Clair looked at Parris. Then she held fast to Thomas.

He read her question. "She was on the boat, too."

Clair shook her head in denial.

"I was one of the maids," Parris said, backing up her lie. Until she had figured out what had happened to her, she wasn't going to tell these two anything.

Clair seemed to accept her falsehood. In fact, from that point on, Parris felt she'd just been placed beneath the woman's concern. Clair completely ignored her.

Thomas never even bothered to look at Parris. His arms closed around Clair as they took one slow step after another along the edge of the water, and Parris dragged five or six steps behind.

She remembered how still and stiff Clair had looked and her heart went out to the woman. No wonder she didn't pay attention to Parris. Good grief, she'd just returned from the dead! By all rights, she should be in an ambulance and on her way to the hospital. If they didn't find civilization soon, they might all die of starvation and overexposure to the sun.

She licked her dry lips. Were there more like Clair and Thomas around? If Clair was to be believed, the ship had sunk because of Sol, whoever he was, and so far, these were the only two survivors. Parris continued searching the shoreline, but saw nothing resembling a human.

Every now and then, Thomas stopped and Clair would sink wearily into the wet sand, her head hanging almost to her lap. Parris was almost as tired. Heat, hunger, and thirst were beginning to take their toll. It had been a long night for all of them.

The surf roared in her ears and Parris wondered how she could have ever been foolish enough to think of ending her life. More than anything right now, she wanted to be home, in her own bed. She didn't care if she cried for her parents and her brother. They would want her to live.

"Sweet heaven," Clair moaned.

Clair and Thomas had stopped, and Parris

came to their sides. She followed their gaze, spying what they had seen.

A pale turquoise wooden lawn chair was turned upside down in the sand.

"I was sitting on a chair just like that one before Sol joined us on deck," Clair croaked.

"It's not your fault," Thomas said.

"I should have listened to him. All those people are dead because of me. So many. . . ."

"You made it," Thomas stated softly. "I made it. Parris made it. The chair made it. There are more. You'll see."

They trudged past the chair, skirting it as though it was a dead body. Parris kept her eyes glued to the beach ahead. When she saw a dim, boxlike shape peeping over one of the larger sand dunes, her heartbeat picked up its pace. Her eyes widened. It was a roof! It had to be.

She wanted to shout, to laugh, but neither of her companions had noticed the dark outline yet. What if she was wrong? She didn't want to raise their hopes only to dash them if she was mistaken. Meanwhile, she kept her eyes on the structure.

Slow step by painfully slow step, she watched the roof take shape. Just as she was about to say something, Thomas turned in that direction.

"You saw it?" Parris asked.

"Yes."

"Why didn't you say something?"

"Because it makes the journey seem longer when it's so far away."

Clair was in another world. She continued staring at the ground, trudging along as Thomas practically carried her over the dunes.

The roof belonged to a weathered cottage, no more than two or three rooms, with a large overhang shading the front from the sun. The way the shade fell right now, Parris surmised it was one or two o'clock in the afternoon.

They went up the steps and Thomas banged on the door with his fist. Nothing happened. "Hello!" he shouted. "Is anyone home?"

Still no answer.

With a strong push of his shoulder, he forced open the door and carried Clair into the darkness. Parris followed, praying there was fresh water—cool, fresh water.

The house was almost as hot as outside. Shuttered windows and closed doors blocked the breeze. Going directly to the back door, Parris propped it open with a chair, then did the same with the door they had just entered. With her last ounce of energy, she threw back the shutters.

Thomas carried Clair to the bedroom off the main area and placed her on the bare mattress. When he stood, he leaned against the wall and closed his eyes. He had walked with Clair, bearing her weight for at least five miles. After his night in the ocean, he had a right to be exhausted.

Her feet dragging, Parris moved toward the kitchen. There had to be running water somewhere.

She found it in the form of an old-fashioned pump that spewed water into a crude metal bucket. She gave it a few jerks, but nothing happened. She felt so damn helpless! Tears formed, threatening to spill down her cheeks.

Then Thomas was beside her, grabbing the bucket and walking out the door. "Stay here and rest," he ordered. "I'll get water to prime the pump."

Parris leaned against the wall, rested her head on her arms, and closed her eyes. Priming the pump. Of course, she'd heard the expression— usually in regard to money—but she never thought anyone actually did it. Apparently, they did.

Moments later, Thomas was back. He poured sea water down the top and began pumping the handle. Suddenly, water gushed out.

With a groan, Parris cupped her hands and drank, uncaring that the water spilled all over. After drinking her fill, she rubbed water over her heated face and neck, then spread it on her hot arms.

Thomas repeated her actions and when he finished, he slicked back his hair and sighed in satisfaction. "Find a glass."

If she'd been herself, Parris would have told him what he could do with his orders. But he'd primed the pump and she was too tired to argue. Opening the only cabinet in the room, she found one crockery mug and gave it to him.

He filled the mug and left the room. Parris

knew he was giving it to Clair. At least someone was thinking. She was too numb to do more than react instinctively.

She slid down to the floor and dropped her head on her bent knees. Instead of falling asleep, her mind relived those horrible moments of last night, when she'd thought she was truly drowning.

And she had lived! She thought of all those other people partying on the yacht who had presumably died. But she had lived. And now she felt guilty for living.

A sob caught in her throat. She lifted her head, squeezing her eyes shut so tears couldn't fall. This wasn't the time. Not now. Not yet. She had to get back to civilization, get rid of the good-looking, masculine mental case and the woman who knew Sol well enough to know he'd blown up the boat. Maybe they were all mental cases—a whole boat full!

She didn't realize Thomas was in the kitchen until he pulled her up and locked her in his arms. Suddenly, she didn't care that he might be crazy. Right now, she needed the touch of another person. She needed the solace that could come only from the living. Once more, tears started to fall, and this time she couldn't stop sniffling.

"We made it, tootsie. Don't cry," he soothed, his hands rubbing up and down her back. "We made it. Right now, that's all that matters. We'll worry about why later."

Parris was unable to keep the sobs from forming, but she refused to give them utterance. She would not cry! Instead, she clung to his shoulders as she had held on to the waterlogged boards in the middle of the ocean.

Thomas pulled away and stared down at her. "I keep asking, but I need to know. Are you all right?"

She nodded, biting her lip.

"Good girl." He let her go, and the air felt cool after the living warmth of his touch. "I'm going to take a look around outside. If I'm right, we shouldn't be more than a quarter of a mile or so from Clair's place. That means that we're less than a mile from town."

Hope replaced her earlier misery. "Are you sure?"

"No, but the landscape looks familiar. It's worth a try."

For the first time she noticed the lines of exhaustion etched around his mouth and eyes. He was dead on his feet, yet he found strength enough to comfort both women.

Too tired to keep up barriers, she placed her hand against his day-old beard, enjoying the scratchiness against her palm. "What can I do to help?"

"Watch Clair. I can't tell if she's hurt or if she's so exhausted she's disoriented."

"Okay." It was the least she could do.

His blue eyes stared into hers, and for just a moment, she was swept away to another, more protected world. He must have seen the longing on her face because he drew her to him. A contentment she hadn't felt in years washed over her and she snuggled closer. His arms tightened as if he enjoyed her closeness as much as she did his.

Then she felt him stiffen. Suddenly he was gone, walking out the door and down the steps to the sand. She felt bereft, but was too tired to analyze the feeling.

It took Parris several minutes to move toward the small bedroom. The springs squeaked as she lowered herself to the edge of the bed. Clair moaned and rolled to her side.

She was a pretty woman with high cheekbones and clear skin. At least her skin looked as if it would be clear once the thin film of sand and dirt was washed away. Parris knew the sunburned side of her face would blister and peel. Her figure was excellent beneath the tattered, saltwater-stiffened dress. It was hard to tell the color of her hair, but Parris thought it had a hint of brass in it. That meant bleached blonde.

Determined not to fall asleep until Thomas returned, she looked around the room. One small window high under the eaves shed dim light into the room. The clapboard exterior was probably the only insulation against the elements. The interior walls were made of thin one-by-fours. The floor, complete with sand, was also wooden.

Other than the iron double bed and a small table, there was nothing else in the room. Not even a closet. The table stood on spindly legs and held one drawer. In an effort to keep herself awake, Parris pulled it open. Inside was a folded newspaper that looked fairly new.

She pulled it out and opened it up. It was an Atlantic City paper. The headline proclaimed that Leon Trotsky was expelled from the USSR. There was a large ad for a circus on the Steel Pier.

Parris stared at the black letters, unable to completely absorb the words. She glanced at the date—June 5, 1929.

It was a fluke. A joke. It was crazy!

It was impossible.

Crumpling the paper, Parris stared at the woman on the bed, her mind whirling in confusion. This couldn't really be happening.

Even while her conscious mind refused to believe it, her unconscious mind accepted the weird fact that she was in 1929.

Everything around her screamed of the past.

Thomas's declarations, unusual suit, and dated speech patterns weren't the only clues. She'd just ignored the rest in order to survive. Looking back, she realized she'd refused to acknowledge that the seacoast had changed drastically. The beach she'd played on had whiter sand, was better manicured and filled with miles of condos or homes interspersed with hotels. From Atlantic City to Cape May Courthouse, there was hardly a spot she could walk for five minutes without at least seeing a building somewhere. And she'd bet the coast looked like that all the way down to Florida. No matter how far they were from Cape May, they should have seen some sign of civilization in a four- or five-hour walk.

And then there was the water and road traffic.

Or the lack of it.

She'd always seen barges from her window at the house. Here, she'd seen one yacht. Period. And there were no cars. That was unusual in itself. The road was just beyond the dunes. At least that was where it was when she lived here.

Then there was the problem of Clair. As much as Parris hated to admit it, Clair had attended the same costume party on the yacht as Thomas. First, she wore a garter belt. Parris had seen it earlier when they rescued her from the sea. Second, she had a hairpin—the wide, spindly kind Parris's grandmother had worn to keep large rolls of hair in place. Clair's hairpin had clung tenaciously to a stiffened curl. A hairpin. Parris knew only a few women who wore garter belts and no one who used hairpins.

If she wasn't in 1929, there was definitely something wrong here. And Parris felt she was the only one not in on the joke—or the information. She was the only one who didn't quite fit in.

Footsteps, one heavy, one not, echoed in the

outer room. It was Thomas, she could tell. He still had one shoe on and one shoe off.

What difference did it make that he might be insane? For that matter, she could be the one off the deep end. Right now, what she needed most was his comforting, warm male body holding her and telling her everything was going to be all right.

When he stood in the doorway of the bedroom, she walked into his embrace, unable to stifle the small mouselike squeak that came from her throat. Gently wrapping his arms around her, he bent his head to hers. They clung to each other and comforted their weary souls.

If Thomas was insane, so was she.

Chapter Three

Thomas pulled away too soon, and again, Parris felt bereft of his warmth and protection as he turned and led her into the front room.

He stared down at her. "You look so damn pale. Are you hurt?"

She shook her head, reassuring him. "No. I'm fine. Just tired. What about you?"

"As long as I've got my shoe, I'm fine."

"What's so special about that shoe?"

"It's mine."

"Now there's a cryptic answer. But it's fine with me if you feel like keeping secrets. I'm too tired to care."

"Thanks, kid."

His weary, boyish grin was enough to warm her insides through a week of winter.

"Did you find out where we are?" she asked.

"I was right. Clair's house is less than half a mile from here; the town's just beyond it."

"Maybe we should go to her house and pick up her car. Then we can come back for her."

"Their—her car is at the docks."

"They only have one?"

"I don't know, but I think that's all they have here. It's the only one I've ever seen. This isn't their permanent residence."

She walked past him toward the front door. She needed to sort out everything she'd learned. She sat on the top step of the porch and leaned against the post. Still trying to calm her chaotic thoughts, she decided she couldn't hide her head in the sand.

"You believe this is the year 1929?"

"Yes." No argument. No explanation. He stood in the doorway, his hands on his lean hips as he watched her absorb his answer.

"What month?"

"June."

"Where are we?"

"Cape May."

"What are you doing here?"

"None of your damn business." He answered so calmly, his words took a moment to sink in.

"What is Clair to you?"

"None of your damn business."

"Look, I've got a problem," she began wearily. "When I went into the water yesterday it was June, 1993. You're telling me it's June, 1929. Which one of us is crazy?"

Thomas didn't move a muscle, but she sensed his tension. "You."

"Thanks for your opinion."

He shrugged. "You asked."

"It could be you, you know." She stared at him. "I think it is."

"It's not." His tone was flat. His beautiful blue eyes were hard.

"You really carry on a scintillating conversation," she retorted sarcastically, at the end of her patience. She wanted to lash out at someone or something for dumping her in the middle of this mess. "Sure you're not related to Gary Cooper, John Wayne, or Clint Eastwood?"

"I don't know any of them."

"None of them?"

"Maybe Gary Cooper," he admitted slowly. "I think he was in a Broadway play last year."

Gary Cooper in a Broadway play? That was almost unimaginable! She stared hard, but she saw nothing in his eyes that spoke of madness— not even the look of a man with a wild imagination.

Thomas walked to the center of the porch. Jamming his hands in his wrinkled and slightly shrunken pants, he gazed out to sea.

Staring at him, she realized that he was probably the only man she'd ever known who could dress in that old-fashioned, sea-shrunken suit and still look as sexy as hell.

She followed his gaze. Because it was the time of the full moon, the waves were higher than normal, but other than that, the late afternoon was peaceful and soothing. There was nothing about the vast ocean to indicate that it had just swallowed up a boatload of people.

"I never really knew how many were aboard. Did you?" she asked, remembering to maintain her pose as a maid on the yacht. She had to know. She'd walked into an ocean to die, yet had lived. Others had gone out on the ocean to enjoy living and had died.

His gaze never faltered. "Including the staff, I'd say about forty-five or so."

"Did you know most of them?"

"Excluding the staff, yes. The owner of the yacht was a member of the mob and a close friend of Al Capone's. The rest were all spoiled, sassy, and daring socialites. Several were millionaires who'd made their fortunes in the stock market."

"Of course! If this is 1929!"

He said nothing.

He was obviously reluctant to carry on a conversation with a woman who sounded crazier with each passing moment.

"If I remember history correctly, sometime in October of this year, the stock market is going to crash," she said conversationally, as if he had asked. "It was called Black Tuesday, and it was the beginning of the Great Depression. They say the crash was caused by too many people buying on margin."

"That's some story," he commented.

Thomas was trying to brush her off, but she wouldn't let him. "People who were—are—wealthy will lose everything they have. Millionaires will jump from their office windows when they realize they're penniless. It will be the beginning of the big depression."

"You're as crazy as a loon."

"Funny, I thought you were the crazy one," she said.

"See how crazy you are?"

He said it with such a deadpan expression that she almost laughed, but she managed to restrain herself. Instead, she grinned.

His expression turned to puzzlement, then closed up once again.

As much as she didn't want to be caught in a time warp, she didn't want him to be crazy either. Deep down, some small part of her needed him to be a hero. A lover.

Her last thought stunned her. She had no idea where it had come from, but she wanted it to go away immediately. This already impossible situation didn't need complicating by dreams of an affair—especially with this man!

Thomas bent down, touching her forehead and making her even more aware of what her body craved. "Why the frown?"

"Just thinking." She brushed away his hand. She didn't need any more contact with him. At least not when she was so vulnerable.

His hand clamped her wrist. "What's that thing?" It was more a demand than a question.

"My watch." She glanced down at her wrist. "It has everything you'd ever want. It even has a stopwatch, a timer, and an alarm clock; it can record appointments two weeks in advance and phone numbers. And I won't mention the calculator."

"It's still running."

"Of course," she answered. "It's waterproof."

Thomas sat down next to her, still holding her wrist. "What's a calculator?"

"It adds, subtracts, multiplies, and divides numbers. It's an electronic adding machine and more." Her heart was beating so quickly she thought it would pop out of her chest. "Would you like to see it work?"

He dropped her wrist as if she'd burned him. "No." He stood up and walked back into the shack. "It's time to go."

Okay, she thought. *So you won't discuss the possibility of a time warp.* Interesting. Could it be that he was as frightened to be in the future as she was to be living in the past?

A sound at the doorway caught her attention and she turned. Thomas was carrying a protesting Clair from the house. He brought her down the front steps, then stood her on her feet.

"You can do it, Clair. Just think about that wonderful big bed of yours. And Bebe will have scones with cream and hot tea waiting for you."

Clair moaned again.

Wearily, Parris stood and walked to Clair's other side. Her mouth watered at the thought of hot tea. Cold tea. Water without salt. Anything wet.

"Come on, Clair. I'll help," she said.

She placed a hand around the woman's slim waist. Again, they began walking down the sandy beach toward the civilization Thomas had promised was waiting just beyond the dunes.

Thomas was right. It wasn't long at all before other buildings became visible in the broad curve of the shallow peninsula. Thomas noticed, too, but shook his head. He didn't want Clair to know yet.

Parris's shoulder hurt from helping Clair walk. Her legs felt like leaded weights; her eyes were glazed in exhaustion.

Clair was in even worse shape. Her head hung down, her limp arm was draped across Parris's shoulders as though they were the best of friends. An occasional moan escaped her cracked lips.

Then Thomas touched Parris's arm and she looked up. A hundred or so yards away was a three-storied Victorian house with a wraparound porch.

Hoping it wasn't a mirage, Parris looked first at Thomas, then at Clair.

"This is it," he murmured softly, and they angled toward the oasis.

The next ten minutes were the longest of Parris's life. By the time they reached the low, stucco wall whose metal gate gave entrance to a back patio, Parris could hardly hold herself up, let alone Clair. They dragged through the gate and up a stepping-stone walkway to the door. Seconds before they reached the door, it swung open. A petite black woman stared at them from the entrance, with her head held high.

"Bebe," Thomas said wearily. "Help me get her to the couch."

In silence, the black woman took Parris's place as they walked Clair into the living room and laid her down on the large, overstuffed sofa.

Her arms like leaden weights at her side, Parris remained standing just inside the doorway. Her muscles were stiff. Exhausted, consumed with thirst, she stood rigid, wondering how she was able to remain upright. Her only answer was that her muscles were too stiff to do anything else.

"What happened, Mr. Elder?" Bebe asked, her words spoken with a French accent. She felt Clair's forehead, cheeks, then throat.

"The yacht went down, Bebe. I found Clair on the beach, and this young woman—her name is Parris—saved her life by pushing the seawater from her lungs. We didn't find anyone else. So far it looks as if Clair, Parris, and I are the only survivors."

"Mr. Sol?" She asked, her voice soft.

"Gone with the others, I guess. Clair thinks he blew up the yacht."

Bebe sighed. Thomas squeezed the maid's shoulder and she nodded. With resignation etched into her face, she shook out the afghan from the back of the couch and covered Clair carefully. "He probably did, Mr. Elder. Mr. Sol wasn't always a well man."

"I understand." He rubbed the back of his neck as if he could rub out the weariness. "You don't have an extra car here so I can get back to my boardinghouse, do you?"

"Yes, sir." She pointed in the direction of the front door. "The keys are on the hall table. The car is in the drive. I just returned from the butcher shop with it."

"Thanks. I'll bring it back in the morning." He shot her a tired smile. "Meanwhile, make sure Clair gets all the water she can handle. And put some cream on her; one side of her face got burned."

"I see that," Bebe said quietly. "I will take care of her. She will be cleaned and in bed in no time."

Thomas walked to Parris and took her hand, leading her out of the room and into the kitchen. There, he gave her another glass of water and drank one himself. Then, grabbing two pieces of chicken sitting on the counter atop a thick pink plate, he handed one to her and bit into his own.

The spicy-sharp scent of fried batter assailed Parris's nostrils, and she almost reeled from a suddenly overwhelming feeling of hunger. She bit into the chicken leg and reveled in the taste. While they ate, Thomas motioned her to follow him. As they walked down the main hall, she had a brief impression of pristine wicker with bright pink, blue, and deep green cushions. A moment later, they were outside.

They had both stripped the chicken down to the bone by the time they reached the drive. Thomas threw his bone over the fence, and Parris followed suit. Then, they stepped into a large black sedan and Parris felt yet another wave of confusion. The car was old enough to be her grandfather's, yet she was sitting in it and Thomas knew how to drive it. They pulled out of the drive onto a shale road, going all of 30 miles an hour, spewing oyster shells everywhere.

Parris closed her eyes, willing herself not to think of anything except getting some sleep. Thomas turned the car and Parris felt the motion, but she refused to open her eyes. She was too tired to absorb any more.

But her eyes flew open a moment later when the car stopped and the engine died.

"This is it," Thomas said, his voice sounding as tired and disgusted as she felt. "We've run out of gas."

"Just my luck," Parris muttered. She stepped out of the car and stared down the street. They were on a paved road, and less than a block away was a hotel. She tried to console herself that at least it would be a short walk.

By the time they reached the rambling Victorian structure and walked around to the house behind it, Parris was exhausted again. She remembered that Thomas had said he had a room in a boardinghouse. The building was tall and narrow, made into several apartments by the looks of it.

Her sneakers dragged on the shale; her shoulders hurt. Her *hair* hurt.

"I'll go in first," Thomas said softly. "As soon as I've opened the door, I'll check to see if the way is clear. When no one is looking, you can slip in the back door."

"Why?"

He looked confused. "What do you mean? I'm getting you into my room."

"Why can't I just walk up with you?"

His tone was filled with disapproval. "It's not seemly for a lady to be seen in a man's room. My landlady might boot me out of my lodgings if she saw you."

"You're kidding."

"No, I'm not. I know this is the enlightened age, but there is still a difference between a lady and a flapper. Mrs. Timmers won't allow a flapper near the rooms."

"We still don't know what year it is."

"We certainly do. Besides, what difference does that make? We still have to get into the room."

"In my time, women and men can share hotel rooms without being married, and no one thinks anything about it."

"I understand it's done discreetly on the West Coast, but certainly not here." He narrowed his gaze and gave her a hard stare. Finally, he said, "Come on."

They turned and began following the stepping-stone walk up to the side of the building, where Parris could make out an inset door. Just as they reached it, Thomas's hand caught Parris's shoulder, halting her.

"Wait here."

She was so exhausted, all she wanted to do was lie down on the sun-warmed sand and close her eyes for a year or so. "I might as well come with you. I doubt anyone's going to see us."

"You might not care about your reputation, but I need mine. Right now, I've got a lot at stake. So stay here and do as I say."

"Chauvinist."

"What's that?"

"Never mind." She waved a hand in the air. "Go on. The sooner we do this your way, the sooner I can get some rest."

Just before disappearing up the stairs, he muttered something under his breath. Parris was too tired to pay attention to him or his moods. With a weary sigh, she leaned against the clapboard wall and closed her eyes. Her feet were so numb, she didn't know if she could stand much longer.

She dozed, unaware that Thomas had returned until he touched her shoulder. Forcing her eyes open, she stared up at him. He was still drop dead gorgeous and he wasn't a figment of her imagination.

"Follow me," he said quietly and turned toward the door.

Once inside, he glanced back and saw that she hadn't budged. A look of impatience crossed his face. "Come on!" His voice was a harsh whisper, finally forcing her to move one foot in front of the other.

The hall seemed to be a block long, and almost halfway down, Thomas turned into a shorter hall. Then, he silently trod the stairs to the second story. Parris followed obediently, her reactions instinctive. Finally, she pulled herself up the last few stairs, her knees almost giving out with the enormous effort.

When Thomas looked back, he expelled a deep breath. With quick movements, he pulled her up the last two steps. "This isn't the time to dawdle," he muttered, hurrying her down the hall past several doors before slipping into one and carefully closing it behind them.

With a heartfelt sigh, Parris lay down on the small Victorian sofa, not caring that her feet hung over the edge. It didn't matter that the back was as hard as the floor. But one thing did matter.

"My God, this damn thing is scratchy!" she complained. She sat up and ran a hand over what she'd thought was cut velvet.

Thomas placed a straight-back chair in front of the locked door. "Where have you been, girl? It's horsehair."

Parris's eyes opened wide and she stared at him. "Of course! I've heard of it. I've even seen it, but I never thought I'd be lying on it."

"Are you trying to tell me there's something longer lasting than a horsehair sofa?"

Parris wasn't in the mood for arguing. She wasn't in the mood for anything but sleep. She stood and began walking into the next room—and toward the bed that occupied it. "No, I'm telling you I have never lain on one before."

"That settles it. You must be the one who got hit on the head," he retorted.

"So says a man who's still walking with one left shoe."

With those words, she flopped across the iron bed, making it squeak. The bed felt wonderful, and she closed her eyes and sighed in contentment. Light cotton sheets smelling of salt air and sunshine cooled her face and hands. She was instantly asleep.

Thomas stared down at the sleeping woman in his bed and wondered why in the hell he'd been chosen to find her. The fates or sirens or whoever was supposed to be the mythical queens of the sea must have had a really good laugh over the mismatch.

Oh, she was a looker, all right. With her blonde hair, those big brown eyes, soft skin, and winsome smile, she could charm the birds out of the trees if she wanted to. But she didn't seem to want to much.

She certainly had a weird way of dressing. Thomas almost felt sorry for her. Those funny, clumsy-looking shoes had to be only one step better than going barefoot. And wearing those old pants and a workman's shirt with rolled-up sleeves must be horribly embarrassing for her. Though he had to admit she didn't act embarrassed.

For that matter, she didn't act anything like any of the women he knew. Oh, her movements were feminine enough. That smooth and easygoing sway of her hips and the coy little way she pushed back her hair were pure female. But those same movements were too free and easy, as if she didn't care that she seemed unrestrained in front of a man. What was the matter with her? Didn't she know she was supposed to be more refined in her movements around the opposite sex?

Parris sighed and turned her face toward the wall. Thomas took a step closer to the bed, and a sharp pain shot through his bare foot and zigzagged up his spine. His breath hissed through his teeth. Right then, he wished he'd had her funny-looking shoes when he'd walked on the sand. He wouldn't have blisters now.

Grabbing the pillow off the bed, he threw it on the floor. He'd give her an hour's sleep in the bed before he kicked her off and took it himself. After all, it was his bed. Besides, she was smaller. She could fit on the sofa even if it was cramped. He couldn't begin to fit there.

Having made that decision, he felt better. A man needed to be in command of the world around him.

He slipped off his jacket and shirt and lay down on the hard wooden floor. He wasn't going to take his shoe off until he was wide awake. With that money and the unknowing help of Clair, he'd crack the mob wide open. Without the money, he'd be like any other sop, for he was on sabbatical from *The New York Tribune* to write a story about the mob. From the time he'd gone underground, he'd had to earn his own money and live by his wits. The liquor money had set him up in the position he'd been waiting for. The past year hadn't been in vain.

For a split second, he thought about undressing completely, but as a concession to the woman in his room, he'd keep his pants on. When he awoke, he'd remind himself to give Parris hell for hogging the bed. It was his last thought.

When she awakened, Parris wasn't sure where she was. Sun poured in the window, and a cool breeze drifted through the open lace curtains into the bedroom.

A soft snore reached her ears and she froze. When it came again, she raised her head and peered over the side of the bed. Thomas was sprawled on the floor.

One look at Thomas's handsome face and the events of yesterday slammed into her. Her breath caught in her throat. His beard didn't disguise the strength of his jawline. Dark, stiff lashes any woman would consider herself lucky to have fanned against his cheeks. With a pillow propped under his head, he was curled on his side toward the bed. His tanned torso moved rhythmically with every soft snore.

Her gaze traveled the length of his body. She noticed that he still wore his left shoe. The man had more than his share of eccentricity!

She dropped her head and closed her eyes. She liked his looks. She even liked his smell; he smelled like a man instead of several different brands of soap, deodorant, powder, and after-shave.

Pushing herself off the bed, she rose and looked around, seeing what she hadn't had the strength to see last night. The room was decorated in Victorian style with high ceilings and decorative moldings. The wallpaper was light pink cabbage roses on a pale vanilla background. The iron bedstead was dressed in a quilt of companion colors. Even the small throw rugs scattered over the oak floors were pink.

The next room, either a sitting room or parlor, was done in cherry-wood furniture that looked as uncomfortable as it was formal—the exact opposite of the bedroom.

A table under the window gleamed in the sunlight. On its polished surface was a white bowl filled with fresh tomatoes. A clear-glass salt shaker sat beside the bowl. Parris's mouth watered. It didn't take her two minutes to polish off several tomatoes. With juice running down her arm, she knew it was time to find the bathroom. A hot shower was in order.

After five minutes of searching, she realized that the bathroom must be down the hall. There was nothing she could do but wait. She palmed another plump tomato and the salt shaker and walked back to the bedroom. Propping a pillow against the iron headboard, she lay back and began to eat.

A loud, unhappy groan from the floor warned Parris that, when Prince Charming awakened, he would turn into a troll. Expletives rolled from his mouth as he pulled himself to a sitting position. He cursed again as he stood, holding his tailbone and his shoulder and grimacing. Obviously using the floor as a bed hadn't agreed with him.

"Hello," she said brightly as he turned around and glared at her.

"You took the whole bed."

"You could have moved me."

"You would have yelled."

"I would not."

"Now, you tell me," he said disgustedly.

"You never asked me, so how could I tell you?"

His blue eyes delved angrily into hers. "You really are argumentative."

"Only when I feel I'm right."

He walked over to the tall bureau and picked up a pocket watch, staring at the time. "A real lady wouldn't lower herself to argue."

"Don't show your ignorance," Parris snapped. She didn't need to be told what ladies did. She was one. "What a sexist remark."

He stared at her over his broad, bare shoulder. "What does that mean?"

Parris stood and pretended to brush salt from her jeans. "It means you don't have enough sense to realize that women are equal to men in everything but strength. Whatever rules of behavior you follow are also good enough for a female. No more, no less."

He dropped the watch back on the bureau top. "Is that how it's done in your time?"

"Yes. Thank goodness, your way of thinking finally went out of style somewhere in the seventies. Now women work beside men and earn the same wages and the same respect."

Thomas ran a hand through his salt-laden hair. "Look, I don't really give a damn how men and women work together in your day and age. We're in my time right now. That means you follow my rules until I can find a suitable nuthouse for you."

She stared at him, a shiver dancing down her spine. "What?"

He held up his hands. "Just kidding, tootsie. Don't worry. I have a feeling you're as sane as I am. I'm just not sure what to do with you."

Anger raced through her. "Since I'm not your responsibility, I don't see that you have to do anything with me."

"Oh? And what would you do without me? Where would you sleep? How would you eat? Where would you go?"

She felt her heart trip at the answer to his questions. She didn't know!

He gave a smug, satisfied nod. "I thought so. You haven't gotten that far in your superior thinking, have you? But as soon as you do, you'll think the pants off us men."

Parris smiled sweetly, more than willing to parry his attack. "I bet most women just love to hear you talk tough, even though you're full of hot air."

"Lady, you're sick."

"Maybe," she admitted. "But an illness can be cured. Your problem can't. Like Pavlov's dogs, you've been trained in your way of thinking since birth. It's deeply imbedded in your warped brain."

Thomas snorted and turned to walk out of the room. "I don't know what the hell you're talking about. And I'd bet my left shoe that you don't know either."

If there was anything she'd learned, it was that his left shoe was more important to him than anything else. And his inability to take it off around her was a statement that Thomas didn't trust anyone, especially her, not to steal whatever was in it. "I need to get cleaned up."

"Bathroom's down the hall. Towels are in the bottom drawer."

It was a rude dismissal, but she understood. She'd insulted him. Even she was surprised at her attack. "Thank you so much for your kindness," she said sarcastically.

"Don't mention it."

Parris opened the drawer, pulling out two threadbare towels and a new washcloth.

She was at the door when Thomas called out, "Wait, I have to go with you."

"What for?"

"Because no one knows you're here. If you go in and Mrs. Timmers or one of her cohorts does a bathroom check, it has to be my voice that rings out."

"I'm not taking a shower with you there!"

"It's a bath. And if you don't take it with me in there, you don't take it at all."

She stared at him, her expression thoughtful. "You're enjoying this, aren't you?"

His grin was boyishly disarming. "You betcha, sweetie."

But his endearment sparked her anger again. "Don't patronize me."

Thomas looked genuinely confused. "What are you talking about now?"

Parris took a deep breath and tried to relax. It wasn't his fault. It wasn't even hers. What was wrong in her time was perfectly normal for his era.

"I'm sorry," she said softly. "I guess I'm just suffering from jet lag. I didn't mean to jump at you like that."

He frowned, his confusion still apparent. "What's jet lag?"

"It happens when you travel by jet and pass through different time zones. . . ." His face was a study in amazement. She laughed. "That's a whole other lesson for another day." She gave his arm a conciliatory pat. "Right now, I want a bath so much I'm willing to share the room with you if you won't peek."

"Of course, I won't," he retorted, reaching for his shaving kit, which was just inside the bedroom door. "At least, not when you'll catch me."

Chapter Four

The bathroom floor was covered with cracked linoleum, curling at the edges. In one corner was a large brown gas heater, in the other corner, an old claw-footed porcelain tub. A small pink rug was placed in front of the tub.

Parris grinned. "I should have known it would be pink—in any shade."

"Shhh," Thomas said, looking a little sheepish. "She's a little over the top on the color, but her heart's in the right place."

Trying to ignore his shirtless body, she gave him a sarcastic smile. "I'm sure. After all, she gave you a room."

Turning to the sink, Thomas ignored her remark. "It will take me five minutes to shave. If you want a bath, you'd better get in there before I do."

"Right," she whispered, then turned on the faucets and water trickled out.

"You're getting more water from the sink than I am from the tub."

Without answering, Thomas turned off his spigot and her trickle became a flow.

While waiting for the tub to fill, she took off her shirt and dropped it in the water. Using the bar of soap in the holder, Parris scrubbed the salt water from it, then rinsed it. Using the empty towel holder, Parris draped the material over the rod and hoped it would dry quickly. The soft summer breeze waving the pink curtains ruffled the material.

"Don't wait for the water to fill to the top. This isn't a swimming pool. Take your bath, for cripe's sake!"

"There's not enough water," she whispered back.

"That's plenty. We don't have all day!"

Parris raised her brows. "What's your hurry? Got a hot date?"

"Can't you do as you're told for once?" he whispered, swirling a brush in a soap cup, then lathering his face. "You don't do anything without an argument. If that's the way it is in your time, then I'm glad I'm not living in it."

"Tough words from a man who wears only one shoe." She was growing more and more intrigued with the mystery behind that shoe.

Again, he ignored her bait. Assured he wasn't watching, Parris stripped off her jeans and stood in her French-cut panties and lacy white bra. Testing the water's temperature, she looked at him. "So you accept the fact that I'm from another time?"

She could see his face in the mirror. Even covered with lather, he was handsome. He grimaced.

"I don't have to. All that matters right now is that you believe it."

"And my watch?"

"It's some kind of gimmick," he said. "Maybe bought at Atlantic City's Steel Pier. God knows they sell everything there."

"Do you honestly believe that?" Unsnapping the front of her bra, she threw it in the tub, following it with her panties. Then she stepped into the water and sat down. "Do you think I made up everything I told you?"

Picking up the soap, Parris washed her face, neck, and shoulders. The scent was so different from her usual soap that she smelled it again.

"Ummm."

"What's that for?" Thomas's voice sounded tight, choked.

Parris couldn't see him because her face was covered with suds. "I forgot how great old-fashioned soap smells. In my time, we add face creams and use all kinds of deodorants."

She cleaned off her face and soaped the rest of her body. Working quickly, Parris rinsed her underwear and bra, then hung them over the side of the tub. Then she turned on the water once more and stuck her head under the faucet. It took three shampoos before Parris thought all the sand was washed out. By the last rinse, she was happy and relaxed again.

She leaned back in the tub, resting her head against the curved edge and stretched languorously. "I think I'm going to live," she sighed.

"Get out," Thomas barked, waking her out of her trance.

She looked up in surprise, then froze.

A razor in his upraised hand, Thomas stood watching her, his face still covered in lather. His gaze was glued to her breasts, and his fingers had turned white from gripping the razor. "You're through now." His voice was thick and whispery.

Unconsciously, Parris covered her breasts with her arms. "Turn around."

Thomas's movements were slow as he turned and stared into the mirror. "Go ahead."

She didn't need reminding twice. The look in his eye was downright frightening. Wrapping a towel around her body, she grabbed her soaking underwear. Less than a minute later, she was at the door.

After peeking down the hall, she raced barefoot to Thomas's room. Once inside, she shut the door quickly and quietly. Leaning against it, she took a deep breath to calm her erratic heartbeat.

He'd frightened and excited her more than she cared to admit. There was something more than lust in his dark blue eyes. The look she'd seen baffled her. All she knew was that Thomas wanted her, but he was angry with her, too. And she wasn't sure why.

She needed to get away from there. If she had really traveled to the past, she had to find a way back to her own time. If she'd fallen into a time hole, then surely she could climb out. Maybe if she could piece together the sequence of events that had led her there, she could find that particular thread that tied her time and Thomas's together. Until that moment, she hadn't been able to think about her situation. Everything had happened so quickly, she hadn't had a chance.

The breeze filtering through the window brought goose bumps to her skin. Parris stared down at the underwear she clutched in her hand. With uneven movements, she went to the living room, dragged a chair to the window, and draped her clothing over it.

She'd left her jeans and shirt in the bathroom. Now what? Her sneakers and socks were in a heap on the floor by the bed. With those shoes on her feet, she could walk anywhere—but not if she was wearing only a towel.

Thomas's bureau drawers revealed neatly folded, white handkerchiefs, white boxer shorts and undershirts. No colors, no different styles—nothing to surprise or delight the eye.

Her only hope was the small closet in the corner behind the door. This yielded a more promising selection. There were three summer suits, a white sports jacket with tan slacks, seven ties, five shirts, two pairs of shoes, and two hats.

"You could have known more women, Thomas Elder," she muttered into the confines of the small closet. "Or at least have an occasional visit from a maiden aunt."

She heard a woman's laughter in the hallway and froze. Thomas's deep voice answered, his tone teasing and sweet. She wished he would talk to her that way.

The woman spoke again. Parris tiptoed out of the bedroom toward the door, listening carefully.

"Well, that shirt certainly isn't your usual style, Thomas."

"My sister bought it for me. You know little sisters," he laughed. "She doesn't have your exquisite taste."

His words earned another giggle. "Now, don't you be talking 'bout your little sister that way, Thomas. You know she's too young to have a strong opinion on anything yet. Give her time."

"I'm trying, Mrs. Timmers." His voice had lost its easy tone. "I'm really trying."

"I'm sure you are, Thomas. If only my Miranda wasn't married. Now, she would give you a run for your money. She's as pretty as a summer sunset. A real beauty."

"I bet she looks just like you."

"Well, people do say she takes after me," Mrs. Timmers admitted.

"I can just imagine." Thomas paused for a moment, then spoke again. "I'll just take care of those, Mrs. Timmers. No sense having you do those old work clothes."

"It's no bother, Thomas. Matter of fact, I enjoy doing little things for you. I'll get these back to you tomorrow, all cleaned and pressed. Even if you're working, you need to look your best, Thomas."

Parris knew the object of their discussion had to be her clothing. She'd left it in the bathroom and now the landlady had it.

Thomas rattled the doorknob. Just in case Mrs. Timmers decided to come in, Parris ran back to the bedroom and hid behind the door.

She heard more muffled words and low-pitched laughter; then the living-room door opened and closed. She held her breath, waiting for a single set of footsteps to tell her that Thomas was alone. There were none.

Dots of perspiration popped out on her forehead. She couldn't believe it! Thomas *was* correct about the year. The landlady's acceptance of Thomas's reference to her garments as work clothes was more proof. What if he was also right about her smearing his reputation if she was caught in his room?

She peered through the crack in the door, but her limited view yielded nothing. The suspense built. To her ears, even her breath sounded harsh. Finally, unable to stand the suspense, Parris peeked around the door and into the living room, and the sudden sight of Thomas made her jump.

He stood just inches from her, leaning against the jamb. His grin was as handsome as it was endearing. "Were you worried about me?" he asked teasingly.

His gaze traveled down her body, then back up, dismissing her towel as a shield. His look made her angry. "Not in a million years!" she whispered back fiercely. "What a sneaky thing to do!"

"I didn't do anything."

"You sneaked in here, trying to scare the life out of me."

His smile slipped. "Actually, I thought you might have gone back to where you came from— whatever time that is."

Her anger slowly ebbed away. "Well, I didn't."

"So I see." He stood away from the doorjamb. "Are you hungry?"

Her stomach growled in answer. "Yes. Does your landlady have my clothes?"

"She took them from the bathroom. I didn't have any say-so about it." He passed her, strolling to the small closet—if he could stroll with one shoe on and one shoe off. "We're going to have to find something in my closet for you to wear."

"I doubt it."

"I'm not spending a dollar on a dress unless you're there to try it on. So, unless you've got another idea, you'll wear whatever I have."

So much for negotiation.

Half an hour later they were both dressed.

Thomas looked splendid in his casual sport coat and slacks—and a complete pair of shoes on his feet. He had gone to elaborate detail to hide his shoe in the bedroom without her seeing where. His dark brown hair was parted neatly on the side. And his smile showed his single dimple to perfection.

With his hand on the door, he surveyed her. Apparently he was satisfied, because he gave no criticism. "Ready?"

She nodded, pulling her hat brim a little closer to her eyes. When he opened the door, she stepped out, then waited for him to show her the way. She'd been too tired to pay attention earlier.

Her bra and panties were still damp and felt clammy against her skin. She'd rolled up the sleeves of the white shirt and taped up the bottom of the trousers and jacket sleeves. If no one looked too closely, she'd pass for a young man. Unfortunately, her sneakers looked rather stupid with the outfit, but she had no choice. Thomas's shoes were miles too big for her.

Thomas guided her out of the rear of the house and toward the sidewalk. Striding briskly, they made their way toward the main shopping area.

"I don't have any money."

Thomas guided her across the street by tapping his cane against her thigh. "I'll handle it for now."

"Thanks."

"You'll owe me." He smiled and tipped his hat at a buxom woman walking past them.

They passed two children, who stared at her feet, and she pulled her hat down even lower. "If you were in my time period, I'd help you out all I could."

"Like hell, lady. You'd have left if you had clothes to leave in."

Her gaze darted to him, but still walking briskly, he stared straight ahead.

It was time to lie. "You're wrong."

"Like hell. I've seen panic before."

"Whose?" she asked sweetly, secretly angry that he could read her so easily. "Yours?"

"My reaction was completely different from yours," he said, stopping in front of a modest dress shop. Opening the door, he stood back to allow her to enter.

A young woman was fidgeting with the mannequin in the window. With someone listening, Parris couldn't ask Thomas what his reaction was. She'd have to wait until they were alone again.

The woman, who introduced herself as Emily, was a bit shocked at Parris's masculine attire, but she regained her composure and helped as best she could. Together, Parris and Emily found two dresses suitable for day wear.

Parris had never realized how regimented and formal the Twenties were, although she remembered pictures of her mother and grandmother in hats, gloves, and little purses dangling on chains from their wrists.

In Parris's time, there were basically three kinds of dress: business, casual, or formal. Any of them could be worn at any time of the day. Not so in 1929. There were morning dresses, day dresses, afternoon dresses, evening dresses, cocktail dresses, and another five or six variations. Along with the two dresses, she selected a cream-colored garter belt and two pairs of silk hose.

"Shoes," Parris whispered to Thomas.

He nodded, paid the bill, then wrote his address on the bag. With a winning smile, he instructed Emily to have one dress and the lingerie delivered to the boardinghouse. Parris would wear the other dress.

Two minutes later, he escorted Parris out to the sidewalk. She glanced around, then down. She thought she had been conspicuous before when she'd been wearing his suit. Now, however, she was wearing a gray-and-rose-flowered day dress with sneakers. Only a handful of people sat across the street on the town square park benches, but Parris felt as if the whole world were staring at her.

Thank goodness the shoe store was only four doors away from the dress shop. They stood for a moment while she stared in dismay at the limited and outdated selection in the window.

"My God, these are so old-fashioned!"

"These are the newest styles," Thomas said. "Besides, if what you're wearing is any indication of what you're used to, it's about time you changed your attitude as well as your shoes."

She wanted to challenge him, to tell him what was going on in the world of fashion at the century's end. But he was right: All she had to back up her own casual taste was her sneakers. At that moment, even she thought they suddenly looked like swamp boats in a desert!

In less than a minute, she chose a pair of shoes. There weren't many choices. Plain white pumps with straps across the instep that reminded her of her grandmother's footwear. In fact, her choice was her grandmother's shoe style. Now she knew why.

"Drugstore," she whispered to Thomas.

He frowned. "Why?"

"Razor, comb, makeup, and toothbrush."

He nodded, and they exited and crossed the square to a storefront with the word Luncheonette in big blue letters across the glass window.

The store was divided into two sections. One side had an old-fashioned luncheonette counter and several tables and chairs; the other was filled with shelves holding all sorts of remedies, goodies, and products whose brands Parris had never even heard of. There were several items for women's problems, but not one mentioned premenstrual syndrome or cramps. There were no sanitary pads or tampons either. Granted, she needn't worry about that for another few weeks, and by that time, she might have figured out a way to get back to her own time. Suddenly her own time didn't seem half bad.

Thomas stood by the cashier reading the daily newspaper. Several women sat near the window sipping sodas and giggling. Their eyes were drawn to Thomas again and again. Parris wasn't sure whether he was ignoring them or just didn't notice their glances. Grabbing only what she thought she needed, she met him at the cash register.

He folded his newspaper, then looked down at her collection of toilet articles. "You need all that?"

She nodded, acting as if it were the most natural thing in the world to expect a man to pay. "Of course. I need more, but I got only what was necessary for now." She glanced up at him. She hadn't felt so intimidated by a man since she was a child and her father had scolded her for buying too much candy. "I'll pay you back."

Thomas sighed and reached for his wallet, putting down some money. As the young man rang up her purchases, she watched. Even the size of the bills was larger than in Parris's day. Was anything the same? No scanner. No electronic cash register. The clerk punched hard at the buttons representing the amount, then dragged a stick from the side of the machine toward him. It reminded her of playing the slot machines in Atlantic City. The grand total of her cosmetics and toiletries and Thomas's newspaper was three dollars. Aspirin cost that much in her time!

"You sure don't come cheap, do you?" Thomas muttered as he escorted her out of the building and into the late-afternoon sunshine. He took her arm and wrapped it around his.

"You're a real comedian." She pasted a smile on her lips as they walked to the other end of the square.

"And stop running," he said, purposely holding her hand on his arm and slowing down her pace. "It's unseemly for a lady to rush."

"It's also unhealthy for a man to get too bossy. But that doesn't seem to stop you."

As another couple passed them, Thomas patted her hand and smiled. "Of course not. That's why God made man—to keep women in line."

"Really?" She tried to smile back. It wasn't easy. "And why did God make woman?"

"To take care of men."

Parris blinked, holding back the red flag she momentarily saw. "Then you believe as I do."

"What?"

"That men aren't capable of taking care of themselves." She patted his arm. "Poor dear. Not too bright are you?"

His smile was gone. "Maybe so, but I'm brighter than you are. I have money. You don't."

"You know, for years men thought money was power. But in my mother's generation, women proved them wrong. They could have all the money in the world, but they still couldn't snuggle up to it on a cold winter's night. In fact, money refused to take care of them when they were hungry, ill, or lonely."

"You have a big mouth."

"Thank you. The better to sass you with, my dear."

He stopped on the street. "What the hell does that mean? It sounds like a quote except that it makes no sense at all."

She looked confused. "It's not that difficult. It's a takeoff of a quote from *Little Red Riding Hood*."

The starch seemed to go out of him a little. "Okay. That one I know."

They began walking again, heading toward a small but genteel restaurant at a corner of the square. The closer they got, the slower Thomas walked.

"What is it?" Parris asked. Her stomach was growling and she was growing dizzy with the delicious aromas of spices and food.

"Are you going to watch your tongue?" His words were stated quietly, urgently.

She looked through the wide window and saw a pretty young woman sitting in the corner. Her gray cloche hat and dark hair beautifully framed her dainty, oval face and accented her pale skin. Her white, gray, and pink dress made her look like an advertisement in an old-fashioned magazine.

"Who is she?" Parris didn't want to admit that her spirits plunged with the reality of Thomas's interest in front of her. After all, if she did, she couldn't tell herself that she wasn't interested in him.

"It doesn't matter. Will you behave?"

"I promise."

He led her inside the restaurant, and the owner—a thin, nervous man—led them to a table by the wall. Parris waited a moment for Thomas to pull out her chair. After handing them napkins and pointing to the menu on the wall, the host left.

Instead of sitting across from her, Thomas leaned down and whispered, "I'll be right back."

"I'm ordering without you!" she whispered back. She was so hungry she was ready to snatch food off the passing trays.

"Just wait two minutes," he pleaded, looking hungrily at another diner's platter. "I won't be long."

He walked cockily over to the pretty-as-a-picture young woman. The girl's face could have lit the room as Thomas approached her. An older woman was sitting with her. A slight family resemblance was evident between the two, but not enough for Parris to determine their relationship. The younger woman couldn't contain her happiness at seeing Thomas, but the older woman's expression showed her disapproval.

"It is so good to see you again, Thomas!" the girl exclaimed. "You've been gone from our group at least a week. We thought we'd lost you to a livelier New York City crowd for good."

With his back to Parris, Thomas bent and kissed the girl's outstretched hand. Parris couldn't hear a word he said, only his low, sexy tone of voice, which made him sound very charming.

But the older woman wasn't falling for Thomas's suave manners. "Well, Thomas, have you made your million yet?"

Again Thomas mumbled an answer.

"Well, I certainly hope you're not keeping company with those hooligans anymore. Respectable people must keep proper company. Decent people don't associate with those whose hands are in an illegal till."

"I assure you, Mrs. Morrow, I would be the first one to slap the hand of anyone like that," Thomas said in a ringing tone loud enough for Parris to hear.

Silence hung in the air. Parris looked around at the other faces in the room. Although they pretended otherwise, the customers were listening to every word.

Thomas returned and sat down across from Parris. Ignoring the slate menu on the wall, he picked up the small handwritten menu from the side of the table and perused the small print.

Parris watched him. She was enjoying the threads of his intricate life. This wasn't her reality, she reminded herself.

The owner joined them. "What would you like?" he asked, looking at Thomas.

"Chicken potpie."

Parris glanced up at the man. "I'll have the same."

"And to drink?"

Thomas ignored her. "A cherry soda."

"A Diet Coke."

She saw surprise in Thomas's eyes and the owner's shock. Obviously, Diet Coke wasn't a drink in this time. "I'm sorry. I meant Coca-Cola."

The man relaxed a little, but he still looked at her warily.

"What the hell's a Diet Coke?" Thomas asked when the owner left. "It sounds horrible."

"We drink it all the time, and it tastes delicious."

"I thought you said you'd be careful," he said.

"I thought I was, but I don't know everything. After all, this isn't my time."

"Obviously," he said disgustedly. "Do you eat with a knife and fork?"

"Yes."

"Thank God for some things," he muttered, still not looking relieved.

Before Parris could retort, their meal was delivered to their table. Obviously, the specialty of the day was kept hot and ready. A farmhand's portion of the chicken potpie was on her plate, and the smell made her dizzy with hunger. She picked up her fork with a shaking hand. It had been two days since she'd eaten more than some tomatoes and one piece of chicken.

Just as she raised her filled fork to her mouth, Mrs. Morrow and her charming companion stopped at their table. "Don't forget, Thomas," the young woman's lilting voice ordered playfully. "My mother and I expect you at our party tomorrow night."

"I won't, Victoria." He promised with a smile that was as charming as it was false.

"And please, bring your cousin with you." Victoria's eyes focused inquisitively on Parris. "I am sure she'll enjoy meeting new friends."

"I certainly would," Parris purred before Thomas could answer.

"But she promised to sit with the child of a friend," Thomas interjected.

"Oh, our other cousin can do it, Thomas," Parris chided, laying on a thick Southern accent. She reached over and patted his arm. "Mind your manners, cousin, or you'll have these fine folks thinkin' you're ashamed of me."

"Never that, cousin. But you know how tired you've been lately."

"Of course, but I'll rest up all day." She smiled broadly at Victoria and her mother. "And thank you so much for inviting me. I haven't had a chance to socialize much."

Victoria looked confused. "I thought you just arrived."

Parris opened her eyes wide. "I did. That's why I haven't been out much."

Victoria laughed—and to Parris's chagrin, she laughed beautifully.

Thomas was livid.

"That's settled then," Mrs. Morrow said. "We'll see you both tomorrow night."

"Of course," Thomas said smoothly. "Thank you for inviting us."

Like the lead float in a parade, Mrs. Morrow turned and, Victoria following close behind, led the way out of the restaurant.

Chapter Five

It did Parris's heart good to watch Thomas squirm. So far, he had been in charge of their topsy-turvy lives and she was the one who didn't know how to survive or what to do.

Thomas sat back with a frown. His appetite hadn't been affected by their disagreement. His plate was completely clean. Parris's wasn't far from being the same. After motioning to the owner for two more orders of the same dish, he stared hard at Parris. Knowing what he was about to say, she gave him an even look in return.

"You're not going to the Morrows' party."

It wasn't easy, but she pretended to smile. "Because you say so?"

"Mainly."

"Do you love her?"

His eyes narrowed. "None of your business."

"You keep saying that as if it's your favorite

expression," she commented. "But it is my business, if you're asking me to ignore an invitation."

It took him a moment to answer. "You wouldn't have been invited if I hadn't said you were my cousin."

"That doesn't matter much now, does it?"

"You're not going." He looked like a stubborn mule. All he needed was for his ears to prick up and Parris would have laughed her way through the whole episode. Only his ears didn't and he was dead serious.

Parris took her last bite of food and leaned back, giving him all her attention. "Why are you helping me with these clothes and toiletries?" she asked conversationally.

He was obviously taken off guard by the change of subject. He shrugged, looking a little uncomfortable. "I don't know. You helped me in the water. I vaguely remember your voice and touch when my hand was slipping from the wood. And then you saved Clair's life. I guess I feel a little beholden."

She smiled again. "How nice."

"What's on your mind, tootsie?"

Parris cocked her head. "Now I wonder what makes you call Victoria by her name and me tootsie?"

His stiffness increased. "Victoria is a lady."

She bridled at that comment. "You don't know me well enough to decide whether or not I'm a lady."

"Oh, yes, I do. A lady would never have dressed the way you did, let alone done the things you've done."

The owner returned with two more plates and placed them on the table. He gave Parris and Thomas a strange look, then reluctantly walked away.

Parris ignored him, caught up in the byplay with this Neanderthal. "I see," she mused thoughtfully. "Then you're saying that Victoria is a hothouse orchid and I'm not."

"Yes." He looked pleased that she understood.

She smiled brightly in relief. "Thank goodness!"

"What the hell are you talking about now?" He narrowed his eyes, ready to go to war over his flower. "If I were you, Parris, I wouldn't say anything against Victoria. She's not here to defend herself."

"What would she say if she were?"

"Probably nothing. She's not used to street fighting. Victoria would be confused and upset by your aggressiveness. She's just not that type of woman."

"If I was the same type of woman as Victoria, Mr. Elder, I wouldn't be here. I'd be dead and so would you and Clair." She smiled, but there was no mirth in her gaze. "So you see, there are some positive aspects to my particular type of person."

Relaxing slightly, Thomas picked up a fork-ful of food and took a big bite. After he swallowed, he said, "I never said differently. I wasn't insulting you."

She ignored his attempt to placate her. "And I have a funny feeling about your Victoria. If she's an innocent, I'd be amazed. As one woman looking at another, I think she plays at being naive, and as long as it works, she'll continue to do that."

Thomas's usually full lips straightened into a thin line. "I don't give a bee's knees what you think. You're wrong."

"I'm right, but you're too bullheaded to admit it."

Thomas dropped his napkin on the table and pulled several dollars out of his pocket. "It's time to leave."

Parris followed suit, placing her napkin on the table, too. "Fine with me."

They stood and walked out of the restaurant like military sergeants. Parris just wished that they hadn't been in such a hurry to prove a point. She had left most of her second helping of food and she was still hungry.

Twilight began settling over the coastline as they walked toward the boardinghouse. Parris longed to look at twilight in her own time instead of in this cockeyed year with this cock-eyed man.

Tears threatened to fall. She was allowed to feel deserted and lonely, wasn't she? *She* was the one who had the problem, not Mr. Chauvinist. *She* was the one who had lost her family, not

Mr. Charming. *She* was the one who was caught in a time warp, alienated from everything familiar, not Mr. Wealthy.

She sniffled and Thomas stopped walking, taking her arm to slow her down. "What's the matter now?"

She sniffled again. "Nothing."

Thomas heaved a hefty sigh. "All right," he said in a resigned voice. "I'm sorry if I hurt your feelings. I didn't mean to compare you unfavorably with Victoria."

She knew a lie when she heard one. "Yes, you did. You meant to put me in my place and you succeeded."

"You're imagining things."

"God, I wish I were!" Her despair was overtaken by anger. "I'm the outcast." She gave a look of disgust. "What the hell am I doing talking to you? You have as much sensitivity as an eggplant."

His jaw clenched. "That's enough of the insults."

"Not half as much as you deserve, you Neanderthal. Not half as much!" She clenched her hands at her sides to keep from slamming them into his stomach. "You've taken one quick look and decided that you know all about me—how tough, how stupid, how resourceful, how feminine I am. Well, I have a news flash for you. You don't know Jack Sprite about me! You don't even have the intelligence to find out!"

Glaring at him wasn't going to hurt him any

more than her words. He looked shocked, but she was sure it was because she was probably the only female who had ever dared tell him off!

She turned on her thick, square heel, strode down the sidewalk, passed the boardinghouse, and headed toward the beach.

"Wait!" she heard Thomas call out, but she wasn't about to let him answer her tirade. Her anger had finally burned away all the feelings of insecurity she'd felt since yesterday. She'd needed that so she could find her balance once more. Two weeks ago, she'd lost her family. Yesterday she'd lost her own life and time. She had a right to be upset, angry, frustrated.

She reached the beach, slipped off her shoes, and began walking parallel to the water. Darkness had descended and long shadows disappeared into evening.

Still angry at everything, including Thomas, she justified her emotions. She had a right to feel sad. After all, she'd lost more than anyone alive—at least anyone she knew about.

Beachside houses and hotels disappeared, trailing behind her like sparkling diamonds on the sand. Her head bent, she watched the water play tag with her feet as she walked along the shoreline.

The depression she'd felt before enveloped her like a shroud. After almost a mile, she looked up and stopped walking. It took her a moment to recognize the narrow-fronted three-story house on the beach. The pretty gingerbread facade and fish-scale shingles were a vivid blue accented with white. Someone was lighting a gas-powered wall sconce in the living room and the gentle light filtered through the golden-colored windows.

That was her parents' house. *Her* house. Just 48 hours ago, she'd left that front door to sit on the beach and contemplate her life. And now, she was in a different time looking at her home instead of living in it. It didn't seem possible.

Oh, there were a few changes time—or the lack of it—had made. In Parris's time, the trim was painted the same blue, but some of the wooden fish-scale shingles had been lost, so they had been replaced with asbestos look-alikes. And the beachfront was at least 100 yards longer because the shore had not yet been eaten away by the hungry sea.

She sat on the sand and stared at the house from a distance. Everything in her wanted to go home. Everything in her wanted the safety and warmth of her personal things around her. She had to tell herself that this was *not* home— this was a stranger's home and wouldn't be her family's vacation home for another 40 years.

Although she itched to crawl forward and peek in the windows, Parris clenched sand in her hands and squeezed. It slipped between her fingers and slid from her palms to mingle with the rest of the beach.

So did her tears.

*   *   *

His hands jammed in his pockets, Thomas strode down the sidewalk. The woman was a real problem—a deranged female who had somehow escaped from the crazy house and managed to edge her way into his life.

He was too angry and frustrated to think logically. Right now, he needed distance from the irrational woman who claimed she'd been tossed there from another time.

Anger kept his feet moving toward Clair's car. He had told himself that he would put gas in the tank and drive it back to her. After all, they seemed to be the only survivors of the wreck. Maybe she knew someone else who had made it. Maybe. . . .

He grabbed the gasoline can out of the trunk and began the long trek toward the service station on the other side of town. Cape May hadn't grown enough to have two stations. Thomas wasn't sure it ever would.

By the time he reached the dimly lit station, his anger was reduced to a simmer, and he could once more think of Parris without wanting to choke the hell out of her. It bothered him that she brought out such a strong reaction in him. Pretty women were certainly nice, but they shouldn't deter a man from his goals in life. Female relatives took enough time, effort, and thought. He didn't need a complete stranger taking from him, too.

She probably had a family somewhere and

had escaped from their attic when no one was looking. After all, he had plenty of reasons to believe that she had problems. Her smart mouth was only the first indication. If he needed more proof, her deranged story about traveling from the future should have done it for him. And that didn't include that wild stunt she had used to get Clair to breathe again.

Because he couldn't logically account for her wristwatch, he found her more of a problem than he cared to admit. He'd never seen anything like that before, and he was sure he hadn't heard of a calculator, even if he could figure out what it was. Where had it come from? When she had explained her circumstances, the look in her brown eyes told him she was telling the truth. But that was impossible.

He filled the gas can and flipped an extra quarter to the boy on duty, then headed back to the automobile. It was night, although the stars were only beginning to peep out from behind the clouds.

Walking at a leisurely pace, Thomas stared up at the sky. One of the things he hated about living in New York was that he couldn't see the stars. Some professor from New York University said that the city lights blocked out the starlight. But Thomas believed that no self-respecting star wanted to shine where starving children and women roamed, seeking anything edible to stay alive—or where gangsters were glorified in some daily tabloids like shootists or gunslingers had been in the dime novels at the turn of the century.

Well, that wasn't his ambition. All he wanted to do was expose the mob for what it really was. That wasn't much to ask for, was it? No, a small voice said, just as murdering Charlie's killer wasn't.

When he reached the car, it took him less than three minutes to empty the can into the tank and turn the engine over. He headed toward Clair's home, which was in the opposite direction from that which Parris had taken. Good. He was still too angry to deal with her.

He was certain that, without money, she had no place to go. Sooner or later, she would wind up back in his room, suitably deflated and humble. He just hoped she'd sneak in and not let anyone see her.

Instead of giving him pleasure, the thought of Parris created an ache in his chest. He did what he was best at when it came to the emotional department. He ignored his feelings. But his body didn't ignore how pretty she was or what a great figure she had when she'd stretched out in the tub earlier that morning. His body even responded to hearing her mouth off. She was a challenge, a fun challenge. He felt the stirrings inside him and knew what they meant and who had instigated them. Parris. One more thing to blame her for.

The moon was even brighter over Clair's house than it was in town. He pulled into the driveway and turned off the ignition, then stared at the living-room windows, but gauzy curtains filtered his view of the room, making it look magical.

As a kid, he had walked dark streets and looked into windows of beautiful homes. He was sure that everybody had nicer houses, warmer fires, better furniture, and happier times than he had. And that was *before* his ninth birthday when his damn father had walked out the door and disappeared.

His mother had worked hard as a seamstress in a shirt factory during the day. After work she would return home, collect his sister from a neighbor's apartment, then cook dinner for her family. After dinner, to make skimpy ends meet, she'd sit by the light of one bright lamp and sew for the neighbors.

He'd always thought he should have been born rich, but when he was nine years old and said it aloud, his father had laughed so hard tears had come to his eyes. "Son," he'd said after catching his breath, "I was the one who was supposed to be rich. Instead, your little sister will probably be richer than any of us. With her green eyes, creamy skin, and pale hair, she'll have more opportunities than you and me will ever dream of!"

Thomas had stared at his little two-year-old sister sitting across the table with a noodle hanging from her mouth and wondered how she would ever attain those riches. "Any woman with half a brain and a little cunning can feather

her nest mighty warm," was his father's bitter remark.

Two days later, his father was gone. Thomas had mulled over that scene a lot since then. When he was young, he'd waited for his father to return so he could ask him one more question. If that was true, then why wasn't his mother rich? She was the most beautiful woman he knew, yet she worked night and day and never had more than a penny in her pocket. It wasn't until much later that Thomas realized his father's own slanted viewpoint wasn't law and that his bitterness had been the reason for his lashing out at society— and the other sex—for his own problems.

Thomas had found out as a teenager that his dad had moved to Chicago, where he ran numbers for the mob. The sorry bastard had also acquired a younger, prettier woman to live with and money to blow on anything he wanted. All this while Thomas and his little sister watched their mother work two and three jobs and grow old before her time. . . .

Meanwhile, his sister had followed in exactly the pattern his father had predicted. On one hand, Thomas couldn't blame her for wanting the better things in life. But did she have to get them from a man who had ostracized her from society because he refused to marry her? Did she have to live with a murdering gangster who had killed more than a few people, including Charlie—and flaunted his crimes in front of the press and police?

Jerking his hand, he pulled the keys out of the ignition and stepped from the car. This wasn't the time to think of his sister. She'd made her decisions and he'd made his. This wasn't the time to think of killing a man. He'd get to do that, he knew. But first, he had other priorities.

Thomas knocked firmly and waited for Bebe to open the double front doors.

The maid's honey-dark skin glowed golden in the light.

He smiled. As usual, Bebe never smiled back. "Is Clair all right?"

"She's fine as rain," Bebe stated dryly, standing aside to allow him entrance before closing the door. "She's been waiting for you."

"Well, I'm here now," he stated, walking toward the living room. "Where is she?"

Clair stood in the study off the great hall. "She's here, seeing if she can drink herself into a stupor." She raised a full snifter in salute to him. "Greetings, Thomas. I thought you'd never get here. I have a thousand questions."

Thomas walked past her and into the dark-paneled room, heading toward the decanters and plump crystal glasses on a rosewood tea cart.

"You look no worse for wear," he observed. "Question away." He poured himself some of Sol's favorite brandy—or so Clair had said it was on board ship.

"Did you report the ship's sinking to anyone?"

"Nope," he stated before sipping the golden liquid. It rolled on his tongue lovingly. He had to hand it to Sol. He'd had excellent taste.

"Neither did I, but now we have to. And quickly. We've waited too long already."

"Why? Has someone else been found?" As far as he knew, no one had been, but Clair was obviously up to something, and he'd bet that, whatever it was, it was a move that would be in her favor.

"No. But I can't file insurance claims unless Sol's dead, and I can't prove that he is unless you act as a witness and tell the police what happened. Well, what might have happened," she amended.

Thomas remained silent.

Clair gulped her drink and poured another. She tilted he head and golden light from the lamp sheened her face. One side was red and blistered, the other as creamy and smooth as ever. The sun had highlighted her personality— split. "Sol didn't really mean to do it, you know."

"Really?" he asked with a disbelieving drawl.

"He'd been sick for the past year, and his illness depressed him. But the pain in his stomach went away when he drank, so he drank more and more." Clair walked to the window and looked out. "The last time we were on Ben Warren's yacht, Sol said he could blow it up easily."

"How?"

"All he had to do was put a gallon of gasoline down the bilge, then wait for the fumes to collect. After fifteen minutes or so, if he lit a match to those fumes, it would be the equivalent of placing eight or ten sticks of dynamite inside the hull."

His stomach turned over with Clair's explanation. Thomas pretended to take another sip. It made all the sense in the world—and over 40 people had lost their lives because of a depressed man.

"So, he did it on this trip."

Clair placed her drink on an antique side table. "I didn't think he'd *ever* do it! Ever!"

"Or you would have done what?" he asked in a conversational tone. If his stomach had knotted earlier, it was in several knots now.

"I would have stopped him!" Clair turned to him, her hands clenching each other. "Don't you see? I might have been able to stop him and then no one would—"

"Be dead?"

"No! No one would *know* he was so damn crazy!" Her wail echoed in the room. "Then I'd be able to run part of his business and people might think he'd trained me for it!"

Thomas's fingers tightened around the bulbous glass. "But, because he blew up the damn boat, you might not be able to?"

Clair never noticed his tension. She was too wrapped up in her own. "Right! So now we have to pretend that the boat just blew up and we don't know why. We don't even know why we lived and all those people died!"

"*You* lived because Parris was able to get the water out of your lungs."

"Yes, of course," Clair said, brushing the deed aside. "And I'll thank her for it soon. Maybe I'll send her a gift. Or something."

"I can't wait to see what the perfect something is that one sends to a woman who saved one's life." His tone was dry. His stomach still wanted to heave.

"I'll think of something. But right now, I have several problems that I hope you can help me with."

Thomas downed his entire glass of brandy. "And what would they be?"

"I have one of Sol's . . . contacts on his way here. He'll be visiting sometime after the next week for ten days. During that time, I need to convince him that I can do what Sol did at the, uh, private casino in Atlantic City."

"The company you need the liquor for."

"Yes."

Thomas's ears pricked up. His stomach even stopped its churning for a moment. He knew Sol controlled more than one speakeasy, but he'd only been allowed access to one. Clair, although she loved to talk, was always cautious about Sol's part in the mob. Besides, speakeasies weren't the same as casinos. Not the same at all. One was to drink and dance in, not too unusual a thing in that day and time. New York had almost 10,000 of them. But casinos had gambling and high rollers. "What private casino? And what did he do? Exactly."

Clair sighed, pulled out a lace handkerchief,

and daintily held it to her nose. "He ran the Alley Cat Club."

"Really? I thought it was a speakeasy, not a full-fledged gambling establishment." Thomas had known Sol ran the place. He had linked Sol to the mob-sanctioned club. Rumor had it that a big boss owned it. It was very selective and he'd tried to get in once or twice with no luck.

Clair nodded. "And he didn't really run it. I did."

"*You* did?"

She nodded again. There was a twinkle in her eye. "It never entered your head that a woman could run something that well, did it?"

"Never."

Her grin widened and there was the shine of pride in her eyes. "You thought I was only good in the hay."

He matched her grin although his mind was elsewhere. "You were great in the hay, but I should have known you'd be a good business-woman. You have a certain edge."

"I've been handling everything ever since Sol got sick almost a year ago. His second-in-command, Mark, used to run it. He taught me as much as he could, then backed away about seven months ago and pretended that Sol was still in top form. That way he wouldn't be dragged down when Sol lost everything. Mark didn't like clubs anyway. But the only people who know that now are the ones who work with me in the office. Everyone else thinks Sol made the decisions and I was only the messenger girl."

Thomas's mind was reeling. He'd known the woman was wily and clever. But he never would have guessed how well she could run things. As he thought back, he realized that he'd never bothered looking at her as anything else other than a connection. It was a bad move on his part. A very bad move. All this time and right under his nose. . . .

Rumors about the elite club abounded. Everyone who knew about casinos also knew they created more income for the mob than any other kind of club on the East Coast. He'd heard that the Alley Cat had made big improvements in the past two or three months; he just hadn't put the information together enough to recognize what the improvements might entail. Thomas had no reason to doubt Clair's story. In fact, he believed it more readily than he could believe that Sol was responsible. Sol's habits had proved he was unreliable.

He knew damn well that no matter how much he disliked Clair personally, he'd never let her know until his own quest was successfully completed. This opportunity couldn't have worked out better if he'd tried. "How can I help?"

Clair dropped her handkerchief. With a smile that was slow and sultry, she walked toward him, resting her hand on his chest. "I knew I could count on you."

"Cut the crap, Clair. You want what I can do for you, not my body."

Her smile broadened, her long-nailed finger tapping a rib lightly. "Don't be stupid, Thomas. I want both."

His stomach tightened again. "What do you want most right now?" He grinned, but it took every ounce of his guts to do so. If she asked him to make love to her, he was up a creek.

Her gaze turned hard, and she looked over his shoulder as if she could see something he couldn't. "I want to run that casino. I've put my heart and soul into it."

Relief made his knees weak. "How can I help?"

"For starters, I need imported Irish whiskey for my guest."

"You should be able to get that through the speakeasy end of the business."

"I should. But I got a call yesterday from one of the guys who, uh, helps me out. He heard about the boat's sinking and Sol's not returning yet. He's backing away, and now he says he won't bring any more until he gets clearance from the man."

"What man?" he pressed.

"Al Capone," she said reluctantly. "Although I think he means that he'll take orders from a man, but not a woman. And I need it there before the big man arrives. It'll show I'm still doing a good job."

So Al Capone was the guest. "That's a tall order."

"I know but I don't have any choice. Mr.

Capone loves his liquor, and since he'll be here for almost two weeks, I need enough to keep him happy while I convince him that I'm capable of handling the casino. He wants the good stuff, not the rotgut we serve the gamblers."

The blood that had coursed through his veins earlier in anger now coursed through Thomas in ecstasy. This was his moment. This was the break that he had been waiting for. Before he had seen Sol's deterioration, he had thought Sol had killed Charlie. But when he'd asked around, he learned differently. His sister's boyfriend was Charlie's murderer—and that man was one of the top five men close to Capone. Perhaps he'd accompany Capone to Atlantic City. Thomas stared down at the woman standing in front of him. Suddenly, she was beautiful again. But this time, he knew her mind was as conniving and as evil as slime under a rock. That realization was like a shock of icy-cold water reminding him of when he'd fallen into the ocean. She was necessary to him, but he would have to be sure he balanced her responses to him so he would be involved with her as little as possible.

This was his chance and he wasn't going to blow it. "I'll get the liquor. What's the deadline?"

"They won't let me know the exact time until a day before they arrive, but it's about seven or eight days from now."

He nodded, his mind going over all the possibilities. He might have to buy the liquor outright. It didn't matter. He'd do whatever he had to in order to reach his goal. "Now I have a request to make."

Her eyes gleamed with her own jumping to conclusions. "Whatever could that be?"

"I need you to give Parris room and board here." The idea had just formed and he was saying it aloud. But there was no time to think it through. "You'll need a secretary anyway, if you're going to prove to the big man that you have everything under control."

Clair looked blank. "Parris?"

Thomas raised one eyebrow. "The woman who saved your life."

"Oh."

"She needs a place to stay."

Her brow wrinkled as if she was trying to think. "I don't know, Thomas. I'm sure she's a nice girl and everything. . . ."

"More than that, my sweet Clair. She's the girl who was on board when your dear, departed husband blew up the damn boat. It might pay to keep her on your good side."

He had lied softly, knowing damn well Parris wouldn't do anything. Clair's frown lessened as she realized what he was saying. "Besides, then it looks as if there were two of you helping to run the casino: you with the brains and her handling the details."

She bristled at that. "No one worked his ass off as hard or as well as I did! No one! And some of those jerks know it! *They* were stunned by some of the things I managed in that place. It wasn't by accident that I made the profits I did!"

"Are you willing to tell Al Capone that you did it all on your own at the same time that you took care of your poor Sol, who was suffering from ill health?" he goaded, hoping he'd hit some nerve that would make her agree with him. He needed Parris there.

"Sol never suffered from neglect," Clair defended. "I always took the best of care of him. He never complained!"

Thomas shook his head and stared down at the floor, pretending he believed her, but wasn't sure anyone else would. He didn't know much about Capone's personality, but he could speculate. After all, he'd spent the last year learning about the mob.

"I know you're capable and smart, Clair. That's easy to see. But do you think Capone is always a fair man? He strikes me as the kind of guy who secretly believes that it would take *two* women to replace one stupid man in a man's world. Whether or not it's true doesn't matter. That just seems to be the way the man thinks."

Clair's fist hit the top of the highly polished desk. "Damn it! I'm smarter than most of them, but they never believe that a woman can do *anything* they can do. It's not fair."

He held back the laugh that threatened to spill out. *Fair?* Since when had a bunch of mobsters who killed, raped, and sold dope, women, and hooch been considered fair? Where the hell could her head be that she would even dream of such a thing?

"I know that," he scoffed. "You have the intelligence to go far in this world," he soothed. "And you are one of the most beautiful women I've ever seen. That's a heady combination."

Instead of his words mollifying her, she stared at him, her eyes narrowed. "Who's prettier?"

Damn. She really *was* competitive. She'd give Capone a run for his money, no doubt about it. "I'm not sure I remember. After all, you shine with both assets, and the moment I saw you, I stopped looking at any other woman."

"Try."

It was a demand. His mind raced—he had to choose the right rival or she would think his whole line was to butter her up. He knew Clair, and the rival she was looking for had to have been on board the yacht the other evening. He made a wild guess. "The girl accompanying our esteemed host, for one."

"Virginia?"

"I didn't get her name," he lied. "She was a nice looker, but had a blank expression on her face most of the time."

Clair smiled in satisfaction. "That's because what little brain she had was fried. She was on heroin."

Thomas was shocked. Heroin was one stiff drug, usually only used by the poor and those already half dead. Not by the wealthy. Never by those who had no life to obliterate. "Who gave it to her?"

"I did. But I didn't start her habit, I only cultivated it. Occasionally, Ben Warren used it himself."

"Occasionally?"

She nodded. "Not everyone gets hooked right away, Thomas," she chided.

The telephone's shrill ring made Clair jumped. Her nerves were reacting the same way Thomas's were; they were both too tightly wound.

"I'll get that in the other room," she murmured, walking toward the door. "Make yourself at home. I'll be right back."

"Take your time," Thomas said to her back as she left the room and closed the door quietly behind her.

He mulled over her story. It had sounded very familiar, except that he'd heard it about another woman—Clair.

Bebe had told him that Clair had sold makeup behind the counter of a five-and-ten before Sol met her at a party where she'd been a paid escort. It must have been lust at first sight, because Thomas knew Sol had made her over from her clothes to her makeup. That had been about six years ago.

Finding a man with money, power, and position was every Cinderella's dream, and Clair must have thought she had fallen into the lap of luxury. He wondered how long it had taken her to realize that the trappings were all on the surface. Sol liked to beat up women, especially after he drank himself into impotency. Thomas had also heard that Clair loved sex and would have whomever she wanted, then numb herself with heroin to endure Sol's beatings when he found out. Some cycle.

Bile rose in his throat. To Clair that kind of life was normal. She didn't see the dirty, disgusting world that Thomas saw.

Clair reentered the room and he tried to look relaxed. It wasn't smart to let Clair know anything. He hadn't trusted her in the past; he didn't see any reason to now.

"I'm going to have a small party at the club this week," she confided.

"Is that what you want to do right now?"

"Of course," she looked surprised. "I like parties. After all, I'm not *sure* that Sol is dead."

"But you're going to file for his insurance policy anyway."

"Yes, but the people who come to the party will not be insurance agents."

"Of course not," he stated dryly.

She walked toward him like a cat after its prey. "And you, Thomas. What is it that you like to do? Put pretty girls in other women's houses so you won't feel bad about using them?"

There was a teasing note in her voice, but Thomas knew better. She was asking an outright question and she wanted an upfront answer. "No. I want to make sure that the path I'm picking isn't littered with any more dead bodies.

Yours and mine included."

"What does that mean?"

"It means that I have a few ambitions of my own, and I don't want this boat incident to get in my way any more than you want it to come between you and Capone. My solution is to keep Parris on our side by giving her a helping hand so she's indebted to us. That just seems like a good working arrangement to me." He set his glass on the desk and turned toward the door, pretending to leave. "However, if it doesn't sound good to you, then I'll just make other arrangements."

"Wait!"

He turned, a bored look on his face. "Yes?"

Clair stood, her chin up, challenging him. Then, suddenly her daring was gone. "You're right, of course. I've got too many fronts that I'm fighting on already to worry about her. She'll be fine here, and I'll coach her on the easier matters at the club. Is she willing?"

"Yes." It was a lie, but he had no choice. She couldn't stay in hiding at his boardinghouse forever. Besides, he needed another pair of eyes and ears here at Clair's if Capone was really coming to visit. He needed every scrap of information he could gather. "I'll talk to her tomorrow and get back to you then."

"Fine. Call me."

She walked toward him again, and this time he had the feeling he knew what a fox felt like on the hunt. Placing her hand against his cheek, she smiled. "And then come by when we can have more . . . time."

He grinned, relieved he'd gotten off the hook so easily. "I will," he promised in a deliberately husky voice. "But business calls right now."

"I understand," she soothed, while looking disappointed that her prey had escaped her grasp. "Bebe will drive you to Sol's car at the dock. You can use it until I need it. Meanwhile, I'm calling the police and reporting the accident."

"Thanks. My car is still sitting under that oak tree on Main Street, waiting for a new part from Detroit. It shouldn't take more than another two weeks."

"That's all right. I can't drive both cars," Clair said, dismissing the subject with a wave of her hand. "I just want the investigation to be over quickly."

"It shouldn't take long."

"It won't," she promised with a confident tone in her voice.

He didn't doubt her for a moment. Sol had run the casino in Atlantic City, so he had to have had contacts all over the country, let alone in a small town like this. There wouldn't be too many questions asked.

"I'll let you know if I hear anything about survivors."

She smiled, but her look wasn't pleasant. "Of course."

Thomas left the room, knowing she watched his back even more carefully than he did. He could feel the slings and arrows of her gaze right between his shoulder blades.

Bebe met him in the large entryway and walked with him out to the car. Without a word, she climbed in beside him, and they took off down the road. Obviously it had been arranged for her to go with him even before Clair had told him he could use Sol's car.

As soon as they were far enough from the house that Thomas felt safe, he glanced at Bebe. "Are you okay, kid?"

He could see her smile even in the darkness. "I'm very fine, thank you."

"Is it more difficult since Sol is gone?"

Her smile left. "Yes."

"You know she's been running that casino?"

"If I had, I would have told you. Occasionally, Sol sent me with her to check on her movements and report back to him."

"And did you?"

"Yes, of course."

"And was he appreciative?"

"But, of course. He told me to add money to my account. I did."

Thomas cursed under his breath. Bebe placed a gentle hand on his arm. "It is a bargain with the devil I have struck, Thomas. But I knew that before I took this position. I am not sorry. Charlie was worth it."

He took a breath and tried to calm down. They'd had the same discussion before, and it had never changed things then. Why would it now? "When do you return to France?"

She removed her hand and placed both hands in her lap. "I am planning to leave in another two months, about the same time you wind up your own investigation. But if things get too hot, I may leave sooner."

Thomas pulled up to the dock where Sol's car was parked. Thomas looked around, and saw no one.

Bebe pointed toward the front line. "There it is," she said, as if he hadn't see it.

Bebe handed him the keys.

He whistled appreciatively at the cherry-red car with spoke wheels. "I've always loved looking at this beautiful machine, but I never expected to drive it. I feel as if I fell in a pile of dung that smells sweeter than I could have ever imagined."

"That, my dear friend, is why so many stay in the gutter. The stench of dung soon smells like perfume to the unwary."

Her words were wisdom personified. He opened the door and stepped out of the car. Bebe scooted along the leather interior.

"Will you be all right?" Thomas asked one last time. He knew her too well to try to tell her what to do. She was an independent woman who had ghosts of her own chasing her thoughts through the corridors of hell.

"I will be fine. I hope your friend is better tomorrow."

"How did you know she isn't now?"

"On my way back from delivering Clair's letter to the police, I saw her walking the high end of the beach. She did not look happy."

So Clair had already put the boat report in motion before he got to the house. He should have known.

Thomas shrugged off the feeling of guilt and unease for leaving Parris. "Who is?" He gave a light thump to the side of the car. "You know where to reach me if you need me. Please take care of yourself and I will see you in a few days."

Bebe smiled, but did not answer. With smooth skill, she placed the car in reverse and backed away from the dock. Thomas watched the headlights disappear down the road.

Instead of driving toward the boardinghouse, he pocketed the keys; then he turned and walked down the beach. Maybe he should check to make sure Parris was all right before he went home.

After all, he told himself, now that he had found a place for her to live, he needed to tell her what her duties were. He had washed her back; now she would wash his. Besides, crazy or not, it was essential that she watch Clair. . . .

Chapter Six

Thomas walked half a block in the soft sand before he finally stopped and took off his shoes and socks. His body cried out for a soft bed and 24 hours of darkness in which to enjoy it. But he knew better. There were things to do first. Like finding Parris.

He hadn't gone far when he spotted her sitting alone in the sand, facing the Hempstead house. He continued toward her.

They had built the house the past spring and Thomas had watched it go up. He'd left New York a year ago, following a mob member he'd befriended to Philadelphia, then to Atlantic City before settling in Cape May about four months ago. And he was beginning to feel a part of this community. It didn't seem to matter that he had convinced himself he was heading back to New York's bustling streets as soon as his story—

his quest—was completed. Instead, his mind pretended he was going to remain there. He was becoming involved with these people and their lives. Who was he kidding? He already *was* involved!

Thomas stopped several yards from Parris. Holding his shoes, he stared hard. The golden glow of lights from the Hempstead house reflected on her melancholy face. Even from where he stood, he could tell she'd been crying. Tears glistened against her pale cheeks like a trail of sparkling diamonds.

A wire tightened around his heart. She looked so sad—and so very, very vulnerable. Her toughness was an act, a facade that kept the world from getting too close. If what she said was true, she really had lost everything. Oh, not in the way that he had lost it, where he could go back and relive and relieve those painful memories. But in another way. Unfinished business. It was hard to imagine being in a different time and place. From her point of view, this place wouldn't look like it did now. Nothing remained the same, even his old neighborhood. His mind couldn't help but ask the next question. What would this place look like in her time? How was it different?

Emotionally, he pulled himself away from the woman. Damn it! Hadn't he collected enough female lame ducks? What was he supposed to do? Have a harem of them and still not have one to love him?

He marched purposefully toward her. She didn't acknowledge his nearness, but he knew by her stiff posture that she was aware of his presence.

Once by her side, he forgot his purpose and stood quietly, giving her time to collect herself.

"I thought you'd be asleep by now." Her voice was low and husky, playing sensuously on his nerves more than he wanted to admit.

He didn't answer.

Finally she looked up and locked eyes with him. He never should have allowed that. His glimpse of her bruised soul mirrored in her eyes tightened the wire around his heart so much he could barely breathe from the pain.

She looked back at the house. "That's my family's house."

"The Hempstead house?"

Parris nodded. "Yes. It's funny, but in my time, they still call it that. It was built in 1929 by the Hempstead family. When Mr. Hempstead died a year later, Mrs. Hempstead continued to live it in, raising her three children by taking in boarders. When they were grown, she sold the house and retired to Ocean City to live with her sister."

"Mr. Hempstead is alive."

She sighed heavily. "Then maybe I'm wrong."

Thomas sat down next to her. "No, you're not wrong and you know it. Why lie now?"

Parris uncrossed her legs and drew them up to her, circling her knees with her arms.

"Because I don't want to argue. Because you don't believe me."

It was a simple statement, and one that aimed its dart home with accuracy. He dropped his shoes and rested his arms on top of his bent legs. "Yes, I do."

She turned and stared up at him. The moonlight glowed on her skin, giving her an almost ghostly pallor. For the first time he realized just how absolutely beautiful she was. Truly beautiful. So beautiful she touched his soul. He swallowed hard.

"Why are you lying?"

"I'm not. I believe you."

She stared at the house again. "You're just saying that."

"No."

"Then if you believe me, do you have any idea how I can get back to my own time?"

"None at all."

"If Einstein were here, he'd know."

Thomas wrinkled his brow. "Who's Einstein?"

Parris began writing in the sand, her finger denting it with regularity. "He's a very famous scientist who formulated the theory of relativity. But he's in Germany until a few years before the Second World War. He won't be here until 1933."

"And he could help you?"

She nodded. "He believed in time travel. He was even working on a formula for it, but I don't think it ever came to anything."

Suddenly what she said sank into his thick skull. "Second World War?"

Again, she nodded. "With Germany and Japan when they attack us at Pearl Harbor in 1941. Canada and Great Britain are in the war before we are, though, and a lot of our guys become pilots in their air forces instead of ours."

Thomas felt his throat tighten. "Air force?"

"You know. The branch of the military devoted to air warfare."

As he absorbed these new thoughts, Thomas sifted sand through his fingers. If she was right, the possibilities were endless. Just the thought of taking air power so seriously as to have an entire branch of the military devoted to it showed how legitimate the airplane's progress was. "Do you know who's going to win the World Series this year?"

"That doesn't deserve an answer."

But Thomas was warming to the idea. "Why not?"

"You're trying to make a fortune on a fluke— my fluke."

"What's wrong with that?"

"I don't know, but something is."

"Do you think if someone had a crystal ball and could look into the future, he or she wouldn't use it because something was wrong with it?"

She shook her head, denying his reasoning. "It's taking advantage of a situation by gaining information that no one else has."

"Of course," Thomas agreed. "Our stock market is based on the same principal. So is getting ahead in business, or taking tests where one person has studied more than another."

"That's not what I mean and you know it!"

"It certainly is," Thomas answered. "There's no reason good enough to withhold a few facts about the future that I might be able to use. I'm *not* using it to buy or trade drugs or alcohol. In fact, I'm not using it for anything illegal." *Much.* If he bet a little money with the mob, would that make him wrong?

The sound of the ocean bumping against the sandy shore penetrated their private world. Parris rocked back and forth with its rhythm.

Thomas waited for her answer. He needed as much money as he could get to play with the big boys and win their confidence enough to expose them. He needed it so bad. It would free him—finally allow him to. . . .

"Thomas?" Parris began hesitantly. "Have you ever heard of paradox as it pertains to the future?"

What in the world was she talking about now? he wondered. "Nope."

"It's a theory that says you cannot go back in time and change anything without dire consequences in the future."

"If that's the case," he said dryly, but with a small smile, "I want to assure you that, in the grand scheme of things, there's very little difference between someone amassing thousands or someone amassing millions."

Rita Clay Estrada

But she wouldn't be swayed from her original thought. "Do you believe me?" she asked. "Really believe me?"

"Yes." He wasn't lying. He touched her shoulder, stroking the side of her arm.

His palm grew hot as if his hand had been scalded. Still, he didn't remove his fingers because the thought of not touching her hurt more.

"I believe you," he repeated.

Tears formed in her eyes and a small smile barely tilted the corners of her mouth. "Thank you."

Her unsullied sadness seeped into his thoughts, pushing away the dirt of the world he'd been in for the past year. Clair and Sol and the mob's world.

"You're welcome," he said softly. "Please don't cry. I don't know what to do when a beautiful woman cries."

Parris gave a shaky laugh. "Beautiful or not, I don't think any man knows what to do then."

His hand skimmed up her arm to rest on her shoulder. She was so slender. With her assertive outlook and outspokenness, it was easy to forget just how tiny she was.

His palm rubbed her neck. "You're shaking. Is it me?"

"Partly," she admitted. "The rest of the reason is in that house." She turned back and stared at it. "More than anything in the world, I want to be in there with my own family around me. In my own time."

"I wish you could be there, too." His hand touched her pale face, following the contour of her high cheekbone.

"Doesn't it make sense," she said slowly, "that if I got here through whatever the hole in time was, I would be able to get back the same way?"

"How?" he asked, still mesmerized by the golden moonlight glow of her skin.

"I don't know, but there has to be a way. There just has to be!"

"What happened that night that made it so special from all the other nights you *didn't* travel through time?"

"Nothing much. The weather report said that there was a tropical storm brewing, but I didn't pay attention. Instead, I was sitting right about here, facing the ocean, when I decided that I didn't want to live. I stood up and walked into the ocean. When it got waist high, I began swimming. I swam until I needed to catch my breath. Then, I rolled over and floated, realizing for the first time just how far out I was."

She closed her eyes and Thomas ached to pull her into his arms. He told himself that he only wanted to comfort her. That's all. Instead, he held her hands.

She continued, but her eyes remained closed. A small tear escaped, running down her cheek.

"I got scared, and for the first time in two weeks, I decided I wanted to live." Parris's lashes fluttered; then she looked at him with brown diamond eyes. "I was so frightened I could hardly breathe. But it was too late. The storm had come inland and the water was so choppy. No matter how hard I tried, I couldn't swim back to shore."

Thomas wished there was some way he could stop her tears. But he knew better. Women's reactions weren't mysterious; but he didn't always understand the reasons for those emotions. But he knew that she needed to talk.

"What made you so sad that you'd try such a thing?"

"My parents and brother died," she said simply, and he felt her pain as if it were his own. Slowly, haltingly, she gave him the details of her story.

He was stunned by his own response. Tears stung his eyes as she spoke of her family's closeness, that intangible but steel-strong support they gave each other. He felt jealous and relieved at the same time. Jealous, because she had experienced the kind of family he'd always dreamed of having. But he was relieved because he knew it really *was* possible to have a family like that. It wasn't just a pipe dream.

Trying to commit suicide was wrong, but he understood her reasons for it. The heaviness in her heart was pretty unbearable. He wasn't sure he wouldn't have reacted the same way if he'd lost so much love in his life, but it was hard to miss what he hadn't had. Until hearing her story, he had thought his craving for a close-knit family had been illusive and indescribable. But she had pointed directly to his own wants and placed a name on them, forming them into something he could see and tag. Damn.

Her fingers clasped his hands tightly. "I want them back, Thomas. I want them back so bad I ache."

"I know," he said, finally giving into his own wishes and pulling her into his lap.

It was as if he'd given her permission to let go. Her sobs wracked both their bodies. Crooning, he hugged her close, her cheek pressing into the hollow of his shoulder, and kissed the top of her head. "Cry, sweetie. Let it all out."

Her arms wrapped around his neck tightly. Finally, the dam had broken and her sorrow flooded out all other emotions.

His heart broke with the sound of her anguish. Thomas rocked her back and forth, holding her as tenderly as a newborn baby. It was a long time before her tears faded to hiccoughs, then to sighs. Still they sat entwined on the cooling sand, feeling the night breeze against their damp skin.

He wished he could do something to make her well and happy again, but he knew he couldn't. If she was anything like his sister, she needed to get this out of her system before they could change their relationship.

Change their relationship? He was stunned at the unexpected turn his thoughts had taken. What was the matter with him? He didn't want to change their relationship. He *needed* to keep distance between them in order for his life to stay uncomplicated—unfettered—unchallenged. It was easier to do his job that way. The mob tried to find everyone's soft spot and take advantage of it. If they thought she was close to him, then she would be in danger, too. He wouldn't be safe until his story was out and those men were in jail.

He pulled his head away from hers, forcing himself to relax his grip on her slim waist. "It's all right," he said, but this time, although he wasn't shouting, he wasn't whispering either.

Parris wiped her eyes. "I'm sorry. I didn't mean to do that. I know how awkward it is when someone is crying on your shoulder."

"Well," he said, gritting his teeth to keep from holding her tighter. "It's done now and I'm still here to help in the mop-up." Thomas pulled a handkerchief from his back pocket and handed it to her.

"Thanks," she mumbled, obviously embarrassed. After wiping her eyes, she handed the wadded cloth back to him and pulled farther away, preparing to leave his lap.

Suddenly, he didn't give a damn that she wasn't supposed to infringe on his personal life. In fact, he wanted her in his life. She *belonged* in it. At least for the moment. He knew it was lust. He knew it well. As an excuse, he told himself that everyone needed a little lust in his life. Including him.

Parris made a move to stand. "Wait," he said, and she looked up at him with brown eyes that he could swim in. "Don't go."

A small, sad smile crossed her face and she caressed his jaw, turning heat to fire. "I'm not a substitute."

"I didn't say you were." His voice sounded hoarse.

"You didn't have to." Her other hand came up and cradled his face.

He stared at her mouth. It had to be the most kissable mouth he'd ever seen. Why hadn't he noticed it before?

"It's plain as the lust in your eyes that you want Victoria or Clair. My bad luck is that I just happen to be near when the feeling moves you."

Victoria was everything a woman should be— and more. She was his measuring stick for success—or for what constituted first prize for the winner in the game of life. And if he won her in marriage, he'd consider himself lucky every day of his life.

But he didn't feel the lust for Victoria that he felt for Parris right now. That gave him a twinge of guilt, but he didn't have time to think it through. As for Clair, he was sorry he'd ever played the game with her. She was a viper, not a playmate. No. Parris was the one who captured his basic emotions.

He cleared his throat. "That's not true. You don't know what goes on in my mind."

Parris continued as if he hadn't spoken. "And I need to find a way back to my time. I need to know that I'm not really Dorothy stuck in the Land of Oz. I need to be there. Now."

She pushed off his lap and stood. Her new dress was all wrinkled. Sand clung to the hem and she brushed it loose. Wind danced around them, throwing sand in his face. He had no choice but to stand, too.

The almost-full moon hung overhead, and with unspoken consent, they picked up their shoes and began the long trek back to the parking lot and pier.

Suddenly, Thomas felt bone weary. He hadn't recuperated yet from his fight with the sea. He glanced sideways at Parris. Her head was bowed, her hands dangling at her side as she trudged through the thick sand. Obviously, she felt the same way.

Tomorrow, he would explain to her about Clair's offer of bed and board. He'd phrase it in such a way that she would feel as pleased as an orphan finding her mother. He didn't know exactly *what* he would say yet, but he'd think of something. He always did.

Halfway to the car, Parris stumbled. Thomas reached out to steady her, his fingers wrapping around her arm as he pulled her toward him. Gasping, she bumped into his chest. They both stood still. Her palms rested on his chest; his hands held her arms.

With this lady, it didn't pay to ask, and it was

obvious that Parris wasn't going to offer. Slowly, he bent his head, seeking what he wanted most—her kiss.

Her full mouth parted invitingly and he claimed it. A warning siren went off in his head, but it wasn't loud enough to overcome the sound of passion ringing in his ears. She was feminine, soft, warm, vulnerable, and exciting. He felt every vibrant inch of her pressed against him, and his body called out in the ancient song of lust. His hands slipped down to circle her waist, pulling her as close to him as he could. She accommodated him, and exhilaration coursed through his blood, almost lifting him into the sky like an Independence Day rocket.

When she pulled away, he was stunned. He'd never experienced a reaction like that before. Never. He couldn't be flying higher if he was a kite in a summer storm.

In wonder, his thumb traced the path his lips had touched.

Parris sighed and her warm breath caressed his hand. "I was afraid of that," she said softly.

"So was I."

His thumb touched her teeth and she bit lightly before answering. "This isn't going to work, you know."

"I *don't* know that. As far as I'm concerned, it just did."

"You're wrong."

"Are you always so opinionated?"

"Yes," she answered pulling away. "And if you

tell me you think it's a masculine trait, I'll walk away right now."

He grinned. He hadn't known he liked to debate, until now. "I would never admit that to an opinionated woman."

Her laughter, low and sexy, caught him in the gut. "I knew you were smart. It just took time to prove it to me."

They continued toward the pier, not speaking. They didn't have to. The calm rhythm of the ocean's waves was their cadence as they reached the tarmac, put on their shoes, and walked to the car. Parris might be an opinionated woman, but she followed well, too. Without asking a lot of questions, she realized that he was leading and complied without balking. He opened her door and the indescribable scent of real leather wafted from the interior. Parris slipped into the front seat and waited patiently for him to climb in and drive away.

"Is this yours?"

"No. Mine broke down and I'm waiting for a part."

"Is it Sol's?"

He was surprised. "How did you know?"

"This looks like a man's car. Besides, you said Sol's car was parked at the dock."

He gave a grunt, then paid attention to his driving.

Once at the boardinghouse, he parked by the side entrance, and they quietly repeated the pattern they had followed yesterday. Parris seemed to understand that she couldn't be seen, and she was as stealthy as the best gumshoe.

They reached Thomas's room, and she took off her shoes so the noise wouldn't alert his landlady below. On the chair by the window sat the packages from the shops they had visited.

Parris turned worried eyes to Thomas. "She knows you're buying clothes for a woman. Will she be angry?"

"No. Curious, maybe."

Like an excited child, she ripped into the bags, pulling out her purchases and checking them over again. Finally satisfied, she turned, stood on tiptoe and kissed his cheek.

He wanted more.

"Thank you again," she said softly. "I really do appreciate all you've done."

Her full, parted mouth took the focus of his attention. "Sure I can't persuade you. . . ."

"I'm sure."

"All right." He sighed heavily. "But I demand the right to sleep in my own bed. I'll share it with you. I'm not gentlemanly enough to sleep on the hard floor again."

She stared at him a long, silent moment, and he could feel the anticipation of touching her starting a chain reaction in his body.

"Fair enough."

Without another word, he walked out of the room and down the hall to the bathroom.

He needed a cold bath or a lobotomy. He was

feeling so confused by his reaction to her, he wasn't sure which.

Parris slipped off her dress and underwear and set them aside on the other chair. The hose were silk—sweet sensuous, slippery, cooling silk. Not even the most expensive, sheerest nylon compared to the feeling of those. No wonder it took a world war to make women give them up.

She reached for her T-shirt and slipped it on, using it as a nightgown.

Now what? Was she supposed to go to sleep or wait for him to return so they could lock up? She didn't know, so she did what she wanted—she lay down on the double bed, gauging the amount of room she would have by sharing the mattress with him. Not much.

For some reason, she didn't care. The memory of his kiss made her stomach flutter again. She thought she'd been in love once or twice, and her nerves had done some funny things then. But it was nothing like her intense reaction to Thomas. In all her adult years, she'd never felt quite that way. Certainly it wasn't love; she didn't know him well enough for that. And she wasn't sure it was lust either. So what was it? And why was she denying herself a night in his arms?

The answer came immediately. *She was afraid she wouldn't measure up to his idea of a woman.* It was that simple and that complicated. No matter how much she might believe that she was a liberated female, the thought of that handsome devil laughing, or *not* being turned on by her, gave her the willies. She'd never recover from that ego bashing. Better to turn off all these thoughts than go through the humiliation of not being desired.

She closed her eyes.

No! her mind cried out. Her body was stiff with holding back her impulse to go to Thomas. Suddenly, she sat up on the side of the bed. Was she insane to deny herself a small piece of happiness? After all, she might be stuck in this time forever. Then she might never meet another man she would want to be with, and Thomas might not be free anymore.

Or better still, she might find a way back to her own time, and then all this would be behind her. She'd always regret not making love to the most handsome, frustrating man she'd ever met, in this time period or in any other.

With that thought planted firmly in her mind, she walked out of their small bedroom, through the living room and to the door. She opened it cautiously and peered around the molding. Mrs. Timmers stood at the far end of the hall, her back to Parris as she checked the linen closet, putting away sheets. Just as quietly, Parris closed the door and started to counted. When she got to 30, she felt the door push toward her.

The landlady was trying to get into the room. Panic immobilized Parris, and for a moment, she couldn't think. Instinct took over. Bolting, she headed into the bedroom, then dived and slid across the wood floor until she was under the bed.

Mrs. Timmers's heavy tread vibrated on the floor as she walked into the room, and Parris held her breath, waiting for the woman to leave. The landlady's slippered feet were planted at the foot of the bed for several long moments, and Parris wondered what she had left out that had caught the landlady's eye. It didn't matter what it was as long as Parris wasn't available to confirm her presence in a male boarder's room.

The woman leaned down and scratched a protruding vein on the side of her ankle. Parris had to release her breath slowly and inhale equally as slowly so she wouldn't make any noise. Her lungs clamored for air. She was sure anyone within 100 yards could hear her heart thumping, echoing like a hollow drum.

After what seemed like an hour, but was probably only a matter of minutes, the landlady shuffled out of the room. The door was closed quietly behind her.

Parris stayed where she was, praying the woman was really gone, but unwilling to trust her own senses. Besides, the ringing in her ears blocked out everything.

Two minutes later, Parris was sure that Mrs. Timmers was gone. Just in case she wasn't, Parris crawled out carefully, keeping her eye on the door.

Her adrenaline pumped so hard, she pressed

a hand to her mouth to suppress the giggle that would give her presence away.

Her jeans and shirt were on the bed, clean and neatly pressed. Mrs. Timmers obviously did one heck of a job on laundry. Parris wondered why she had stood at the bed so long; then she spotted what had held the landlady's interest. On top of the blouse sat a small plastic container holding Parris's driver's license, library card, two credit cards, and a picture of her family taken the last time they were together. Mrs. Timmers had obviously removed the holder from Parris's jeans when she had laundered them.

Her skin flushed, then heated with possibilities. The dates on her license and library card were too far into the future for the landlady to believe they were real. So what would she believe? That they were falsified documents? That would be the obvious assumption. Would she go to the police? Tell someone else? What reason was there for using dates so far in the future on phony documents?

Parris couldn't think—couldn't reason out the problem when she was panic-stricken. Suddenly, she wanted a man's arms around her, comforting her. She was so tired of fighting the world for her own space in which to live. Just for a little while, she wanted someone else to solve her problems because she couldn't solve them herself.

And that thought amazed her, too. She'd always been so strong, so capable—so ready to tackle anything. What was the matter with her?

Before she realized it, Parris left the room and scurried down the hall to the bathroom. Without knocking, she tried the door. It was unlocked. She walked in, closed it quietly behind her, and stared at Thomas lying in the tub.

His eyes were closed, his brow etched in a scowl. She wanted him to hold her—to tell her that everything would be all right. She craved for him to make love to her until she couldn't remember the thousands of problems assaulting her.

In return, she would give him all the love she was capable of giving—even if it was only for the moment.

Chapter Seven

Thomas's thick lashes fluttered, then opened to show eyes as troubled and as sea blue as they were earlier. Then his dark brows rose inquiringly. "Trying to tempt me or just drive me crazy?"

"The former, I hope." Her voice was a whisper.

His gaze drifted down her legs to her bare feet, then up again, resting briefly on her breasts. "I thought you didn't want my advances."

His low, husky tone slid down her spine like a sensuous caress, and she took an unsteady step toward him. "I do now."

"Why?" Although his gaze was hot, he sounded so detached he could have been talking about the weather.

Taking a deep breath, she slowly approached

him, slipping her T-shirt over her head. By the time she reached the side of the tub, she stood in French-cut panties, and then they disappeared.

His eyes widened. "I've died and gone to heaven," he murmured.

She smiled. Her worry that Thomas might not like what he saw was put to rest. In one smooth motion, she stepped into the half-filled tub and straddled his legs, facing him. "The water's chilly," she murmured, not really caring.

"I don't feel the cold anymore." His heart-warming grin was slow in coming. "Is it my birthday? Is that why I'm being rewarded?"

She shook her head. "No, that's why *I'm* being rewarded."

"It's *your* birthday?"

"I've been through hell and deserve a reward," she corrected, lowering herself to sit on his thighs. Just before her weight rested on his, she hesitated.

"Don't stop there," he said, circling her waist and pulling her even closer to his hard stomach.

"I don't want to hurt you."

"That's refreshing," he commented dryly, with an edge of roughness in his tone. "But I think I should be contemplating that question." He positioned her firmly on his lap, his eyes boring into hers. "Are you a virgin?"

She felt a blush creep up her neck. But she answered as if it was the most natural question in the world. "If I was, Thomas Elder, I wouldn't have made the first advance." She mentally held her breath for his answer.

"God, I'm glad." He lightly kissed the top of her breast.

She sucked in her breath, forcing out the word. "Why?"

"Because this isn't the time or place to teach a novice." His lips moved lower until he finally captured a pouting nipple between his lips.

Her breath caught in her throat at the exquisite torture. She sought his chest and felt the springiness of the hair beneath her palms. The water engulfed her hands, warming her wrists. Warming her insides. Warming her heart. Her breath came in short gasps; the feel of him, of his very being, made her light-headed.

His hips rocked and she swayed with him. Her hand clasped him, seeking to give him the same pleasure he was so intent on giving her. Instead, he took charge once more. Holding her waist, Thomas lifted her up, then back down, fitting her to him exactly.

His teeth flashed. "Beautiful body. Beautiful breasts."

"Shhh," she whispered into his ear, teasing him with her breath. "Your landlady is somewhere in the hall."

"Then we'll be as quiet as lovers in the back seat of a buggy parked behind a rectory."

She wanted to laugh at that comparison, but he didn't give her a chance. Instead, his mouth completely covered her breast, teasing the dark areola with the heat of his moist tongue. His hand cupped her other breast, his nimble fingers lingering to lovingly stroke her nipple.

She sighed raggedly. "Mmmm."

"Me, too," he whispered.

She opened her eyes and stared at him. His look spoke more than words could ever say; his touch was more electric than the lightning storm the night she found him.

Thomas tugged on a strand of her hair, bringing her mouth to his. His lips covered hers softly, gently. He seemed to savor her movements as much as he instigated them. He held still, his mouth seeking, then finding the pulse in her throat.

Tears threatened to spill over. Making love with Thomas was important to her, but just as important was the imprint of another person verifying she was alive and whole and steeped in reality. In living.

His hands weren't a dream. His mouth wasn't a dream. His body, strong and supple and working magic on hers, was as real as her own. Mixed with the excitement of being with Thomas was another emotion—relief.

She'd never made love to a man in her dreams before. She doubted if she had begun now. That meant she wasn't dreaming and all this was really happening. She was here. She was alive.

His lips trailing down her neck to her breast distracted her once more. "Yes," she whispered, her hips moving enough to cause small waves of water to lap against their bodies.

"Sweet lightning," he exclaimed softly, tightening his buttocks and thrusting forward to touch deep inside her, igniting another flame that lit her eyes with promise.

Parris arched her back, her hand seeking, then finding and stroking his shaft. Suddenly, everything was centered in her midsection, coiling, tightening into a hard ball of searing fire. She felt the water weave its spell as she stiffened with the first onslaught of a climax that began a warning roar in her ears.

Thomas must have felt the beginning of her tiny explosions, too. His hands tightened on her waist as he ground her against him, accentuating the pleasure that flowed through every pore of her body. Her hands clenched his shoulders as she leaned toward him, her mouth devouring his, her intense passion sparking his.

Minutes later, she lay limp against his chest, her breath light and feeble. His hands caressed her back and hips, traveling up and down, then soothing her sides.

He kissed her cheek. "Thank you."

She chuckled, then muffled the sound with her hand. "You're welcome."

"Why are we in the tub? We should be in bed where it's dry and comfortable."

"As opposed to wet and wonderful?" she quipped, slowly pulling away from him and standing. She grabbed the towel from the rack and wrapped it around herself, the end neatly tucked into the top. "The interlude is over. The man wants comfort instead of fantasy." She sighed dramatically.

"That's not right," he answered, his intense gaze devouring every inch of her wet, exposed skin. "If you want wet, I'll make you wet, and without a tub full of water."

Leaning down, she whispered in his ear, "I'll meet you in the room."

She stepped daintily from the tub and opened the door. After peering cautiously down the long hall, Parris disappeared.

Thomas leaned back and closed his eyes. His position might have passed for the same one he had been in when Parris had entered the bathroom. But everything was different. Everything.

This was almost the end of the Roaring Twenties, as some of his esteemed colleagues of the press called the decade. Everything was wild and crazy and filled with chaos. Women were fighting for emancipation in all phases of life, including work and sex. The world was changing so drastically, it turned lives upside down.

But Thomas never would have believed anyone who tried to tell him what the past two insane days would be like. Including the past half hour.

Parris puzzled him. No matter what he expected from her, she did something completely different. She was a pain in the butt, yet she was endearing. She reminded him of his sister, but she also reminded him of the most sensuous woman he'd ever met . . . and that woman was the most successful madam in Philadelphia.

With decisive action, he stepped from the tub, pulled the plug, and absently listened to the gurgle as the water drained. He cursed softly as he realized Parris had left with his towel. Taking the shirt he'd discarded earlier, he dried himself off, tied the ends around his waist, and went out the door and down the hall.

Now that he'd had a taste of her, he wanted more. He needed to hold her all night long. All too soon, she'd be living with Clair.

He also needed to tell her about that plan—which wasn't going to be easy.

In bed Parris waited for Thomas. Her newly cleaned and pressed clothes were hanging in the closet; her driver's license and pictures sat on the dresser top.

She still wanted Thomas's arms around her, reassuring her that all would be well. She still wanted to be back in her own time. She still wanted to wake up and assure herself that this nightmare was over.

The door opened and Thomas stood there, his dress shirt tied around his waist like an Indian breechclout. A soft giggle worked its way out, then was followed by a chuckle, then a muted laugh.

His stern glare wasn't honest enough to remain

that way. Slowly, his own smile peeked out, carving a dimple in his cheek. He came toward her, his hands on his hips, the front-tied sleeves swaying back and forth with each step.

"So you think I look funny?"

She nodded, still trying to control her mirth.

"And you obviously believe I did this to amuse you?"

She nodded again, her hand covering her mouth in an effort to stifle the laughter.

"Well, little lady, think again. You walked off with my towel." He edged around the side of the bed. "And now, you owe me a favor."

"And what would that be?"

He stopped by the side of the bed, his hands still on his hips. "I'm not sure yet, but I'll think of some horrible deed that needs to be done."

She stared at him boldly before her gaze slowly drifted down his body, then back up again. "Take it off."

He did.

Then they made deep, satisfying love.

Late-morning sun streamed through the open window and kissed Parris's face with warmth. Yawning and stretching, she awoke with the most wonderful sense of well-being. It wasn't as if she didn't know what had happened two weeks ago. It was as if she'd known, grieved, and gone on with her life. Her life with Thomas Elder.

That thought made her eyes pop open, and she

stared at the empty space next to her. Thomas was gone.

She slipped from bed and grabbed her T-shirt off the floor, pulling it over her head as she walked barefoot toward the other room. When she reached the door, she halted, charmed by the picture Thomas made. He stood by the window, dressed in deep gray slacks with minimum pleats sitting low on his hips. Still bare chested, he had a starched shirt dangling from his hand. Sunlight poured through the lace curtains, flowing over his body like liquid. His other hand held her wallet inset. He stared at it as if it would speak any moment, and his frown grew even deeper.

"Thomas?"

He looked up, then back down at her driver's license. "Where was this?"

"In my back pocket."

"It's real." He didn't ask—he knew the answer.

"Yes."

He flipped the plastic with his thumb. "And this is your family."

She knew the photo. Her parents, brother, and she were seated around an umbrellaed table at Rockefeller Center. They'd spent two days in New York and had just come from a Broadway show. They were all laughing, so very happy. "Yes. It was taken several years ago, just before I started college."

"Those are the cars of the future."

She walked over to him and glanced around

his shoulder. She'd never noticed before, but in the background was a taxi stand where several cabs were lined up—all various shapes and sizes.

She chuckled. "Some are, and some are as old as the hills."

He dropped the plastic on the table and turned to her, his distant gaze the color of blue ice. "I forgot to tell you last night, but you'll be staying at Clair's home for a while. She needs a secretary and I thought you would fill the bill."

Suddenly she drew a blank—as if she was missing a piece of some puzzle. She refused to acknowledge the hurt she also felt. She'd deal with that later, privately. "Clair? When did this happen?"

"Last night."

"And you're just now getting around to telling me?"

He slipped into his shirt and began buttoning it. "You didn't seem to be too interested in listening to much of anything last night, so I thought I'd tell you this morning."

"*Tell* being the operative word," she stated, trying to control her reeling emotions. "And you consented to this without my permission or my input."

"Input?" he asked. "What a funny word." He picked up his cuff links and put one through his cuff. "I didn't think either one of us had a choice. My landlady doesn't allow women in the room. You don't have a job. I have work to do.

All those things add up to your accepting Clair's kind offer."

"I see. We're going to pretend that I didn't come from another time, that last night didn't happen, that neither Clair nor Victoria are bitches—different in form—but bitches none-theless."

Not looking at her, he checked his cuffs, then walked into the bedroom. "That's right, tootsie."

Words wouldn't come to her. Parris stood in the middle of the room, too confused by the chain of events to follow what was happening. One day he made love to her as if she were the most precious thing in the world, and the next day he was as cool to her as if she were a stranger.

Two minutes later, he came back into the room, adjusting his suit coat.

She found her voice. She'd also found her anger. "What the hell is going on here?" she demanded. "And where are you going?"

"Don't act like a shrew, Parris. It's unbecoming." He patted his pockets, double-checking that everything he needed was there.

"Don't you *dare* patronize me," she growled, the sound coming from deep in her throat.

He stared at her and she glared back, refusing to give a mental inch to this man.

Thomas made a sound of disgust. "I don't have time for this. Behave yourself, and when I get back late tonight, I'll take you for a bite to eat, then to Clair's house."

"Go to hell, Tommy."

"Don't call me that."

"Don't ask for favors."

"I'm telling you to be civil," he corrected. "I already got your favor last night. Me and probably a hundred other guys."

He couldn't have aimed truer if he tried. And if she'd been a Victorian maiden, she would be swooning by now.

Instead, she smiled. "That's right. And you didn't make a passing grade." She stepped past him and headed toward the bedroom. "If I were you, I'd polish up my act. You need to remember that sex is a partnership sport. You didn't even make it to the playoffs."

She didn't look back. Instead, she closed the door behind her, then leaned against it. The explosion she expected never came. She heard the front door open, then close. She was alone.

Her shoulders slumped. With shuffled steps, she made it to the bed and plopped on the mattress.

"That son of a bitch," she muttered into the feather pillow. It was the last thing she said for hours. The ever-present tears wouldn't allow her to say more.

Thomas drove toward Atlantic City with purpose, concentrating on the route as if it were paved with gold. The real reason he concentrated was so he wouldn't think of Parris. Parris in her undershirt with her hair mussed enticingly, as if she'd been making love all night. Parris staring at him as if he'd lost his mind. Parris slinging insults with the accuracy of a tournament dart thrower. Parris on the verge of tears, wondering what kind of ogre he was.

"You're one fine son of a bitch," he bit off, letting the words flow in the air.

He knew Parris knew him by that name, too. He also knew she didn't realize why he had behaved so rudely. She couldn't see inside him, his fear. Parris had breached every defense he'd ever built. That alone was reason enough to lash out at her this morning. It wasn't fair, but it was certainly understandable.

No, it wasn't, you jackass, he told himself. He'd emotionally hit her for something that bothered *him.* That made him no better than Sol for beating Clair or his father for blaming his mother for everything that had gone wrong in his life.

Damn, he hated to admit it, but the whole situation wasn't anyone's fault but his. He'd been way out of line when he talked about their lovemaking, and she'd only retaliated with her own sharp words because of his stupid remarks. He had to tell himself that because he didn't want to think that she might be right.

He pushed the gas pedal and the car shot forward. The sleek Bentley with candy-apple-colored spoke wheels purred toward Atlantic City—and maybe some answers.

*   *   *

Anger and frustration burned pink spots on Parris's cheeks as she stepped into the little dress shop where they'd gone yesterday. A bell above the door tinkled and the same woman who had waited on her emerged from the back.

"I'm back," Parris said brightly. "You're Emily, right?"

"Yes," the woman said warmly. "What can I help you with?"

"This time I need something a little more . . . dressy."

The woman smiled. "Right after you left yesterday, I remembered a dress your size we had been holding for another customer. The customer decided against it, but I hadn't had time to put it back on the floor. I think the dress would be perfect for you."

"Show me now," Parris urged, and the woman did.

Twenty minutes later, Parris signed the ticket that held instructions to have it billed and delivered to Thomas.

She repeated the same process at the shoe store, where she bought shoes, a purse, and two pairs of those lovely silk hose. Then she picked up more cosmetics from the drugstore. Those she paid for with the five-dollar bill she'd found in the bottom of Thomas's sock drawer.

Lastly, she ate at a small seaside restaurant. The fish was delicious, the sauce wonderful—served on a bed of rice that had been skillet browned before being strained. She was sure the cooking oil was filled with cholesterol, but she refused to let it bother her. When in Rome. . . .

While sipping her coffee, she stared at the ocean once more. It was comforting to be near it. When she didn't see it for a long time, she missed it. If she couldn't hear it, she felt uncomfortable. Parris wondered if the ocean had something to do with her traveling through time, but she didn't know. She just needed to feel the connection with the large body of water to know that everything would be all right.

Not like her connection with Thomas Elder. The name rippled through her mind far too easily, considering he was a jerk. Any man who could claim to be a virgin was the *only* man who had the right to demand that of his mate. Yet he had used that very thing against her. She wasn't his mate either, so he had no room to talk—or to accuse.

It didn't matter that she'd only been with one other man. To someone like Thomas, one man was as good as 100 men.

She sipped her coffee, trying to forget the evening of love they'd spent together. It was impossible. Those moments had been wonderful, touching, and nothing he said or did could take that memory away from her. For a short time, she pretended that she'd been loved by a man who was wonderful and worthy of love— even if it was only for the moment. That was something many women never experienced, and she felt blessed by it.

She swallowed hard. So what if the man was a bastard in every other regard?

Sighing, she laid money on the table and stood, ready to take the next step. First, she had to look her best for the party at the Morrows'. Early last night she'd decided she wouldn't embarrass Thomas by showing up. But that was before his insults and cruel rejection this morning.

So, if she was to spend the rest of her time in this awkward day and age working for Clair, then she'd leave old Tommy with a bang-up memory to hold dear.

That was the first thought to satisfy her since she'd come out of the water and found herself in a different time.

Thomas steered the Bentley onto Victoria Morrow's street. The moon playfully darted behind the clouds. He could have cared less. He was exhausted from the day's activities and churning up the complicated thoughts about Parris. He wouldn't be going to Victoria's party if he hadn't already committed himself.

He had come straight from Atlantic City. All day long he'd been under pressure. First, he had spent hours talking with the police about the accident report concerning Ben Warren's yacht. They had already begun the paperwork, since the yacht had been registered out of Atlantic City. Clair had been right. There were no other survivors anyone knew about. There had been proof of the ship sinking—lumber littered the coast.

Then for his news article, he talked to gangsters who would just as soon slit his throat as look at him. Despite what he'd heard, there was little discipline in that brotherhood. It was hard to believe that most of the major cities from Chicago to the East Coast were ruled by crime. Most people didn't recognize it until they went into business for themselves or lost a relative to drugs or hootch. More and more young kids were getting suckered into the so-called fraternity, looking for acceptance. Besides, Al Capone and his ilk looked so glamorous, with beautiful women draped on their arms and the newest automobiles in their driveways. By the time the dirty, worm-infested side of the business was known, it was too late for a young kid to back out.

Once Thomas made his appearance at the Morrows', he would pick up Parris from his digs and take her to Clair's home. She needed to get settled as soon as possible. And once she was, maybe he could take the time to find out what her life was like in the nineties. Perhaps she had information that might come in handy later.

He felt awful about their argument this morning, but he couldn't help it. Although he truly believed she was from another era, the impact of that truth hadn't hit him until he saw the picture of her family. He had realized then just how much separated him from Parris. It wasn't clothing, thoughts, money, or even morals. The villain was time. She came from somewhere he only dreamed about, and her sudden appearance was damn frightening.

For a moment, he remembered holding her in his arms, and his stomach tightened at the memory. He'd never known anything like the feelings he'd experienced then. That was scary, too—damned scary.

He pulled up behind another auto and killed the engine. The street was lined with cars—the Morrows' party was obviously in full swing.

Putting thoughts of Parris in the back of his mind, he pasted on his best boyish smile and walked up to the screen door, knocking hard to be heard over the Victrola playing in the parlor.

Victoria walked toward the door, a happy smile showing her delight at seeing him. Her white-and-blue dress reminded him of a Southern belle—an innocent Southern belle. Parris's comments about Victoria came to mind, and he wondered if she was right and this young girl was less naive than he thought. One look into her eyes, and he ditched the idea.

With a flick of her wrist, Victoria unlatched the screen and pushed it open. "Well, it's about time, Mr. Elder. I was beginning to think you might just miss our little party completely." She scolded him with such a beautiful smile.

Thomas entered. "I couldn't think of anything else all day, Victoria," he lied. "I rushed through work to get here as fast as I could."

"Why, Thomas, what a sweet thing to say!" She looped her arm in his and led him toward the dining area. "Your cousin swears that you get caught up in your work, though, and that you hardly have time for family."

A spear of heat coursed through him. It took everything he had to keep his face blank. "Cousin?"

"Of course, silly. Mama invited her. Remember?"

Thomas's gaze searched the double-doored entryway to the dining room. The large mahogany dining table was pushed against one wall, and chairs lined the perimeter of the room. The Oriental rug had been rolled up and put away. Several couples were dancing to a lively tune. Others lounged in chairs or stood in small groups and conversed.

Thomas found Parris immediately. She was laughing up at a young man who looked utterly enchanted with her. She looked beautiful and beguiling. Searing anger flooded through his veins. It took everything he had to force himself not to move toward her, reach for her neck, and stran—

"She's such a charmer, Thomas," Victoria continued. "I swear, I think *everybody's* in love with her."

"I just bet," he bit out. His teeth couldn't have been more clenched than if he were a hungry bulldog with a rabbit between his jaws.

"And my brother, Jeffie? Well, he just thinks she hung the moon."

"She did."

Victoria laughed, and for the first time, Thomas noticed that she seemed to do it on scale. So much for natural. It was another reason for being angry with Parris: She forced him to look at Victoria in a way he hadn't wanted to do.

Forcing a smile, he turned to her. "Would you keep that young man company for just a moment, Victoria?" he asked. "I have to discuss some family business with my cousin."

"That's my brother. He hasn't left her side all evening." Her smile disappeared, replaced with a slightly fake look of concern. "I hope it's nothing serious."

Thomas leaned forward, brushing her hair with his lips. "Her mother's not well."

Victoria pulled back. "Mother? I thought I heard her say that her mother died, and she was raised by *your* mother."

Damn! He thought he'd have a few moments to find out what story she'd concocted. "Her mother is dead, but she thinks of my mother as her mother, and I want to tell her what the doctor said."

"Ohhh," Victoria said, giving his arm a sympathetic squeeze. "By all means."

They walked over and Victoria wound her arm around her brother's. "Come on, Jeffie," she said to the reluctant young man. "Thomas needs to talk to his cousin."

Parris waited until they were out of earshot. Her smile was bland. Her gaze settled somewhere over Thomas's shoulder. "Thomas needs to talk to his cousin about what?"

"What the hell are you doing here?" His whisper shook with agitation. "And how in the world did you find the Morrows' house?"

"I was invited. Remember?" She smiled sweetly, but he could hear the bitterness in her voice. "And I asked Emily at the dress shop. She gave me explicit instructions. By the way, thank you so much for the dress. And shoes. And hose."

Whatever it had cost for her to look the way she did, the money was well spent. Under any other circumstances, she would have been able to charm every penny from him. But he wasn't going to tell her that. "I didn't pay for them."

"The bill is in the mail." She stood and smoothed her skirt. "It couldn't happen to a bigger stinker."

"That's unfair!"

"Nothing's fair. Including my being stuck with you. But that's the way fate dealt this hand. I'm only doing the best I can."

She finally faced him. "By the way, the police came and searched your room today. If I hadn't left when I did, they would have found not only my clothes and identification, but me, too. And what a story I could have concocted for your landlady! It would have been the bee's knees," she stated sarcastically, and he felt his own frustration and anger building again.

She held up her hand as if she was placing words on a marquee. "How about 'Woman kidnapped off boat to be love slave for demented cousin?' Or 'Amnesiac wanders into the arms of lover only to find his mass-murder graves.'"

"You're nuts. Do you know that?"

Her smile was as sad as he felt. "We all are. For every far-out story, there's a *National Enquirer* to print it."

He frowned, confused by her reference. "*National Enquirer?*"

"Never mind." She sighed. "Besides, what's important is that the police seem to think that you had something to do with the boat's sinking. Did you have a grudge against Ben Warren?"

Thomas became wary. "I hardly knew the jerk."

"Well, his wife knew you."

"He wasn't married."

"According to the records, Virginia somebody-or-other was his wife."

Thomas stood stock still. "Says who?"

"The police who visited your room. I listened outside the door. When they came out, I hid in the bathroom."

His mind spun with possibilities. So Ben Warren had kept his wife a secret from the mob to protect her. It wasn't much but the *Tribune* would love a touch like that.

Or maybe Parris was lying.

No, he knew better. Oddly enough, in this whole mess, she was probably one of the only two women he trusted. Bebe was the other one, and he knew her reasoning behind seeking vengeance. Bebe, too, had loved Charlie.

Suddenly, Thomas was tired, tired of everything. But he was especially tired of being angry with Parris when he really wanted to hold her in his arms and make love to her until the next full moon.

He held out his hand. "Come on," he said softly. "It's time for us to leave."

Parris withheld her hand for one long moment. "Where are we going?"

"To Clair's. By way of Kansas." He smiled, this time admitting some of his feelings to her. "Or at least by way of the moon."

"Why, cousin," she said with a teasing note to her voice. "I do believe your intentions aren't honorable. And we're not even in the South, where they have kissing cousins."

"Who says?" he declared, steering her out of the room and down the hall. "New Jersey is the only keg state tapped at both ends: New York and Pennsylvania. That accounts for some craziness in families."

"What does that expression mean?"

"That both states drain New Jersey resources and leave their residue behind."

"Dear sweet heaven," Parris murmured, following him through the screen door. The party was still going strong, and they wouldn't be missed. "I'm beginning to understand the problem. That might mean it's time for me to move on."

"Not yet." He calmed his heartbeat. She was only talking. She didn't know how to get back yet. "I get to pick your brain first."

"Wonderful. I finally meet a man who wants me for my mind. My mother would have been so proud."

"That's not *all* I want, but it's a start." His needs seemed to hang in the air between them, giving help and hope to her floundering senses. If his needs were her own, they were once more in harmony.

Chapter Eight

Thomas chose the beach road for the drive to Clair's house, and since the windows were rolled down, the salty night air touched Parris's face. She leaned back, inhaled the fresh scent of the sea, and wondered what would happen next in this grand adventure.

Would she have to force her way back into her own time or would she touch the water and slip into it? She hadn't thought of that before, and the idea of such a simple solution excited her. But she wasn't naive enough to rule out that anything could happen and that returning home might not be so simple at all.

"Are you ready for bed?" Thomas's voice was low and caring, sensuously washing over her as much as the faraway sound of waves soothed her.

"No, just relaxing," she said. "I was as worried

as you probably were tonight. I didn't want to make a mistake with those people, because they might be able to help me later. Someone, somewhere, has a piece of information that might help me figure out how to get back to my own time."

"Don't you like it here?" He sounded as if she'd hurt his feelings.

"Not really," she admitted, unwilling to mention that he was the one good thing about the era, and even then, he didn't care enough about her. "I need to return to the time just before my parents' car accident so I can stop it."

"Do you really think you can do that?"

"Yes."

"How?"

She gave a brittle laugh. "If I knew the answer to that, I'd be doing it now."

"What are you going to do meanwhile?"

"Get prepared."

The car leisurely purred along until they reached the docks. Thomas veered around the parking lot, reluctantly edging the car to the road to Clair's house.

Parris tried to concentrate on the changes in her life, but she couldn't. Every time she stared into the darkness, she saw Thomas as he looked when he was making love to her in the tub. His face tight with passion, his beautiful body slick with water. He'd made love to her so exquisitely knowing what buttons to push, what words to say to evoke her deepest responses.

Almost from the moment they'd met, she'd known that for her, he'd be lethal. That was one of the reasons she'd kept the conversation between them smart and sassy. Until her little foray into the bathroom with him, she'd used words as a wall and she needed to do that again.

Her walls were necessary if she was going to concentrate on getting back to her own time and saving her brother and parents. It was her hope, her reason for living, and getting emotionally involved with Thomas only muddied the water. But until she figured out a way home, she needed Thomas's logical input and help.

Another thought occurred to her. "By the way, why do you want me working for Clair?"

All the way across the seat, she felt his guard go up. "As I told you, you need a place to stay and a job, and she needs a secretary."

"And?"

"And nothing, tootsie." His words were clipped.

Parris crossed her arms and stared straight ahead. "Very well, Tommy. Don't expect me to get out of this car until you tell me why I'm staying in Clair's house. You've got something going on, and until I'm sure what it is, I don't think I want to be a part of it."

The car's headlights illuminated the road ahead, and the dunes on the ocean side looked like dark, dinosaur humps. Parris kept her eyes glued to the darkness beyond the windshield as she tensely waited for Thomas to say something.

"I'm telling you only once. Don't call me Tommy."

"Go to hell, Tommy."

The car skidded to a halt. Thomas turned, his gaze lit by the fire from the dash lights. "No one calls me Tommy. I hate it!"

"Well, you call me tootsie! And I *hate* that name!"

"Why didn't you say so!"

"I said it the only way I know how!" she yelled back.

In the dim recesses of the car, Parris watched Thomas lean back and close his eyes. She was weary, too, and she would have liked nothing more than to rest her head against his shoulder and relax her guard for just a little while. But despite her earlier thought, she knew that depending on him wasn't the answer. Her self-reliance would solve the problems confronting her. But, oh, it would be nice if there were two of them in this boat heading across the sea of life. Two instead of one. . . .

Thomas pulled her to him, curving his arm around her shoulder. "All right, let's talk." He leaned back again, obviously content with her near him. So was Parris.

"Clair's husband ran a business in Atlantic City. Now that he's gone, she wants to manage it. In order to do that, she needs a secretary. You fit that bill."

"What business?"

"A speakeasy and casino."

"I didn't know gambling or drinking was allowed there now."

"Now?"

She nodded. "In my time, Atlantic City is one of the gambling capitals of the country."

He frowned. "What kind of gambling?"

"The usual—craps, blackjack, slot machines."

"And drinking?"

"Prohibition will be repealed in a few years and the country will begin drinking with a vengeance."

Thomas sighed. "And I just figured out how to make money."

"Life's a bitch," she said, quoting a saying from her own time. "And then you marry one."

His deep chuckle reverberated against her ear. "God, you're crazy!"

"Thank you," she said when he stopped laughing. "Tell me why you want to know what Clair is doing."

He suddenly sobered. "How did you know?"

"Don't dodge the question. Tell me the truth or you can forget this setup."

"Okay," he answered reluctantly. "But if you tell anyone, both our lives aren't worth a buffalo nickel."

She breathed in his unique scent and wondered how anyone could not be attracted to him. "Promise."

"I'm a reporter for the *New York Tribune*. I'm working undercover on a story that will put Al Capone's mob behind bars or have me wearing cement overshoes—one or the other."

Cement overshoes—the words chilled her. The saying might have been trite in her time, but she bet that it was new, and accurate, in this time. Now that he'd said he was a newspaper reporter, everything made a lot more sense.

Still, she needed confirmation. "You're not a gangster?"

He sighed heavily, as if it were a burden to admit. "I feel like it half the time, but no, I'm not a gangster."

"I'm glad," she whispered, her hand reaching out to rest on top of his. He turned his hand over and clasped her fingers, weaving them between his. Warmth flowed through her, and she leaned back and enjoyed the feeling.

She should have known that something was up with Thomas. Although he knew Clair well, he really wasn't the type to fit in with her crowd. He didn't have that uncouthness and ruthlessness she thought gangsters should have. And since he didn't, she didn't want to see him get hurt or end up dead because of the mob.

"I hate to tell you this," she said, "but no one will get Capone until several years from now, when he's finally caught by the IRS."

Thomas looked at her. "He is?" His voice rang with excitement. "How?"

"They will nab him for tax evasion and put him in jail." She furrowed her brow, trying to remember the details of the old *Untouchables* television series. She hadn't seen the newer version, so she had to go strictly by memory—which wasn't that good. "I think he ends up in Alcatraz." She remembered some of the movies of her era—including the one her brother played in. "It seems to me that he dies of syphilis. Then, there's John Dillinger, who dies outside a movie theater somewhere. He's gunned down by the FBI."

"What else do you remember?"

"I don't know," she admitted. "My knowledge of history isn't that fine honed. But I remember bits and pieces."

"Name some."

Parris thought a few minutes, her mind concentrating on her memories rather than his hand on her back and his warm breath feathering her brow, but it wasn't easy. "Well, I told you about Black Tuesday, the stock market crash sometime in October of this year. Too many people buy on margin—I think right now, the margin is ten percent—and sometimes that money is borrowed, so people aren't really millionaires except on paper. However, many manage to make it through the crash and become millionaires later after the Great Depression."

"How long does the depression last?"

"Until World War Two."

Thomas, deep in thought, absently kissed the top of her head. She warmed under his touch. Parris wondered if he knew what he was doing. She forced her thoughts back to the questions at hand.

"What costs the most money in your day?" Thomas asked.

"I don't know. Let's see. Rolls Royce's Silver Cloud, Mercedes Benz cars. Stamps. Real estate, especially in New York, Connecticut, downtown Chicago, and anywhere in California. Actually, the South grows by leaps and bounds."

"If you remember anything else, let me know."

"Why? What do you plan to do with the information?"

"I'm not sure."

Parris puzzled over it a moment. "I can see you making a killing on the stock market or in real estate if you were going forward in time with me. But you aren't."

"You don't know that." His voice was tight.

Parris laughed in disbelief. "Neither do you. You hadn't even thought about it until I just mentioned it."

"Don't be so sure of yourself, Parris. You're no mind reader."

"And you're paper thin when it comes to some things, Thomas Elder."

He sighed, sitting up in his seat. It was the signal that their peaceful interlude was over. "I think it's time we get going before we're at each other's throats again."

Regretfully, he was right. They seemed to be able to shoot sparks off one another quicker than flint. Parris ran her hand through her hair in an attempt to straighten it. She didn't need to get involved with this man. All her energies should be focused on getting back to her own time.

Still, she noticed that Thomas was as reluctant as she was to face the present. It took him forever to reach for the ignition key and turn it. He pumped the gas pedal before the engine raced in the dark, filling the car with sound.

"By the by," Thomas said, his frown deepening as he looked at her. "This being a part of Clair's household could be risky. Very risky. Especially if they find out who I am."

She gave a half smile. "I know."

"You can call it quits now and I won't hold it against you. In fact, the more I think of it, the more I like the idea of maybe getting Victoria's mother to put you up for a while. I think she'd love it." The frown marks between his brows eased. "Yes. That's it. I'll move you there."

"Why do that?" she asked, surprised that he'd hook her up with Victoria when he hadn't wanted them even to speak to each other earlier.

"I don't want you to be a part of this. They're dirty people, tootsie, and sometimes their dirt can rub off."

"If I help Clair, will it help you with your story?"

"Yes, but that's not the point. You could be in danger. These aren't the same type of men we left at the party just now. These Joes don't care if they have to get rid of you. They just do it."

"I'm aware of that, Thomas. In fact, this isn't

175

your decision; it's mine. If I decide to do it, you have to go along with it."

He looked belligerent. "Who says so?"

"I just did," she stated calmly. "Didn't you hear me?"

He drove on in silence for a little while, and Parris knew he was thinking of all the things he wanted to say, but wouldn't. Now that she knew what he was doing, he would try to keep her on his side. Finally he said, "Are you sure?"

"I'm sure."

"Stay out of Clair's business matters. Just do the job she tells you to do, and then, keep your nose clean."

"Sounds simple enough," she said dryly, wondering how she could do both. Not that it mattered. She'd do what she wanted to do to help.

"I don't have my clothes," she said, hoping he'd turn the car around and take her back to his place. Then it would be too late to return to Clair's and she'd have one more night with him.

"I'll bring them first thing in the morning," he promised.

Her heart plummeted. It was her last excuse.

In a matter of minutes, they were in Clair's driveway. Bebe, stoic as ever, answered the door and ushered them in.

Talk was one thing, but doing was another. Parris could feel the tension tighten every nerve in her body as she stepped into the living room. She sensed that Bebe and Thomas were nervous, too.

Clair was waiting, a half-filled glass in her hand. Parris had the feeling that this drink wasn't her first. Perhaps that was a plus.

"It's about time," she snapped. "I thought you were supposed to bring her earlier this evening."

The palm of his hand was hot on the small of Parris's back as he moved her forward. "The Morrows' party was tonight."

"Why you bother with those stuffy people, I'll never know," Clair stated before downing the last of her drink. "They don't have a bit of fun in them."

"And you obviously have too much—all in the name of liquor."

Clair ignored him as she walked into what appeared to be an office. They followed. Thomas left Parris's side to head to the tea cart used as a bar. When Clair lifted the cut-glass bottle, Thomas put his hand on top of it and held it down.

"You can do whatever you want—as long as it's after this interview."

"Says who?"

"Me."

His tone was strong, challenging. For a moment, Parris was sure Clair would hit him. Instead, the older woman carefully placed the bottle back on the cart and turned her angry eyes on Thomas.

He sighed. "Listen carefully, Clair. I was at the police station in Atlantic City today. They seem to think that there might be a link between you and the accident. The word is Sol blew up the boat."

"That's a lie!" Clair spat. "I told the Cape May police that someone on board had threatened to do it, but that I didn't know who it was."

"You should have played ignorant, Clair," Thomas admonished. "I told them what they already suspected. It works better that way. I also said that all you really knew was that you were with me on deck. Right or not. They went through my room today, but it was strictly a formality. What matters is that we've made up a reasonable story and that it is believed. Otherwise you'll lose managing the club."

"Damn." Her tone was harsh.

"Do what you must to make them believe you. Parris will help substantiate our story."

Clair turned vicious, taking out her frustrations on Parris. "And what is it you do that makes Thomas want you in our lives? Anything I can guess?"

Parris kept her gaze steady. "Obviously I can't compete with you on the liquor level. You're in a class by yourself."

Clair's chin rose. "In that case, you must be one hot cookie straight from the oven, dear. Obviously brains aren't part of the package."

Parris was trading insults with a drunk. Great. Just what she needed. If she didn't get the upper hand, she'd be walking out of there before she was ready.

"This isn't going to work," Parris stated, turning to leave. "I'm not putting up with a drunk just to help an old friend. She'll ruin anything anybody's got planned before giving it a chance. I don't want to be around to watch another ship sink, metaphorically speaking, of course."

For a moment, Thomas's blue eyes flamed in anger, then suddenly he caught on.

"You promised you'd do this for me." His words were a statement.

"Not under these conditions. Use my expertise somewhere else. Not here."

Clair wasn't as drunk as she pretended. They now had all her attention. "Where would you go?"

Thomas and Parris ignored her, concentrating on each other, the only two actors in a very important play.

"Don't you think I should take the offer from the West Coast? They were sending me a plane ticket to get there."

"I know," Thomas stated wearily. "But I need you here. Clair needs you here. At least until"— he hesitated a moment before continuing—"the guests are settled."

"Why are you doing this for her?" Parris was blunt, and out of the corner of her eye, she could see Clair flinch, then turn toward Thomas as if she, too, was waiting for his answer.

"I feel responsible. I was getting ready to do some business with Sol and never noticed he was going over the deep end. I should have seen the same signs in him that Clair did, and I should have acted on them. If the gentlemen find out, they'll wonder why she's in the position of power she is. They'll consider it a bad decision to leave her there."

"Now, wait a minute," Clair began, but Thomas ignored her.

Following his lead, Parris did, too. "But if she's not worried, why should I be? My boss won't care about her problems—or yours for that matter. He just wants things to run smoothly."

"Who's your boss?" Clair's voice was demanding.

"A sweet gentleman named Roach," Parris answered absently. If Clair's expression was anything to go by, the bait was better than Parris had first thought. Clair's eyes were as big as the full moon. The other woman didn't notice that Thomas had a surprised look as well.

"Look," Clair began in a placating tone. "I was too distraught to pay attention to what you were doing here. I need your secretarial skills, Parris, and I would love it if you helped me out." She laughed lightly, but Parris heard the forced emotion. "Besides, I could use another woman's companionship. It's so lonely here. Not like New York at all."

Parris stared at her. "No more drinking on the job then. We've got our work cut out for us; we don't need alcohol messing things up."

"Of course," Clair murmured, placing her glass on the tea tray and moving away. "I'll have

Bebe show you to your room."

Clair looked at Thomas; then with a sigh, she left the room.

Thomas had refused to look back. Instead, he stared at a painting of Sol on the wall behind the desk. It not only made the man look handsome, but also refined. That put the artist in the same class as a fairy-tale illustrator.

Parris waited until she heard Clair's voice down the hall before saying, "Good job."

Thomas still didn't look at her. "Thanks. See you tonight."

"How?"

"I'll find you."

Before Parris could answer, Clair was in the doorway, Bebe standing quietly behind her. With a backward look over her shoulder at Thomas, Parris followed Bebe out of the room.

At the end of a hall, Bebe ushered her into a room. It was clean and airy, with open windows covered with daffodil-yellow chintz curtains, and a matching yellow chenille spread on the bed reminded Parris of her grandmother's home. She walked to the window and stared out. A light breeze ruffled the curtains and they billowed lightly around her as her skin cooled.

"I'll find a gown and a robe for you," Bebe stated from the open closet. "There should be one or two extras around here."

"I don't need them." Parris's gaze sought the ocean. She hated gowns; they always tangled in her legs. She heard the waves and prayed that when dawn came she'd be able to see them, too.

"Maybe not tonight," Bebe said, pulling an extra blanket from the top shelf. "But you will tomorrow. We have people coming and going. It would be prudent to wear something to cover your body if you plan on leaving the room." Bebe hesitated. "Sometimes, even if you don't."

Parris looked over her shoulder. "At night?"

"Some business associates stay overnight to do business. It is easier than lodging in a hotel. This way they can talk until early in the morning and not be . . . overheard."

"I see," Parris said slowly, absorbing all the information and wondering if she was going to make it through the night.

Bebe turned and began to leave. "Bebe?" Parris hesitated, then plunged on. It was better to find out the situation now rather than later. "Have you been with Clair long?"

Her expression was guarded. "A year."

"What's it like to work with her?"

Bebe retreated even farther. "She's a hard task-master, but she is fair."

Curiosity made Parris press even more. "Was her husband fair, too?"

"But of course. Did you expect less?"

Parris walked over to the iron bed and sat down. "How long have you know Thomas?"

"You should ask the gentleman that."

"Do you enjoy his company?"

Her expression was as closed as a vault door. "You should not be asking me these questions, Miss Parris. I think maybe you should ask Monsieur Elder. I am sure he will be 'appy to tell what he would wish you to know." Her French accent seemed thicker than before. Parris wondered if it was due to stress or one of Bebe's ways of pointing out the differences between them.

Parris smiled. "Obviously, we both know more about him than we care to discuss," she murmured. "Listen, Bebe. I need all the help I can get in trying to get through this time period. If there's anything you know that can make it easier, please help me out."

Bebe stood by the door, ready to flee. But Parris knew her interest was piqued by the conversation. "What do you mean, *time period*?"

It was Parris's turn to be reticent. "I mean, well, ever since the boat sank, it's been a tough time. Nothing seems to be the same."

"And do you come from 'ere?"

"No. I'm from Philadelphia. But my parents owned a summer home not far from here."

"On the beach?"

"Yes." She stood. "But it's not there now."

"How interesting," Bebe stared hard at her, and Parris felt as if she was seeing right through her. "Did it flood?"

Thoughts of her family brought that old familiar sadness with it. Suddenly, she wanted to be held and comforted. "Not exactly."

She wanted Thomas. Where was he? Was he making love to Clair? That thought hurt so much she could hardly catch her breath. "I think I'm tired now."

Bebe turned toward the door. "Please call me if you need anything. My room is across from yours."

"Bebe." Parris stood and walked to the black woman. "Thank you for your help tonight."

"You are very welcome, Miss Parris."

"And call me Parris. I'm an employee here, just like you."

Bebe looked surprised, but she nodded in agreement.

"Bebe," Parris began slowly, unsure of how much to tell the woman. "I can't explain it all right now, but I need a friend."

"Monsieur Elder is your friend."

"Yes, but he won't be here. You will."

Very, very slowly, Bebe allowed a smile to tilt her lips. With a petite figure, cafe-au-lait skin and huge brown eyes, she was absolutely beautiful. "I will try."

Parris took her hands in hers. "Thank you."

A bump against the windowpane made both women turn. Thomas, one leg over the sill, looked at them. A grin spread across his features as he looked at their entwined hands. "Help me, will you?"

Keeping her laughter as silent as possible, Parris clasped his hand and pulled him inside. Her heart was buoyant again. He *wasn't* in Clair's arms. In fact, judging from the wicked look in his eyes as he stared down at her, he hadn't been with the other woman at all.

He grinned and one dimple slashed his cheek. "Miss me?"

"Immensely."

"Good. I'm hanging around for a while and I want you to be happy about it."

"As long as you behave yourself," she whispered back.

His brows rose. "I was hoping not to."

"That's my kind of behaving."

She earned his chuckle as a reward. The door closed quietly behind them, and Parris turned around.

Thomas lightly kissed her ear before whispering in it. "Bebe just left. We're alone. I want you."

She arched her neck to give him better access, her breathing as light and airy as his touch. "Why?"

He didn't move, and reluctantly she looked at him. His expression was dark, thoughtful. Her stomach pitched.

"Parris, I want you to understand that I love being with you, but I'm not looking for a long-term commitment. Just a little fun."

She pretended his words didn't hurt. "Why are you telling me this?"

"Because I'm worried that you might misunderstand. I'm really intrigued by you. In fact, I like you too much to hurt you."

She looked hard at him, refusing to allow her hurt to show. No matter what the time period, men hadn't evolved that much. Men in her day tried to qualify relationships, too. That didn't keep her emotions from plunging to dark depths. Jealousy was a hard taskmaster, one she couldn't control. "Do you like Victoria too much to hurt her, too?"

He stiffened. "That's different, and you know it."

"Right." Parris pulled away, unwilling to acknowledge how much she ached. He wanted to have his fun with her and to keep his respect for Victoria. Well, she wasn't going to be anyone's substitute. "Then I suggest we both go our separate ways and you won't hurt anybody."

The silence was so thick that Parris was sure she was knee-deep in it. But she refused to turn around and look at him. She knew she'd burst into tears.

Finally, he spoke. "I need to talk to you about tonight."

"We'll talk tomorrow."

"No."

Suddenly, she looked at him. "Yes," she stated. "Now leave the way you came in. I'll see you tomorrow."

He looked as if he was going to argue. Then without another word, he left the way he came.

The room was empty without him, but not

as empty as her bed was. That was all right, she told herself. She'd been right in kicking him out. If she had let him stay, she would be crying harder than she was right now. . . .

Chapter Nine

After crying herself to sleep, Parris had thought she'd resolved her man problems. But she realized she was wrong when she awoke in the middle of the night and stared at the ceiling. At best, what little rest she had gotten had been fitful, and no matter how hard she tried she couldn't fall back to sleep.

Damn that man! Thomas needed to learn a lesson that was not easy to teach. He'd made the mistake of categorizing women—all women. Victoria was the sweet, virginal love of his life—fantasy or otherwise. And Parris was assigned the role of the earthy, gal pal who was all right to want, but not all right to marry.

Clair wasn't a factor at all. If she had been, Parris was sure she would have seen sexual byplay between Thomas and her, but there hadn't been any.

She didn't know where Bebe came in, but it was pretty obvious that although she and Thomas liked and respected each other, there was nothing sexual going on. So that left Thomas's harem of two, which was one too many.

"It's a tough choice, boyo, but you'd better make the right one," she muttered, conversely wishing that Thomas was there to hold her, if only for a little while.

Purposely, she chose another topic to dwell on. Her next problem was even more immediate. She was going to be a secretary. Dear sweet heaven, she *had* one, but she'd never *been* one! Aside from following orders, what did a secretary do?

Parris thought back to the beginning of her career, when she'd shared a new typist with two other accountants. Barbara had been the model of efficiency, even when she was rattled by the amount of work that had to be done. She was so good that she had become a full-fledged secretary within months.

Aside from the normal computer management jobs and accounting procedures, what else had Barbara done? Parris suddenly remembered what she liked most about Barbara: She had had experience with the people in the office and made her knowledge available to Parris. Parris had been overwhelmed when she'd started her new job. Fresh out of college, Parris was unsure of anything that didn't directly deal with accounting. Barbara had set up a routine to follow, then gently moved Parris into it. Barbara's practices also fit into the general office's system, which made Parris's mainstreaming into the office staff a lot easier.

But that hadn't been all Barbara had done. She'd kept her ear out for office gossip and information, then passed to Parris all the pertinent data, as well as likes and dislikes of the upper management and more lucrative clients. It had worked in Parris's favor more than a few times in her past six years with the company.

In fact, until that moment, Parris hadn't realized just how much she'd relied on her secretary and how much she owed her. Rumor was that Parris was going to be offered a partnership, and in all honesty, half of that partnership was due to Barbara's looking out for her boss's interest.

Right now, acting as Clair's secretary seemed hopeless, and she was sure that by the end of the day, Clair would fire her. But Parris had no choice. Besides, Thomas—complicated, in-love-with-another-woman Thomas—needed her. And she would help because she needed to give something to him in return for all his help. Whether he liked it or not.

Besides, it was nice to feel needed again. Even if the man who needed her was a genuine stinker.

She hated feeling like a dog in the manger, but she did. As much as she wanted all of Thomas's attention and loving, she also wanted to go home. And if she ever made it back to her time, he would have to carry on without her. Wasn't it better not to have his emotions on her conscience, too? An inner voice told her she was right, but her heart still felt lonely without him.

Go figure.

With a heavy sigh, Parris pulled up the sheets, took a deep breath of the damp, sea air, and finally fell asleep.

True to his word, Thomas had sent all her belongings over and Bebe had brought them into her room sometime in the early morning, because everything was on a chair, in the closet, or in the bathroom when she awoke in the morning. After eating a hasty breakfast and waiting for Clair to get up, Parris and Clair finally set out for the hour-long trip to Atlantic City. Parris loved being behind the wheel, so she didn't mind chauffeuring Clair.

They arrived at the Alley Cat Club a little after noon. Clair, her sunburned face caked with thick makeup, directed Parris around to the alley, where double steel doors were propped open by two badly dented metal trash cans.

"This will do," Clair said, sliding in her seat until she was at the car door.

Parris glanced at her in the rearview mirror, then cut the engine. Until then, she hadn't noticed just how small the old rearview mirrors were. Times had changed.

They both got out of the car, and Parris followed the older woman inside, stepping over a mop left on the wet floor. They were in a none-too-clean restaurant kitchen. Enormous gas-stove tops were caked with grease; the wood worktable running the length of the room was equally filthy. Parris wondered how many people had suffered with bouts of food poisoning from eating food prepared there.

Clair marched through the swinging doors and into the dining room, Parris hot on her heels. Dirt and disorder were left behind once the doors swung closed behind them. Plush black carpeting covered the entire room except the postage-stamp-size dance floor in the center of the cavernous room. There were alcoves throughout, making each booth area private and protected. A few even had royal-blue velvet drapes that could be drawn for even more privacy. Around the perimeter of the dance floor and small stage for the band were various gaming tables, scaled to fit lengthwise from the floor to alcoves, fanning like a sunburst.

"Danny, where are you?" Clair's voice was firm, filled with authority.

"In the back office, Clair," a man's voice called. They followed the sound to another hall jutting off the front lobby, passing the rest rooms as they went.

Another large room, Parris determined. But this one had a ceiling that was twice as high as the club's ceiling. No windows here, either.

Tall, old-fashioned black telephones and pads of paper filled several tables that were lined up in the front of the room. In the back was another door. Parris still followed Clair. Once inside those portals, the decor changed again.

This was obviously the heart of the club, where behind-the-scenes decisions and negotiations were handled. This room was decorated as if it were a library in one of the wealthiest homes in America. Floor-to-ceiling glass book shelves lined two walls, and the third was a rich, red brick, with a fireplace in the center. The last wall was papered in a deep red-brown-and-blue-paisley pattern. Parris could make out two narrow doors that had been wallpapered to disguise the openings. Good taste apparently knew no bounds. Even gangsters had taste.

Clair smiled tightly. "Good morning, gentlemen."

Three men—one wearing a dark brown suit that blended with his swarthy coloring, and the other two in rolled-up shirtsleeves—stood facing them. Parris could feel their hostility.

"Who's that with you?"

"My secretary, Danny."

"My, my," the man in the suit sneered. "Aren't we the Wall Street executive?"

"At least she's respectable. Not like others I know."

"Since when did you get a secretary?" Danny asked belligerently, staring at Parris as if she were a bug.

"She's been working at our house with Sol and me. Now that Sol's . . . gone, I'm bringing her here to work." Clair circled the desk. "So cut the crap, Danny. We know too many secrets about each other to bullshit."

Parris continued to stare back, alternating her gaze among the three men. Clair's words must have struck a chord, because they all began to relax.

"How long have you had a secretary?" Danny asked.

"Privately? Longer than you've had those two," Clair retaliated. "How was the take this past week?"

Parris realized Clair and Sol must have taken off work to be on the yacht. And Danny was second-in-command.

"Over our quota. Don't worry. The figures look good. Have you got the new set of books?"

"You'll get them next week." Clair pulled out a key from her purse and opened the bottom drawer. Slipping out a file, she began reading.

Danny didn't hide his impatience, but his tone of voice was a different matter. "When's the big man coming in?" he asked solicitously.

"He canceled this week. He'll be here in another week or two," Clair murmured vaguely, her gaze on the file's papers.

"And when do his men come in?"

"A few days before."

Parris watched glances flow between Danny and his two friends. "Except for the books, we're ready."

"Good." Clair closed the file, replaced it in the drawer, and locked it. "Now, I told the cook to have a crew in to clean up that kitchen. What happened?"

Danny looked irritated. "Nothing. We just don't have the time to baby-sit a cleaning crew. Besides, it's clean where they cook. Nobody sees the kitchen, so why bother?"

"Because we could be cited for a dirty kitchen. You know that."

"By who? The cops are on our payroll."

"But not every city official is, Danny. The mayor and some of the city council aren't," Clair stated as if speaking to an idiot. "We don't take chances on having someone poke his nose in where it's not wanted. You also don't park in a no-parking zone or in front of a fire hydrant. Only small-town punks trying to thumb their noses to show how big they are pull stunts like that. Otherwise, it's not smart."

Danny looked irritated, but he kept his own counsel. His friends, though, were easier to read. They obviously thought Clair was stupid for paying attention to such small details.

Clair sat down in the plush leather chair and began going through the morning mail. "Okay, let's get to work. It's going to be a long day."

The rest of the day *was* long. Some of the paperwork had been completed by 7:30 that night, which was just about the same time that the band struck up. The chef brought in dinner and set a small, cloth-covered table by the hidden doors. The food smelled delicious and tempted Parris's palate, but she hadn't forgotten the state of the kitchen. Her appetite was stingy at best.

Danny joined them, ate in silence, then left.

"Are you following all this?" Clair asked quietly.

Parris nodded. Clair's change from bitchy, helpless female to woman executive, then to more-than-competent co-worker was nothing less than astounding. And Parris felt herself responding with admiration to her new boss. Despite knowing what the business was, she had to admit she worked well with Clair.

However, if Parris had thought that her generation was striving for equality, she hadn't realized until now how far women had come. Women in Clair's time period were so far down the totem pole that only the true game players could survive.

"Danny's two men don't agree with a thing you say, Clair. As a matter of fact, I think they're a mirror of Danny's own feelings. Birds of a feather. . . ."

"I know." Clair leaned back and stared into a cup of coffee laced with cream. "We'll just have to be careful and keep an eye on them."

"You're right about the kitchen." Parris's voice was so soft it was almost a whisper.

"I know, but I'm not sure if I should press the point."

"Do it," Parris confirmed. "I'll watch the crew and keep them in the kitchen area. One of Danny's henchmen can watch me."

Clair's gaze lit with admiration. "Wonderful idea. I'll get the chef to organize the workers. And that also means I'll only have to deal with two men instead of three for a day. Maybe for once I won't feel so outnumbered."

"Certainly not intellectually," Parris stated dryly, for the moment feeling unusually close to the woman and her problems with the business world.

They both laughed.

After dinner, the casino workers began dribbling in. Parris could tell by the sounds beyond the office door that the nighttime activities were gearing up.

Still, they had work to finish. Parris typed letters on an ancient Underwood typewriter kept in a closet hidden behind the wallpaper. Her fingers hurt from pounding the keys hard enough to make an imprint on the paper. There was no correct button, tape, or liquid to eliminate errors. She had to begin again with every major mistake, which was frustrating.

Filing wasn't any easier. All files were kept in a cabinet inside the closet, and they were numbered rather than labeled. Only those who were familiar with the files knew the system, and Parris wondered what they were trying to hide. If the police confiscated the records, they'd go through each scrap of paper. So why hide them under file numbers?

But when she asked Clair, the answer was simple. "It's not for the police. It's so the workers can't come in and pull a file for information. *They'd* have to look through each file."

Parris was learning.

When they left the casino at one in the morning, the guests were still swinging. New Orleans jazz tunes played while dancers zigzagged across the small dance floor. The gambling tables were manned by men and women dressed in tuxedos or long gowns. Classy. Very classy.

If Parris had had the energy, she would have loved to people watch. As it was, all she could think of was the hour-long ride home she still had ahead of her.

That night, she was asleep in bed within ten minutes of arriving home.

That first day of work began a pattern that developed six days a week over the next two weeks. Parris learned more about the casino business than she would have ever imagined. Her mind reeled from the facts and figures, and being a CPA came in handier than she cared to admit. Two sets of business books were kept: one for the mob and one as a front for the restaurant and dry nightclub. There was no bar that the customers could see. Drinks were mixed in a room behind the dance floor, then brought to the table by waitresses in French-maid costumes. In case of a raid, the contents of all the glasses would be poured into the flower vases on the table.

What surprised her most was that she and Clair got on so well. They seemed to understand each other's needs well enough that explanations usually weren't necessary. And in a career that was dominated by men, they were the only ones they could relax with. Parris had to laugh when she thought of her situation. Adversity made strange bedfellows.

In all that time, she never saw Thomas. She had expected him to check on her, or at least to let her know what was going on with the police or if his landlady had said anything about seeing Parris's identification. He'd acted as if he'd wanted her to watch Clair; then he never came around to inquire about what she might have learned. She was completely baffled, she told herself, refusing to acknowledge the deep hurt that was just below the surface of her emotions.

Every spare minute she thought of him, she also wondered if he was with Victoria. Even though the thought brought an ache to her heart, the idea also lingered in her mind to tease and taunt her.

"Damn the man," she thought every early morning when she went to sleep.

"Damn the man," she thought every late morning when she awoke.

Obviously, she had a little emotional conflict to work out. And as soon as she had a minute or two to herself, she'd have a nervous breakdown.

Damn the man!

Over their usual coffee and rolls late one morning two weeks after Parris had started her job, Clair and she read sections of the paper in silence, which had also become part of their ritual.

"Chanel is having a showing in New York," Clair murmured.

"She's tops."

"You know her styles?"

Parris looked up. "She's an institution in the industry. Her perfume alone is a household name."

Clair stared down at the newspaper again. "The Waldorf Astoria Hotel was torn down to make way for the tallest building in the world. Something called the Empire State Building."

"I know."

"RCA stock is soaring."

"Any dividends?"

"No," said Clair. "But it's selling at three hundred dollars a share. Maybe I should buy it now."

"Wait a while, Clair. Save your money and put it into the stock market after November. You'll make a killing then."

Clair continued to read the paper. "The game of bridge is really catching on."

Parris glanced up. "Do you play?"

"No, but I've always wanted to learn. Do you?"

"Yes. My roommate in college always needed a fourth, and I was elected. It was a great way to learn. But I haven't played for a long time."

"College?"

"Just a year." It was a lie, but better that than try to explain.

Clair put the paper down. "We'll have a house-guest tomorrow."

Parris lowered the paper. "Al Capone?"

Clair nodded, her expression solemn, but there was excitement in her eyes.

Parris's own heart beat fast at the thought of really meeting the legendary gangster, but she remained outwardly calm. "Do we do anything special?"

"Just give him the best room in the house and let him tell us what we don't know."

"Or what he thinks we don't know?" Parris raised her coffee cup to her lips.

Clair laughed. "That's about right. But, my, I do love powerful men."

Bebe set small bowls of jam on the table between them, then reached for the coffee-pot. Parris watched her putter around and decided it was time to end this present situation of worker and servant. "Sit down, Bebe. Join us for coffee."

Both Clair and Bebe looked at her, obviously startled by her command.

Parris took a deep breath. It was time for the beginning of an explanation. "Look, both of you.

Where I come from, race is not the dividing line between friends and workers. Class is, and Bebe is probably one of the classiest ladies I've ever met." She turned to Bebe. "And I want to be your friend, not someone you pour coffee for. So, unless Clair wants both of us to move into the kitchen, sit down and tell me about yourself."

Bebe glanced at Clair's shocked face, then back at Parris. "Just where, exactly, are you from?"

"Obviously not here," Parris retorted. "Where are *you* from?"

"Lyon, France."

"And did you sing there?" Parris asked, determined to draw out Bebe.

"How did you know I sang?"

"I've heard you in the kitchen when you thought no one was listening. You've got the best voice I've heard in years. Better than Sarah Vaughn or Bessie Smith."

Bebe's eyes widened. "You *know* about Bessie Smith?"

"Of course," Parris answered, wondering how she would explain Sarah, who was probably just a child at that time.

Bebe smiled one of her rare smiles. "I heard her last year when I was in New York visiting my sister. She was getting ready to record 'Fat Man's Blues.'" Bebe shook her head in wonder. "Can that lady sing."

"Someday are you going home to sing, too?"

Bebe nodded her head; then her gaze became guarded. "Someday," she hedged before standing. "But right now, I have work to do."

When she left the room, Clair leaned forward. "What the hell did you do that for?"

"Because I want to get to know her better. I'd bet my bottom dollar that woman is going to become somebody special, someday."

"Maybe so," Clair whispered angrily. "But right now, she knows her place and is a good servant. Don't try that again."

"Clair, Bebe doesn't have a special place, and neither do you or I. But if you insist on keeping us segregated then I will abide by your wishes. I'll take my breakfast in the kitchen, where employees can feel comfortable together. It's less informal anyway."

"You're a stubborn bitch!"

Parris smiled, hiding her own frustration with the situation. "I know. My mother said words to that effect herself. Only *she* meant them as a compliment."

A quick exit was discreetly called for, and Parris took it. She walked back to her room, checking her watch to ensure that she was still on time. In another hour or so, they would be driving to Atlantic City for the final touches on the club before Al Capone's henchmen saw it. According to Danny, two or three men had arrived in town early that morning and were supposed to check everything out before Capone showed up.

All the excitement would take her mind off the inadequacies of the time period. But Parris vowed that if she ever got back to her own era, she'd remember how wonderfully far the country and society had come in such a short time. She'd had no idea that the Industrial Age and human rights were as new as they were. If she thought things were tough in her time, it was twice as bad in this one. So much for the romance of the Roaring Twenties. In this time, romance was soaring hormones and a distinct lack of caring for anyone or anything. And the stock-market crash and Depression hadn't even happened yet! Talk about dehumanizing times a-coming!

As usual, she became homesick for her own time and space. She even became homesick for television—the one modern advancement most of her peers loved to debunk. She'd give a good bottle of bootleg scotch to watch an hour of *I Love Lucy* reruns for the zillionth time.

And when those homesick memories ran their patterned race in her head, thoughts of Thomas invaded—following her into everything she did and thought. Knowing he was working on his story didn't help much. She knew he wasn't doing it night and day. That realization brought others that hurt. She couldn't win for losing.

Thomas squinted into the night sky, then leaned against the car's fender and waited for the rowboat heading toward him to pull into the makeshift dock. It had been the worst two weeks of his life, but tonight would make most of it worthwhile.

From the time he had taken Parris to Clair's house, he'd done nothing but dodge questions, from his landlady badgering him about Parris's identification and the date on it, to the police asking him about Parris's new clothing hanging in his closet. He had told them he was storing them for her while she found a place to live and settled into a new job in Atlantic City. He was just thankful that they hadn't examined the rooms or his belongings too closely, or they might have found his shoe and the stash of money. He didn't know how he would have explained that!

But he had been certain of one thing—the mob's power. Once he had stated that Parris was a secretary at the Alley Cat Club, the police had backed off completely. That had raised a few questions in Thomas's mind. How many cops were in the mob's pockets? And how many of them were just plain scared of taking on the mob? Probably the entire force. So who in the hell did he think he was to go up against them? *A fool,* a little voice shouted. *A complete fool!*

His arms folded across his chest, he squinted out to sea. It was windier than usual, and the going was tough. A larger, fisherman-type boat floated 200 or 300 yards from shore, unable or unwilling to come any closer. Another, much smaller boat slowly wending its way to shore was almost at its destination. If Thomas didn't know better, he'd swear the men on the rowboat were purposely stalling for time. But why? They didn't get paid until they brought the case of premium scotch to land. And he wasn't stupid enough to have more than the agreed-upon amount of money in his pocket.

Finally, a man jumped off and tossed the rope around a rickety post at the water's edge.

Thomas waited until the boat was secured. "Where is it?"

The weathered man glared, then nodded his head toward the bottom of the boat. "It's all there."

The hair on the back of Thomas's neck stiffened. With studied nonchalance, he pushed away from the fender and walked toward the boat.

The burly man halted him at the bow. "Money first."

Thomas grinned, reaching into his jacket pocket. "That's no problem." He pulled out an envelope and tossed it on the sand. "That's yours, and this is mine."

When the man bent down to pick up the envelope, Thomas leaned over the side of the boat and slipped his hands in the side of the wooden crate. Pulling hard, he succeeded in getting it out of the boat. He swung around to angle back to the car.

But the fishy-smelling man was a step ahead of him, a knife in his hand. "Put it back," he said throatily.

Thomas stood with the case between them. "Not a chance." He tightened his grip on the wooden handles. "You get your money, and I get the whiskey. Fair deal."

The man gave an malevolent, toothless grin. "Fair is when I can sell this here case over and over again." The smile disappeared. "Put it back. Now."

Thomas kept the case between himself and the knife, walking back toward the car, one agonizingly slow step at a time. "I don't want to fight, but I will if I have to. Then you'll have hell to pay. This whiskey belongs to Al Capone now." Thomas nodded to the envelope sticking out of the man's pants pocket. "That's his money, this is his whiskey. You have a problem with that, talk to the boss tomorrow."

When the toothless man lunged, Thomas held tightly to the wooden box and thrust it toward him. But he hadn't been quick enough. The knife deflected off the wood and plunged into his forearm, then ripped a six- or seven-inch gash as the other man fell with a grunt, the knife still in his hand.

Thomas hissed between his teeth, loosening his grip on one side of the wooden case. A bottle dropped heavily on the grungy man's back and broke. He yelled, then rolled. Thomas, his arm quickly numbing, dropped the case on the hood of the car and turned around to face the jackass.

But the jackass moved quicker than Thomas thought he could. He was back, the knife aimed at Thomas's chest.

Kicking, Thomas hit the man's elbow, jerking the knife from his hand and sending it flying into the darkness. A fist collided with his stomach, forcing air from his lungs. Another fist plowed into his shoulder. Thomas blinked, calling on every saint he could think of to help him.

Reacting instinctively, Thomas kicked the man again, hitting his shin. A scream echoed in the damp air. Groping and finding the knife in the sand, Thomas tried to catch his breath. As Thomas slowly sank by the wheel well of his car, he watched the fisherman crawl toward the boat. Several grunts and groans later, the boat floated out to sea.

Hoping to fill his lungs with air, Thomas kept taking large gulps. Parris's face floated into his vision. She suddenly resembled an angel. He closed his eyes to hold the beautiful image as long as he could while waiting for the pain to triumph. Just as he knew it would, every bone in his body cried out.

Thankfully, he didn't have to wait for the entire inventory of aches and pains to slam into his gut.

He blacked out.

Chapter Ten

The banging on the door in the middle of the night was enough to wake the dead—let alone three women. Clair, Bebe, and Parris all met in the broad foyer and stared at the door as if it would magically open. Clair held a small, steel gun in her hand.

A knock reverberated through the house again. Parris held on tight to the ties of her robe as she watched Bebe cautiously walk to the front door.

Parris's mind raced. Could there be a gangster war going on outside? Was that how Al Capone made an entrance? Did someone have a grudge against Clair? Anything was possible. She wasn't the only one thinking those thoughts if the look on the other two women's faces was any indication.

Clair moved to the entrance of the living room, her weapon pointed toward the door. After she nodded to Bebe, the black woman opened it.

Blue-uniformed policemen stood on either side of a drooping and disheveled Thomas. His smile, though wry, was still endearing. And it was aimed at Clair.

Parris hurt with the effort of forcing herself to stay where she was. She wanted to run to him, to check and make sure he was all right. She wanted to kiss and soothe his brow. But she didn't. Instead, she stood and watched as the other two women rushed to his side, replacing the policemen as they helped Thomas over the threshold and toward the couch. The police followed slowly behind, their gaze bouncing everywhere as they took note of Clair's expensive decor. Parris could imagine them describing the interior to their wives.

"What happened?" Clair demanded, her voice tight and high pitched. She touched the bandage that wrapped his arm. "Who did this?"

"Some fishermen decided they wanted war, and I was the dispute."

Bebe got a glass of brandy and handed it to Thomas. The policemen didn't say a word about the liquor. "What is this? Dispute?"

Thomas sipped the golden liquid, then answered. "They wanted me dead or hurt, but I don't know why."

Parris still stood in the entrance of the living room, her hands clenched into fists and tucked in the pockets of her borrowed white satin robe.

One of the policemen cleared his throat as if preparing for a recital. "I'm sorry we're barging in so late, ma'am. We got a call to stop some bootleggers on the Point. By the time we got to the, uh, designated spot, Mr. Elder here was out cold. We took him to the doc's house and had Mr. Elder's ribs and hands bandaged. He then asked to be brought here."

"It's all right, officer," Clair assured him in her vulnerable-woman role. "I know that Mr. Elder would never harm us. He was a very good friend of my, my"—she reached for a handkerchief in her robe pocket—"my dearly, departed husband." Her words ended on a sob.

If Parris thought she'd just heard the most trite words in the English language, she was the only one who thought so. Obviously, this woman was a consummate actress. Bebe reached across and patted her employer's hand, while the police looked both sad and uncomfortable.

The other policeman spoke for them both. "We're sorry, ma'am. If you need us, just call the station. We can be out here within the hour."

Clair stood, her eyes wide and her gaze as innocent and earnest as a virgin's. "Thank you so much, officers. You've been such a help." With Oscar-winning talent and a finesse Parris envied, Clair ushered them to the door.

Bebe took the empty glass from Thomas and poured another brandy. When she sat down next to him, she took a sip of the liquor before handing the glass to him. "What happened? Was it the bootleggers?" Her voice was low, confident in her questioning.

"Yes. They were stalling for some reason. One of them tried to make it seem as if they wanted their liquor back, but there was something else going on." Thomas took a swig of the brandy. "When I mentioned Al Capone's name, the weasel didn't even flinch."

"Maybe he didn't recognize it," Clair volunteered as she came back into the room.

"No. That's not it." Thomas looked straight at Parris, who tried not to back into the hallway before running away. "And why weren't *you* surprised that I was escorted into the house?"

"I was," Parris said.

"You didn't act like it."

"Am I convicted on my performance—or lack of it?"

Bebe raised her hand in the air like a traffic cop. "Both of you, stop it. This is not the moment to argue. This is the time to solve riddles. Yes?"

Parris stiffened, waiting for him to accuse her again. She wanted to run to him and make sure that he was all right. She wanted to push Clair and Bebe out of the way and hold him for herself, soothing away his hurt. But she couldn't do either of those things. With the exception of Thomas's long, hard stare, which she returned, neither of them said anything.

"Let me get some aspirin," Clair murmured, feeling his head as if he'd caught cold and had a fever instead of bruises from the brawl.

"What happened to the liquor?" Parris finally asked.

"One bottle hit the fisherman in the back and broke. I gave two more to each of the policemen. The rest are in the back of my car."

Parris raised a brow. "*Sol's* car?"

"The same." His voice was clipped, his blue-eyed gaze steel hard.

Parris's smile was equally hard. With her hands still clenched in the pockets of her robe, she turned and headed down the hallway.

"Sweet dreams," she said over her shoulder. She didn't care if he knew she wasn't aiming her thoughtful wish toward him.

"Thank you. The same to you," he said loudly. Obviously, he was determined to have the last word.

"You're welcome!" she shouted just before entering her bedroom. A giggle erupted in her throat, but she couldn't allow it to bubble forth until she closed her door.

When the giggle came, it was a cross between laughter and tears. For two solid weeks, she had been thinking of him doing all kinds of wild things, but she hadn't thought of him setting up a deal for bootlegging whiskey. Damn him! Why couldn't he have let her know he was all right? Two full weeks had gone by, and if he hadn't got hurt tonight, it might have been even longer!

She knew he'd been working on his story, but that was the same reason he'd become involved with Clair and perhaps Bebe. In the long run, that was how he became involved with her! She wondered if he had convinced other women to help him, and she knew how involved he could get and what type of woman he would approach. She'd seen many of them in the casino.

So had he found some woman to help him? Had he been spending time with Victoria?

Soft shuffling and occasional low murmurs in the hallway told Parris the women were putting Thomas into the spare bedroom next to hers.

The sounds seemed personal, and she felt as if she was eavesdropping on a private conversation. With quick, decisive movements, Parris shed her robe, turned off the lamp, and climbed into bed. She was *not* going to allow that man to disrupt her life or thoughts.

It was odd, but now that she knew where Thomas was and that he was safe, she couldn't sleep. Her eyes wide open, she stared at the curtains ruffling in the breeze.

Damn that man! Ever since she'd met him her life had been in turmoil! For all she knew, he was the cause of her coming into this time!

It wasn't until dawn crept through the windows that she closed her eyes and slept.

Damn that woman!

Thomas lay in bed breathing shallowly so his ribs wouldn't hurt. The doctor had said they weren't cracked, but they were bruised so badly that they needed to be strapped for a while. And he had wrapped them so tightly that Thomas could hardly breathe. On the other hand, he knew that the doc had done what was best. He'd even applied Absorbine Jr., his mother's old cure-all. His hands were bruised and scraped, but he had no broken bones, and the slash on his arm was only superficial, requiring a few stitches and a gulp of good whiskey. Thank you, sweet Jesus.

If only he could heal his mind as quickly and probably as well. Something was going on around him, and someone was out to get him. It was obvious from the police searching his room and the fisherman trying to gyp him that someone was warning him off. But who? And why? In the grand scheme of things in the underworld, he hadn't *done* anything different or meaner or cut anyone out of a deal!

And no one knew what he wanted to do. No one knew except for Bebe that his sister's boyfriend was on his hit list and that, if he could get close enough to kill the bastard, he would achieve his goal.

He remembered the angry look in Parris's eyes as she stared at him across the living room. Her disapproval of him hit his very core. He hadn't realized just how much he wanted her approval until then. Her dirty look had said it all: She thought he was stupid and not worth giving the time of day to. Suddenly, he felt so cold and so alone. He wondered what he'd done to deserve her contempt. He couldn't find an answer.

Her look had made him feel empty. It was as if she could see inside him and found him inadequate, not quite a man. Not only was he stunned by her reaction to him, but he was stunned at his reaction to her opinion.

He was *hurt*, for God's sake! He *could* have been killed! She might have acted a little worried! Clair and Bebe were worried. If he had told Victoria, she would not only have been worried, but frightened for him, too. Instead, Parris was angry—just plain angry.

Maybe he should have visited her sometime during these past two weeks. Maybe then he'd know what was on her mind. Instead, he'd purposely stayed away from her so she could acclimate herself to her new surroundings without his interference or influence. It had been a sacrifice, but he'd done it anyway. Besides, he'd had his own problems.

Who was he kidding? Himself? How stupid he was! He even lied to himself!

He knew why Parris was angry, and he didn't blame her. He hadn't taken the time to explain everything to her; he'd just assumed she would blindly follow his lead and then sweetly hand him whatever information he wanted without question. He should have known from the things she'd said that she wasn't docile or stupid.

And he didn't like the fact that he'd missed her more than he ever thought possible. In fact, he resented it. It didn't make sense. He was supposed to be in love with Victoria Morrow and to get information from Clair by using Parris. After all, Parris was working at the club and would be able to tell him the major moves of most of the players in this part of the mob. She could even tell him the names of those coming from Chicago, and if his sister's boyfriend would be one of them, which Bebe wouldn't know and Clair wouldn't say.

Nothing was working out the way it was supposed to.

If he didn't feel so damn bad, he'd go to her room. He could only admit to himself that he wanted to be with Parris. He'd give all the money hidden in the heel of the shoe back in his room to be able to lay his head on her breast. He wanted to hold her close and sleep deeply for just one damn night.

He knew he had to apologize so things could go back to being the way they were before he'd told her that he wasn't interested in a long-term commitment.

It had been a bald-faced lie born out of panic. She was getting too close to him. Becoming too lovable . . . too necessary. He couldn't afford to have someone that close to him again. It hurt when something went wrong or the relationship blew up, which it always did. Parris wasn't the kind of woman a man could walk away from.

Suppressing a groan, Thomas sat up and edged off the bed. Carefully, he walked to his door and opened it. Everyone was in bed and the house was quiet. He walked down the hall as quietly as he could, biting his cheek to keep from moaning aloud with every jolt to his ribs.

Once he reached Parris's door, he opened it as quietly as he had opened his own. The room was dark, but he could make out her figure leaning on pillows propped against the headboard. Watery moonlight outlined her against the crisp white sheets.

Thomas took a step inside the room and closed the door behind him. "I just want you to know that I'm sorry if I hurt your feelings the last time we saw each other."

"Forget it." Her voice was cool. Chilled. Goading.

"And that I only acted that way because you were so sweet and I didn't want to hurt you."

"Thanks for being such a caring individual and sharing that piece of information with me." Her tone was syrupy sweet, sarcastic. Heated sarcasm.

She cared. She still cared. That gave him satisfaction.

"And I want you to also know that I've missed you. Staying away was one of the hardest things I've ever done."

"Too bad."

She was cold again. Good. It meant she was emotionally involved in this conversation whether she wanted to be or not.

"I just wanted you to know," he said, reaching for the knob and hoping she'd stop him. She didn't.

With a heavy sigh, he reluctantly turned to go.

"Thomas?" Her voice was soft and low.

He turned quickly, a twinge of pain in his ribs telling him how quickly he had done so. But he ignored the pain. "Yes?"

"Go to hell."

It was said so sweetly that it took a minute for him to realize what she'd said. Anger welled in him as her words sank in. "You stupid twit." His voice was equally soft but angry. "I came to apologize and you act as if you were personally insulted. Well, I'm sorry if I hurt your feelings, but for someone who claims to be liberated, you're just a pretender. You're no different from any other woman."

Before she could counterattack, he left the room and went down the hallway. By the time he climbed in bed, his entire body ached. If he had been completely alone in his room at the boardinghouse, he would have cried.

Turning out the light, Thomas stared out the window. His eyes burned, but would not close. His heart ached. He kicked himself over and over for letting his mouth get the better of him and letting his pride get even further in the way of what he wanted.

He wanted information on the Alley Cat Club.

He wanted to know what Al Capone was doing here.

He wanted to kill his sister's lover.

He wanted to be friends with Parris.

In fact, his friendship with Parris was the most important of all. Everything else came in second.

Once he'd admitted that to himself, it was as if a weight had been lifted from his chest. He'd finally told himself the truth.

And just where in the hell did that leave him? Knowing his brain knew what his body had known all along wasn't a great revelation.

He'd goofed. He'd alienated the woman he wanted to be with. He knew he deserved to kick his own butt; however, he had no idea what to do to bring her back to him. In all honesty, he hadn't had too much of a problem with women before. They came to him and, after a while, moved on. It was usually his choosing and his timing.

But Parris was different. She wanted him, he could tell. But instead of being dutifully submissive, she wanted their being together to be on equal terms—and sometimes those so-called equal terms were her terms.

Damn the woman!

If he were younger, he'd go find the nearest willing woman. But he was older and more discriminating. He no longer fell into every willing female's bed. Suddenly, he wished he could. Then he might be able to choose one of many women to make love to right this minute.

That brought his thoughts to Clair. He'd been drawn to her at first, then repulsed. But circumstances being what they were, his needs and inclinations had changed again. Now, there he was, relying on Clair for help and understanding and wanting Parris to tumble into his bed.

As much as he wanted Parris, though, their lovemaking would have to wait until he felt better. What he wanted was to have her hold him, to have her stroke him as if she cared, to have her care for him as if she meant it.

Instead, she'd given him directions to his old address. He'd been living in hell for the past year.

If nothing else, Parris reminded him of the time when he wasn't thinking of revenge. A time when he believed he could do most anything and do it well. His sister, his father, and Capone's gang had taught him differently, and aside from all the other reasons to hate the man, his loss in his belief in himself was just one more.

He punched the down pillow and rolled over, only to wrench a rib. Sucking in air, he lay still until the pain eased. God, he wished Parris was with him!

His time away from her had been hell for another reason—one he didn't care to admit. But now that he had time to reflect, he might as well go all the way.

He tried to put his deep-seated feelings into words. It wasn't easy, especially for a man who believed in actions over words.

The truth was that he expected her to disappear into her own time at any given moment. He might not believe in organized religion, because time and effort in that direction had never paid off for him. But that didn't mean he didn't believe in God. On the contrary. He believed in God with all his heart. The world he lived in proved God existed. It was *man* who had screwed the world up with death and famine and poverty. And since God did exist, it only stood to reason in Thomas's mind that He had goofed when He'd thrown Parris into this time frame. And as soon as He discovered it, He'd yank her back into her own era. And when that happened, Thomas would be without her. For that reason, and that reason alone, he couldn't afford to get too close to her. Her absence would hurt him, so why kill himself by becoming more involved?

There. He'd finally put his thoughts into words. After he'd done that, he'd wondered if she had disappeared. He didn't think so. There was no noise that sounded like an explosion echoing through the house. No giant wave crashed through the windows. No poof of smoke that terminated her time here. Nothing.

So why did he feel such an indescribable urge to go check on her?

He lay still, waiting for the feeling to pass. It didn't.

Just as he was about to curse under his breath and walk down the hall to her room, his door opened.

Parris slid silently inside the room, closed the door, and walked to the foot of his bed. Her hands gripped the footpost as she stared at him.

Relief flooded him, making his bones feel like jelly.

She stared at him a full minute before speaking. "Don't think I came here to apologize."

"I don't."

"Don't think I need your company either."

"I don't."

"I just wanted you to know that I was worried about you."

"You couldn't convince me of that."

"It's true." Her fingers tightened on the wood. "I just didn't know what to say. By the time I figured it out, both Clair and Bebe were doing such a good job fussing over you that I figured you didn't need another woman worshiping at your feet."

"You were wrong."

She shrugged and her gown strap slid off one white shoulder. "Maybe. Maybe not."

"Clair and Bebe—" He wasn't sure what to say. He wanted to explain how much Parris meant to him so she wouldn't shut him out again, but the words wouldn't come. Instead, he said, "You were so cold." His words sounded like a child's accusation.

"I didn't mean to be."

"It hurt."

"I didn't mean to hurt you either."

"You didn't care."

She smiled slowly and sweetly, melting his heart before she even spoke. "Poor baby."

Thomas grinned, only partially satisfied by her response. He patted the empty side of the bed. "Come sleep with me."

She looked at his hand, then back at him. He could get lost in those mystical dark eyes of hers.

She tilted her head. "Nothing else." It was a statement.

"Nothing else." It was a promise.

Lightning quick, she rounded the side of the bed and slid between the crisp sheets. Then she lay as still as Thomas. The warmth of their bodies mingled in the small space between them, heating the emptiness there.

Thomas sighed. "I wanted you here earlier."

"We don't always get what we want."

"Come closer."

"Nothing else."

"Nothing else."

Parris moved over. Her leg touched his and her arm grazed his. He felt tingly and wonderful. Thomas was amazed that he couldn't ever remember feeling such anticipation. In this free-wheeling, jumble-tumble, sex-is-free world, he'd never ached, physically ached, as he did to hold this woman.

"What are you doing to me?" His hand reaching for hers, he asked his question. He tried to make it sound as if he really knew.

"The same thing you're doing to me," she said timidly, apparently as astounded by her reaction to him as he was to her.

This time his smile was complete, sweet satisfaction. "Pleasant dreams, as my mother used to say." His voice was a blurred whisper.

"Don't let the bedbugs bite."

"Cheery thought." On that note he drifted off to sleep, Parris's hand held firmly in his. There was a hint of a smile curving his lips.

Chapter Eleven

Thomas tried to get out of bed as quickly and quietly as possible. The stitches in his arm screamed as he moved carefully away from Parris. In sleep, she had curled into him, and he backed away from her, wincing as his ribs protested.

The last he'd heard, Capone's men were due in town today. He had to get dressed and back to work.

When Parris woke, she'd have her own work cut out for her. Clair couldn't be easy to work for, especially if she resented her secretary. Since Parris hadn't said anything about the other woman, their relationship was probably the same as it had been two weeks ago. Thomas felt bad about pairing the two of them, but he'd had no choice. Yet he couldn't have done too badly since they were still together and alive.

He dressed in his dirty suit, wanting to curse that fisherman to the heavens for costing him another $50.00 worth of clothing. He'd find that bastard, and when he did, he'd stomp him into the ground.

After softly kissing Parris's brow, he left the house and headed back to his boardinghouse for a change of clothes.

Parris woke feeling as if she held the world in her hands, only to find her hands were empty. So was the bed. Thomas had obviously sneaked out in the middle of the night, leaving her alone—again.

She glanced at her watch. It was almost noon. In a little while she'd be dressing for work.

Before her emotions could swamp her with tears, she got out of bed and walked to her own room. If a hot bath didn't help, nothing would, she told herself, already knowing what the limited capabilities of a bath were.

Damn him!

By the time Parris and Clair reached the club, Parris's nerves were strung with steel. Thomas Elder could go to hell in a hand basket, and she'd be on the sidelines cheering for the devil!

Danny and his two buddies were there, as usual. Both lizards, as Clair called the men, lounged against the office wall near the closets, while Danny sat on the corner of the desk reading the paper.

"Get off my desk," Clair said, striding around the corner and sitting in a large leather chair.

Sitting on one of the leather chairs grouped around a small table by the side of the door, Parris watched the cat play.

"You don't have to be rude." Danny slid off slowly, as if taunting her. "After all, it's not the end of the world."

"This is my office, my desk. I want access to all of it without having to move your butt to get it."

"My, my," Danny drawled. "Getting testy, aren't we? Could it be that you're nervous about Al Capone's men?"

"No." Clair's voice was clipped and short. "You make me nervous. If you think you're taking over here, better think again, bucko. You're not even in the running."

"You aren't the one to make that judgment."

The teasing was gone, and for the first time since Parris had been working here, she saw Danny's claws completely bared. Normally, he kept his veneer of sophistication intact.

"You may be out on your sweet little ass once Mr. Capone gets here. Even he might see that this club needs a man's hand in the business end to really make a profit."

"You idiot, you don't even know what you're talking about," Clair said casually. She picked up a pencil and held it between her fingers and aimed all her attention at measuring it.

"Boys, leave us alone," Danny stated quietly, sending a silent message to the lounge lizards.

Parris looked at Clair. "Why don't you order my dinner for nine tonight?"

Parris nodded and left, closing the door behind her. The lizards didn't know what to do, so they hung around the empty bookie's office outside Clair's office.

Parris walked into the recently cleaned kitchen and greeted the chef, who was checking over his supplies in the large refrigerator built into the wall like a bank safe. After giving him instructions for Clair's dinner and having a cup of coffee, she decided she had to get to work and only hoped Danny and Clair had stopped arguing so she could. There were books that had to be double-checked before Capone arrived. Clair's job depended on it. Besides, it would keep her own mind from dwelling on that rat fink Thomas.

The lizards were nowhere to be seen when she returned to the outer office. Although the office door was closed, there was no sound coming from it either. Somewhere in the distance, Parris heard the dull thud of a hammer.

She opened the office door and walked in. It was empty. Well, whatever had passed between the two enemies, it was apparently over.

Walking to the closet door, Parris opened it to get out the books she'd been checking. The hammering got louder.

Although her eyes saw it, her mind didn't believe it.

Suave, sophisticated Danny was standing in the small closet, his back against one wall—and Clair's body, was leaning against the other wall. His suit pants and boxer shorts were around his ankles.

Clair's legs were wrapped around his waist, her strappy high-heeled sandals slinging back and forth against the wall behind them like the tapping of a hammer. Her arms were curved around his shoulders, her eyes closed in ecstasy.

Parris hadn't realized she'd gasped until two pairs of dismayed eyes stared at her.

The hammering stopped as Clair and Danny both waited for her to make a move.

Parris couldn't.

"We'll be out in a minute," Clair said sweetly.

Looking as calm as she could, Parris nodded and then closed the door. Turning, she left the room and entered the main bookie area. The lizards were back, both lounging against the empty tables, their arms crossed, bored looks on their faces. However, they showed their surprise when they saw her come from the office.

Almost immediately, the light tapping began again, and the two men looked even more surprised. Parris couldn't handle it anymore. She exploded into laughter that was so hard she couldn't see through the tears that coursed down her cheeks. She barely made her way to grapple a chair from under a long table and bunch up in it—while listening to the tap, tap, tap of Clair's shoes against the wall as the two lovers completed their act of ecstasy.

"Neither rain nor shine nor flood. . . ." she began, only to laugh again.

Neither of Danny's men said a word, but their faces added to the comical situation. Obviously, they knew what was happening, too, but were trying to ignore it.

The tapping increased. So did Parris's laughter

The tapping sound was replaced by deep scrapes.

Suddenly, the tapping stopped.

Trying to regain her composure, Parris went to the ladies' room, stopping only occasionally to giggle.

Twenty minutes later, Parris had managed to get control of herself, but it hadn't been easy. In fact, every time she thought about standing in the closet doorway and seeing Clair and Danny, she wanted to burst out laughing. Instead, she told herself not to remember.

With dignity, Parris walked back into the bookie room. The office door was open, and she heard Clair's voice giving instructions to the cook, retracting her own orders for dinner.

Parris walked in. It was time to get back to work.

While Parris wheeled out the old typewriter, Clair finished with the chef and excused him.

As he left, Parris noticed Clair had given him the sign to close the office door.

They were alone.

"Parris?"

She pretended to be busy stacking paper and pencils on the arm of the table. "Yes?"

"Everyone has needs."

Parris looked up. She was amazed to see the sad light in Clair's eyes. Clair had always seemed so in control and capable of living without men, except when she was playing a part. In the past two weeks, Parris had seen her slip in and out of her role as a savvy businesswoman. But she had never expected to see this side of her.

"But Danny? You two do nothing but fight."

"I know." Clair gave a sharp smile that disappeared as quickly as it came. "Aggression brings out the sexiness in me."

"Arguing with him turns you on?"

Clair nodded. "Stupid, isn't it? But he's so stimulating when I pit my ideas against his, stand behind them, and then get aggressive with him. I never got that from Sol," she explained sadly. "In fact, I never got that from any man."

"Does Danny know this?"

Her smile peeped out for a moment. "Obviously, he does now."

Parris shrugged, but her grin threatened to bubble over into laughter again every time she thought of the scene she'd witnessed in that closet. "Whatever turns you on."

Clair looked relieved. "Thanks for understanding."

"I'm not sure I do, but it doesn't matter. You're entitled to do whatever you want." Unable to keep it inside anymore, Parris laughed. "But next time, warn me not to open the closet door."

Clair blushed, and Parris was amazed again. "Anyway, I'm sorry I shocked you."

Unable to stop herself, Parris asked, "Will it happen again?"

"Probably."

"I'll be more careful."

"Thanks." Clair handed her a stack of papers. "These are the letters that need answering this week."

Parris reached for them, but couldn't help asking the one question that kept playing in her mind. "Clair, you do know that Danny is trying to get rid of you and manage this club by himself?"

"I know, but that's business."

"Don't you think that making love to a guy who wants to take your place is a little risky?"

"No. Sex isn't business," Clair stated positively. "Business is business."

"Of course," Parris stated dryly. "How could I have been so stupid?"

Clair laughed, but her gaze was already on the books.

Capone's men were due anytime.

Half an hour later, five men opened the door and walked in. All wore suits and all but one had hats in their hands. Clair leaned back in her chair and stared at the one in front. He was a pockmarked, swarthy-complected man who looked even more so because his bowler hat shadowed his face.

Giving up all pretense of typing, Parris watched.

Clair finally stood and shook hands with the man, who called himself Gus Landi. His thick Italian accent made it difficult for Parris to understand everything he said, but she got the gist of it.

After two of the men checked the closets and a third man stood outside the office door, Gus spoke to Clair. "First, you gotta show us Mr. Capone's room. Then you gotta show us the kitchen cupboard, then the club books. We'll take it from there so you won' have to worry 'bout nothin'."

Clair stood and walked around the desk. "I'll be happy to show you my house and you can search it from top to bottom. As for my kitchen, Bebe, my cook, takes care of everything, but I'm sure she'd love to show you whatever you need."

"Anna books." The man repeated the phrase doggedly. It was apparent he didn't want to bother with the rest—that this was his first priority.

"I will hand over the books when Mr. Capone is here. Until then, they remain in my care." Clair's voice was firm.

"I want them now."

Clair looked around. "Is Mr. Capone here?"

"Iz my job."

Clair nodded. "Forgive me, Mr. Landi, but it's my job to protect those books until Mr. Capone gives me permission to do differently. As soon as Mr. Capone tells me, they will be in your hands. I promise."

"We see 'bout dat." He looked at the two men standing on either side of him, then back at Clair. "You sure you want to do this way?"

Although Parris knew Clair was frightened, her actions certainly didn't give it away. "I'm sure."

Mr. Landi smiled. "Okay by me," he said. "Now, where's our table? I'm hungry."

When Clair nodded at Parris, she stepped away from her typewriter and led the men out of the office and into the large dining area. Already, the draped private booths were filling up with the long list of reservations. But one booth was kept closed: It belonged to Clair—or whoever she deemed could use it. Today, it was Mr. Landi's.

"Please have a seat, Mr. Landi. I'll have the waiter bring you a menu."

"Thank you, girlie," he stated, finally handing his hat to one of his henchmen and slipping to a spot in the darkest confines of the booth from which his view of the gaming tables wouldn't be obstructed.

"Parris," she corrected, knowing it wouldn't do any good. She hadn't run across one man of this generation who treated a woman like an equal. It astounded her that Clair could work successfully in this atmosphere. But she did.

Tension permeated the club. The help and staff knew about their esteemed guests and reacted accordingly.

Mr. Landi ate each course at a leisurely pace, his face showing no expression. He never stopped eating, nor did he cork the burgundy wine that seemed to flow from bottle to glass all by itself.

Clair sent Parris to check on the entourage every 15 minutes. Knowing better than to interrupt them, Parris kept tabs on them through the waiters.

The whole experience was nerve-racking for Clair—and for Danny, who continued to pace in the bookie room—and comic to Parris. Although she was Clair's secretary, she did not belong in that time, and those men were ludicrous.

By midnight, Parris's humor had grown thin. She walked into the dining area for what seemed like the millionth time, her gaze darting among the increasing crowd around the tables. Her eyes halted at the craps table. Tuxedo-clad Thomas, with a beautiful redhead at his side, was shooting dice. He gave the woman a wide smile and broad wink as the dice were thrown back to his end of the table. The woman's laughter was low and sexy, grating on Parris's nerves like salt against scored skin.

Parris froze. Even after their confrontation, she had believed he cared for her. She could have sworn it. Because of that, she'd postponed her attempts to return to her own time. He was the only thing that had kept her from trying. As far as she was concerned, there was nothing to recommend this time period except Thomas. And even in her belief in his love, she had been wrong.

Anger geared her into action. Without thinking of the consequences, she walked up behind him. Standing fairly close, she lightly goosed him. Thomas stiffened, then quickly turned around, his expression furious. His eyes widened. A slow blush reddened his cheeks.

"What are you doing here?"

"A friend of mine got me a job here. Remember?" she hissed back. "And pray tell, what is your excuse?"

"I'm working," he answered shortly before turning his back on her once more and picking up the dice again.

Parris felt the redhead's wondering gaze, and it hurt more than she would admit. The woman wasn't angry or territorial; she was curious. Parris's presence didn't seem to bother her at all. The hurt burned off, leaving anger in its place.

Her gaze turned toward the redhead. Her long, full hair didn't seem to match the look of the Twenties at all. It had more of a Nineties' style. And her gown bore the distinct beauty of a Worth. Pleats from the bodice to the thigh-length hem shadowed the ivory-colored dress into a thousand shades of tan. The redhead's skin was clear and smooth and youthful. Her eyes were the most beautiful blue Parris had ever seen, with thick lashes too natural to be mascaraed. She was extremely beautiful and looked slightly familiar.

Parris spoke before she thought. "He'll never be faithful."

The redhead's lips quirked. "He always has been."

Parris jabbed again. "He's a womanizer."

Laughter gleamed in the redhead's eyes. "So I've heard."

"He'll hurt you every chance he gets."

The sadness in the redhead's eyes replaced the mirth. "He already has."

Those words were said so softly that Parris had to strain to hear them. When she did, her own anger dissipated. "Excuse me." Before she broke into tears in front of Thomas's girlfriend, she headed for the kitchen.

"Parris!" Thomas called, but she didn't stop. Nothing would make her stay around and emotionally slice herself into ribbons in front of him.

"Parris!"

She practically ran through the double swinging doors into the chaos of the kitchen. Her eyes were blurred by the tears that wouldn't remain hidden. She was a fool—a big fool! Every sort of a fool! A stupid fool! A fool in love!

"No!" she yelled over the noise and turned toward the doors just as Thomas strode in.

"Damn you!" he shouted, grabbing her shoulders and shaking her. "You don't make a scene in front of the mob! Ever!"

She pushed his hands off her. "Don't lay one single hand on me, you damn creep! Don't *ever* touch me without my permission!"

"Shut up and listen to me!" His stance was aggressive, and his fists clenched at his sides instead of touching her. He took a deep breath and began again. "I'm here on business, which means that I can't chat with you. Do you understand?"

That did it! "No! You understand!" She jabbed her finger into his chest. "You *knew* I was working here! What did you expect me to do, ignore you? Was I supposed to pretend you weren't at the tables? If that's what I'm supposed to do, then you better tell me ahead of time! I'm from a different place. Remember? I don't know all your stupid rules. I'm having a hell of a time just *existing*, you damn, damn. . . ." Her frustration took away all the words she wanted to say. She couldn't think with anger bubbling in her throat.

His anger was apparent, too. His blue eyes were the color of night lightning as they glared at her. With all the noise and commotion going on around them, she still noticed the dark curl that fell on his forehead. Her hand itched to touch it. Maybe grab it and pull!

"Parris," he muttered, running his hand through his hair. "I swear you are so—"

"Sweet? Kind? Confused by your stupidity?"

Before she could say anything else, his mouth covered hers with a kiss that was as harsh and electric as his gaze. Much as she hated herself for it, she reached up and clung to his shoulders, crushing her body against his. His hands clamped on her waist, his fingers tightening in a steely grip. His mouth ground against hers, his tongue creating the movement her body craved to imitate.

"Well, well, well." A deep, sultry voice cut through the banging, chopping, and sizzling sounds of the well-operated kitchen. "So big brother obviously doesn't practice what he preaches."

Thomas pulled away as if Parris had scalded him. He continued to stare at Parris as he answered, the look on his face one of sheer disgust. "Don't be stupid, Patricia."

Stunned, Parris glanced at the other woman. Once more there was mirth in the redhead's eyes, but there was also a glimmer of truth.

"Oh, I'm not stupid, Tom. And you shouldn't be either." Her voice was firm, unafraid of Thomas's anger. She smiled and put out her hand. "Hello, I'm Patricia Elder. Obviously, you've met the other member of our charming family."

Parris automatically followed suit. Her voice caught in her throat and burned before she got out the words. "You're married?"

"No, I'm his little sister." The redhead laughed, making a low, melodious sound.

"Cut it out, Patricia," Thomas said, turning toward the double doors. "Come on. Your *friend* is waiting."

"He's always a bully, but he's sometimes right," Patricia whispered conspiratorially. "I'd better get back to Joey."

Parris was still reeling from the information that this woman *wasn't* Thomas's girlfriend, but his sister! "Joey?"

Patricia nodded, her beautiful smile still in place, but her expression wasn't as spontaneous. "He's at the table with Mr. Landi."

Thomas's fists hit the door, immediately silencing the kitchen for the space of a full moment. At Thomas's fierce glare, the kitchen slowly began functioning again. He turned to the redhead and whispered, "Damn it, Patricia! You don't have to tell the whole world our business!"

"No, only a woman you kiss as if you need her air." She spoke so softly that only Parris heard her answer.

Thomas certainly didn't. He was already walking through the doors into the dining area. Even with 20 people in the kitchen, Parris felt as if she were alone.

Patricia smiled. "Good to meet you, whoever you are. If Tom cares about you as much as I think, you and I ought to get along just fine.

Can you come out and sit with us? I can't sit with Joey. He's here on business."

"Thank you," Parris answered politely, still unable to concentrate on anything but the stinging hurt of Thomas's rejection. Even his kiss had been a form of punishment. She just wasn't sure whom he was punishing. "But I'm working, too, and I'm late getting back to my boss."

Patricia held up her hands. "Hey, good luck. Working in this place can't be easy during the best of times, let alone when the big boss is visiting."

"You know?"

"You bet, sister." Her smile was completely gone, seriousness replacing the fun of teasing her brother. "The whole world stops when Mr. Capone steps into the picture. Nobody can have a life unless it revolves around him." Bitterness didn't sit well with the young woman. But it was honest. "That's what this visit is all about."

"I see." Parris's own emotions were so topsy-turvy that she couldn't figure out how she felt.

"Not hardly," Patricia said with a laugh. "But you'll get the picture. Besides, it's a great time for me to see my big brother. He always seems to be around when I need him. In fact, he seems to be around when I *don't* need him, too."

For the first time, Parris noticed the sadness in those blue eyes, which looked so much like her brother's. "He loves you very much."

Patricia laughed. "I know. If he loved me any more, I'd be smothered to death!"

Parris's brother Jed had been that way with her until she'd put her foot down. She remembered the mixed feelings that love had produced.

Patricia turned toward the doors and looked over her shoulder. "Ready?"

Parris smiled. "Go ahead. I'll be there in a minute," she said. "And by the way, your brother was right when he said you were more beautiful than any movie star."

Her eyes widened. "He said that?"

What was a little lie? Especially when that was exactly what Thomas thought. "Yes."

Patricia smiled. "You're lying," she whispered. "And I love it. Thanks." With a sage look, Patricia left Parris at the kitchen exit.

Parris sighed, leaned against one of the storage cabinets, and closed her eyes, trying to bring her tumultuous emotions in check.

According to Patricia, Thomas was as much a protector to her as Parris's brother had been to her. She remembered her mixed feelings. She had wanted Jed's love, but she wanted to choose her own protector—and her best protector had turned out to be herself. But her brother had had a tough time with that line of thought. It had taken his getting immersed in his own career for him to pull out of her life enough so that they could finally be friends. Then they had become the best of friends.

God! She missed him!

And whether Thomas was Patricia's brother or her protector or both, this escapade into the past had made one thing clear. Parris was her own best judge of what was right and best for her.

It was time to return to her own time.

Chapter Twelve

By the time Clair and Parris reached home, Parris felt as if she'd been wired to the thousands of lights on the Atlantic City Steel Pier. Every nerve in her body hummed so strongly she could hardly analyze her own actions.

Minutes after they walked into Clair's home, Clair had had a brandy, listened to some music, and then gone to bed. Parris immediately did the same.

Slipping out of her clothes—or rather the clothes she'd borrowed from Clair's closet— Parris stood in her nightgown at the bedroom window and stared out at the undulating ocean. The midnight breeze cooled her heated skin, but her nerves were too strung out to relax.

On the spur of the moment, Parris slid over the windowsill and jumped to the sandy grass below.

The wind whipped at her light, satin gown, and with a jauntiness she thought had long deserted her, Parris walked around the side of the house to the brick-enclosed back patio. That entrance was the way she, Thomas, and Clair had entered the house that first time.

Parris skirted the patio and continued walking to the water's edge. The firmly packed wet sand yielded to her footsteps like a padded floor. As the water licked at her bare toes, Parris took a deep breath and slowly exhaled.

It might as well be now. It was time to take a chance and see if she could control her own destiny. More than that, it was time to go home.

With a determined gait, she began jogging into the waves. The icy water swirled around her, raising goose bumps on her flesh. She shivered, then ducked into the water and began to swim.

Finally, she started breathing heavily and looked over her shoulder at the shoreline, which seemed to be as far away as the last time. She rolled over and stared up at the sky. It was clear and beautiful and very unlike the night she'd left her time, when a storm had been brewing and she had found herself in the center of a deep whirlpool.

Her heart fluttered in her breast. This wasn't right. It wasn't the right time of the moon. The weather wasn't the same. *She* wasn't the same. As much as she wanted to go back to her own time, she felt sure it wouldn't happen now. Nothing was the same.

When she'd stepped into the ocean over three weeks ago, she'd felt as if she had no alternative. To her mind, it had been a choice between death on earth or death in the ocean. In her own temporary insanity, she'd believed she'd made the saner choice.

Not so, this time. This time it was all wrong—it felt wrong.

Parris flipped on her stomach and began swimming toward shore. Panic edged her movements as she realized just how far out she was. With each swell of the waves, she pushed herself to reach the shore.

Don't panic, she told herself. *Slow and steady. Be the tortoise, not the hare.* If nothing else, she thought wryly, at least she had confirmed that, more than anything, she wanted to live.

The next time she tried returning to her own time, she'd be sure that all systems were go—whatever those systems were. She needed to think it out, come up with a plan, and work on it systematically. That was the proper course to follow.

Her arms ached. Her breath was short. Still tamping down the panic that was so close to the surface, Parris rolled over on her back and floated. It was calming to know that it was all right to take all the time she wanted to get back to shore. With that thought, she stared up at the star-studded sky and smiled. Life was good. She was alive.

As she floated, she realized she'd been cold

earlier, but was warm now. Something told her that wasn't a good sign, but she was growing too lethargic to care.

Feeling as if she was on a water bed, she closed her eyes. The gently undulating waves were lulling her to sleep better than a baby's lullaby.

"Par-ris!"

She smiled. It was nice falling asleep to Thomas's whispering her name in her ear.

"Par-ris!"

How sweet.

"Par-ris!"

A wave receded and uncovered her ear. She frowned. Her imagination was playing tricks on her. He was shouting instead of whispering. And he sounded irritated.

"Par-ris!"

She lifted her head. More than irritated. He was angry. Well, two could play that game. She'd ignore him.

"Par-ris! Come back!"

Since when did he have the authority to tell her what to do? Hadn't she paid him back? Then she remembered. No. With the exception of enough for another pair of shoes, all the money she'd earned these past two weeks sat in the bottom of her drawer. She had promised herself she'd pay Thomas as soon as she saw him. But she hadn't seen him until last night. And she'd forgotten.

"Par-ris!"

Obviously he wanted his money, or he wouldn't be so irritated.

"Par-ris! Get back here now!"

She opened her eyes. This wasn't a dream. That voice had to be real. She just didn't feel like responding. She was too tired.

"Parris! Come here!"

Thomas's voice was closer now. It took every bit of strength she had to look over her shoulder. Water slapped her in the face, acting as a wake-up call.

"Parris!"

He swam toward her, his strokes odd and unsure.

"Damn the man," she muttered, disturbed from her peaceful rest. She didn't like the feelings that returned to hammer at her. All those questions and doubts. And now the bone-chilling cold.

Parris shivered, then made a halfhearted attempt at swimming toward him. Now she was as irritated as he apparently was.

When they finally met, he was so angry all he could do was stare at her.

"Now that you came out here, do you want to race?" she taunted him.

"Do you know how stupid you are?" he exclaimed angrily.

"Go to hell, Thomas."

"What the hell were you trying to do? Kill yourself?"

"Of course not. If I had wanted to do that, I'd be dead by now."

"Then what are you doing out here?"

"Trying to get back to my own time! *My own family!*"

A rolling wave lifted them, then placed them gently in a valley of water. They could hear each other breathe. Parris was glad she was in the water. It was harder for him to tell whether her face was covered with sea or tears.

Finally, Thomas spoke. "Can you swim?"

"I got this far, didn't I?"

"Can you swim back?"

He wasn't going to win that easily. "If I have to."

"If I have to take you back, you'll be unconscious when I do it."

She believed him. The fire in his eyes was enough to convince her.

Instead, she pushed back a strand of wet hair and nodded. "Okay. I'll try."

"Go ahead," he ordered, finally catching his breath. "I'll be right behind you."

Parris's feet touched the ground, and she realized they'd been floating over a sandbar. One slow step at a time, she headed for shore. Somehow, they were supposed to share the ocean again, and like deja vu, Parris felt as if they were bound together in this time and in another. But the glimpse of the past—or future—was gone instantly.

The long shelf of sand allowed her to walk through the water toward shore, dragging one leg after another. She was so tired she was ready to drop.

Suddenly, Thomas's arm wrapped around her waist, hauling her onto the shore with him. Once they reached the hard, water-packed sand, they both dropped, sitting with their heads between their legs, trying to catch their breath.

Parris looked up. "Why are you here in the middle of the night?"

He shook his head. "I don't know."

"How did you know where I was?"

He shook his head again. "I don't know that either."

Wrapping her arms around her middle, Parris stared out at the ocean. "I'm glad you were."

His arm came around her shoulder, blocking some of the wind from her freezing body. "So am I." He stood. "Come on. You should be dried off and put to bed."

Allowing him to help her up, Parris began the trek back to her bedroom window. "Did you tell Clair where I was?"

"No. I went to your window. When I looked in and didn't see you, I knew that you'd gone out the window. That's why it was open so wide. So I followed your footprints toward the water. The rest was easy. In a long white gown on a dark ocean under a quarter moon, you were fairly easy to spot. Especially since I was looking for you."

Parris climbed through the window, knowing Thomas was close behind her. In the dark, she stripped off her nightgown and reached for another one in the drawer. Clair had bought them by the dozen, and then had given Parris six of them as a gift as well as the clothes Parris wore to the club. Clair was generous in that way, especially since she thought Parris's own clothes weren't suitable for their line of work.

After stripping off his clothes, Thomas grabbed one of the folded towels on her dresser to dry off with. She purposely kept her gaze averted, unwilling to acknowledge how much she missed the sight and feel of his tall, lean body.

She heard the sound of tape being pulled and a deep, hissing sigh. He must have removed the bandage from the stitches. It had to have hurt because he'd been swimming in salt water.

Once they were both dry, Parris knew it was time she confronted Thomas. She was still shaking, more scared by her brush with death than she was willing to admit.

She turned and faced him, but before she realized he was close, his mouth came down and claimed hers. She molded to him, her hands resting on the tight muscles of his upper arms. He felt so good. . . . The kiss was too short. His hands tightened on her waist as he pulled away.

"You scared the hell out of me," he admitted roughly, his voice rasping on every one of her nerve endings. "Until I spotted the white of your gown, I thought you'd drowned."

She rested her head against his lightly haired chest and heard the heavy, thick thud of his heartbeat. "I might have if you hadn't called me."

His hands tightened around her even more. "Don't *ever* do that again."

She looked up at him. His eyes glowed darkly in the moonlight. "Why do you care?" she asked. "Why are you here now?"

With hands that trembled lightly as his fingers curled around her face, he stared at her as if memorizing every tiny feature. "I love you."

For just a moment she believed him and her heart jumped with joy. Then she remembered. "You love every woman you want sex with."

"That's not true," he stated quietly, but with complete conviction. "I've never said those words to another woman before. It's you, Parris. I love you."

Her lashes fluttered closed in sheer ecstasy. He'd said the words she'd been afraid to think. He'd said them despite all they'd been unable to voice. Until now. And she was glad.

She opened her eyes and heart, allowing her feelings to show in her eyes and smiled. "I'm so happy. You see, I love you, too."

His fingers stroked her cheek and jaw as light as air. "Thank God," he said shakily. "I'd hate to think of feeling this way alone."

"You damn near would have if you hadn't spoken up," Parris teased. Her relief shone in her eyes.

"Don't cuss," he admonished softly. "And you couldn't help but love me." He raised an imperious brow. "I'm a lovable guy. Besides, I set out to make you love me."

"You're an egomaniac," she corrected. "That isn't the same thing. However, I'm willing to overlook a few flaws to find your true, redeeming character."

His smile was slow in coming, but worth waiting for. Parris was positive it momentarily lit up the room. "You're as full of blarney as I am."

"Oh, no," she chuckled. "You beat Donald Trump for charm and charisma, and Kennedy for the gift of gab and a way with the ladies."

Thomas looked stunned. "You know about Joseph Kennedy?"

Her smile grew broader. "Better still, I know about his sons. Joseph Jr. dies in the Second World War, John becomes the first Catholic president, Bobby the Attorney General, and when Jack is killed, Bobby runs for president and is assassinated, too. Teddy becomes a senator from Massachusetts and because of a young woman's death, his chances for the presidency are shot."

"My God," Thomas breathed. "It sounds like the family is bitten by snakes."

"I know."

"Who's Donald Trump?"

Parris had had enough of the definitions and explanations. "Never mind." Her hand touched the side of his face. "Besides, I believe you were telling me how much you love me."

There was a wicked gleam in his eyes. "Was I really? You must have been dreaming."

"No, you were if you think for one moment

that I'd settle for three little words without the rest of the ribbons and bows."

"All the frills?"

"That's right. All the frills," she confirmed.

Thomas pulled her closer to him, his fingers tightening on her waist and back. "I love you, Parris. I didn't want to, I tried not to, and I'll probably struggle against it for a long time. But the results are the same. I still love you."

It wasn't a dream. Thomas was there, holding her, telling her what she most wanted to hear. And those same words were aching to spill from her own mouth. "I love you, Thomas Elder, although, for the life of me, I don't know why."

A low deep chuckle reverberated in his chest, and Parris put her head on his heart to hear it rumble. "You'll never learn to keep your mouth shut, will you?"

Circling his waist with her hands, she closed her eyes. He smelled so good—all sea water and mild moonlight. "No."

Burrowing her head deeper into his chest, she smiled lazily. Now that Thomas was with her and had declared his love, she was content. Sleepy exhaustion was overcoming her quickly.

Standing in the middle of the room, in the middle of the night, Parris went to sleep in Thomas's arms.

Thomas could tell by her deep even breathing that she was relaxed. His hands soothed her back and hips, touching the body that he craved to hold for the rest of his life. He wondered how he had gone so long not realizing until that night that she had stolen a piece of him. Victoria was the dream of something young and innocent and status. Parris was the the same dream, but with the necessary touch of reality.

"Promise me you'll never do that again, Parris. I could have lost you." He refused to mention that he could have lost her by her traveling back to her own time. He wasn't ready to face that yet. "You could have drowned in that damn ocean."

Nothing.

"Parris?"

It was then he realized that she had fallen asleep in his arms.

He chuckled. The woman was a marvel. With infinite tenderness, Thomas picked her up and carried her to the bed. Within minutes, they were lying side by side sound asleep.

Bebe's voice filled Parris's ear. "Mr. Capone, he is here. Miss Clair is seeing to his needs."

Parris's eyes popped open. Bebe was bending over the side of the bed, her voice low as she spoke to Thomas. He was wide awake.

"When did he arrive?"

"About twenty minutes ago. I had to alert Miss Clair, then serve coffee. He drove in from Philadelphia this morning."

Holding the sheet, Thomas sat up and threw his legs over the side of the bed. "I'll be out of here in five minutes," he promised. "Did he see the car?"

Bebe nodded. "Yes, but it does not mean anything. He does not know that you are using Sol's car."

"Thanks, Bebe," Thomas said, running a hand through his hair. "I owe you."

"I owe you much more," she said quietly, giving his shoulder a light pat before leaving the room as silently as she had entered.

Parris held her breath as she waited for Thomas to do something. Say something. Last night had been a declaration of love. Did he regret it? Was it something said before the real world threatened to intrude?

Thomas looked over his shoulder, staring into her eyes. The coolness of his glance turned warm, then hot, seeping into her very soul as he slowly smiled. "Good morning."

"Morning." Although she felt the balm of his sun-drenched smile, she still felt anxious and wary.

"Did you sleep well?"

She nodded. Her fingers clutched the top of the sheet that rested just below her chin. "Did you?"

He bent over, his lips brushing against hers. "As long as your cute little butt didn't twitch against me, making me think of things I hadn't thought of before."

"And what could you possibly have been thinking of?"

He pulled back slightly, his gaze losing that teasing quality. "I love you, Parris."

Her breath caught in her throat. "Still?"

He nodded. "Still."

"What happens now?" That question covered a multitude of other questions. Each one bombarded both of them, and neither Thomas nor Parris was capable of putting all the answers together.

"We'll see," Thomas said. His lips grazed her neck, his head dipping even lower to caress the top of her breast. "Later," he murmured against her skin.

But she didn't care. Her hands were already busy pushing aside the sheets so they could touch more freely.

"I have to try to get back, Thomas."

His lips brushed her cleavage. "I know."

"I have to—" She couldn't remember what she had to do. She closed her eyes and reveled in his caresses, only to remember something else. "Bebe might come in again."

He kissed the soft skin beneath each breast, then let his lips trail to just above her navel. "No, she won't."

"Al Capone's in the next room." It was a feeble protest, but one that should be pointed out.

"Only until he gets hungry and goes into the kitchen." He kissed her just below her navel.

Lightning zinged down her spine. Heat radiated through her stomach. "What if Clair comes in?"

His tongue blazed a trail lower. "She'll be jealous." His voice was a whisper as he lifted her legs over his shoulders. "And then she'll shut the door behind her when she backs out."

Liquid heat spread throughout her body as Thomas made love to her with his mouth. Bright sunlight poured through the window, spilling light on his tanned body. Every nerve in her body was tuned to Thomas's touch. Every fiber sang with the need to be with him. Have him inside her. Be a part of him.

"Thomas." Her voice was a whisper, a light breath on the air.

But he heard her. "Not yet."

His tongue teased her more, and her hands clenched the sheets. "Thomas."

"No."

Tension narrowed into a spiral cord that wound around her, holding her captive within the sensations of his touch. His mouth, his fingertips, even the crisp hair on his chest caressed her nerves. There was nothing else in the world but Thomas. Nothing. . . .

"Thomas!" Her whisper was a plea. A demand. A scream that died in the warm morning air.

"Now," he said, finally covering her with his weight. It was an exquisite heaviness—one she craved as much as his touch.

His mouth covered hers, demanding her response. Parris gave it willingly. Her mind was delirious with pleasure.

He entered her in one gentle thrust, commanding every movement so that all she could do was follow.

"Thomas," she whispered.

"I love the way you say my name. Say it again."

"Thomas," she moaned, closing her eyes to feel all the places he stirred within her.

Then, with one thrust, he touched her innermost core. "Thomas. . . ."

Drifting on a cloud, she heard her voice utter his name. She clung to his shoulders as if he was the only solid thing in the universe.

He stiffened, holding her as close as two bodies could get. His warm breath caressed her neck as he traveled to the same cloud and was given the same gift.

And they were both deserving.

Chapter Thirteen

Cigar smoke filtered lazily through the air, saturating everything in the dining room. Standing nervously, with the late afternoon sun blazing through the windows and shining in her eyes, Parris clasped the warmth of Al Capone's lightly calloused hand. "How do you do, Mr. Capone?"

He was a little shorter than she was, perhaps five foot five or six, and much stockier than she had originally thought. This was no actor, but the real thing. And this man did *not* resemble Robert DeNiro in the movie version of *The Untouchables*.

Reality, however, bred strong fear. His breath smelled as stale as his cigar. His eyes were slightly bloodshot. And if she wasn't mistaken, his middle was girdled. His face was pockmarked and a scar down one cheek was proof of his violent nature. The glamour of movie stars wasn't there, but his presence was just as awesome. If he'd been living in her day, the media would have labeled him charismatic, but it wasn't something that came across in photos or interviews.

His eyes evoked fear, that stiletto gaze arcing right through to one's very heart.

It certainly was enough to put Parris on guard.

"What do you do, little one?" he asked.

"I'm Clair's secretary. I help maintain the files and make sure that the books are kept correctly."

"Are you a bookkeeper?"

Parris felt Clair's anxiety, but there was nothing she could do to alleviate it. She looked the short man in the eye. "Yes."

Capone laughed. "A woman bookkeeper working for Capone? That oughtta keep some of those mouthy broads quiet! They're alla time trying to get me to let them in the business."

Parris forced a smile.

Clair reached over and lifted the coffeepot. "More coffee?" she asked sweetly.

"Sure, doll." He leaned back and grinned. Obviously, Mr. Capone was in an expansive mood. "I like coffee almost as much as I like booze."

Clair glanced at Parris. "We'll be going in early today, Parris. But with Mr. Capone there, I don't think we'll need your help today."

"No, no, I changed my mind," Capone said, brandishing his cigar as if painting a gray-colored rainbow. "She can come with us, after all." He grinned. "We may need her help in finding something. Right?"

"Actually, Clair knows exactly where everything is, Mr. Capone. She has her finger on the pulse of the business."

He gave Parris an intense look, then shrugged and smiled. "Maybe. Maybe not."

With those words and a narrow-eyed stare directed at Bebe, who was returning with a fresh pot of coffee, he'd effectively cut off any more conversation. As if on cue, a bulky-looking man entered the room. He was dressed in a brown, double-breasted suit that accommodated his broad build. Parris was sure he also wore a holster strap under his jacket.

Thinking about gangsters and actually seeing them were two different things. Seeing them, Parris decided, took away the glamour and instilled fear. These men actually snuffed out lives, robbed people and businesses, sold women and drugs—and not necessarily in that order.

Yet, here she was, exchanging pleasantries and information with one of the most well-known gangsters in the world. As exciting as the opportunity was, she'd give anything to be back in her own time. She also wanted to ensure she would live that long.

"Are you ready, girlie?" Capone stood and began walking toward the front door. His bodyguard, whose nickname Parris had decided was Big Boy, led the way. Bebe had anticipated their moves and was already at the open door. "We'd better hurry. I want to get this over with."

Clair fell in beside him and Parris followed behind the rather unusual parade. In the driveway, the older woman handed Parris her car keys and then slipped into Capone's car with Big Boy. Obviously, Parris was supposed to drive herself. Having her suspicion confirmed by seeing the outline of a holster as the bodyguard bent into the driver's seat of Capone's car, Parris was happy with the arrangement.

It set the mode for the rest of the day. She was always a step behind the entourage and a step ahead of Danny and his men. It was high anxiety for her and unexpected frustration to Danny, who wanted to talk with Capone about taking over the club. At the rate he was going, he muttered under his breath, he'd be an old man before Capone would hear him.

Parris had to agree—and applauded Clair's tactical maneuvers.

Although Clair pretended subservience to Capone, she was well organized and crammed their time with facts and figures that would boggle the average man's mind. Capone was so busy looking as if he knew what she was throwing at him that he never left her desk.

Parris imagined it was tough for him to admit that a woman was capable of running the club. Clair, understanding the men of her generation, especially Capone, gave him detailed basic information, and never let him know she knew he was ignorant of the facts she was presenting.

Parris ate at her desk while Clair, Capone, and his buddy Mr. Landi ate in the privacy of the dining booth with the blue velvet drapes closed to curious eyes.

Just as Parris finished her own dinner of veal scallopini, Danny strode in. He stopped in front of her desk, his hands inside his full-pleated pants pockets. "How long will she be gone?" he demanded.

"I have no idea," she said calmly.

"Don't you keep track of the busy lady's schedule?"

She stood and placed her fork and knife on the plate. "When she wants me to."

Danny sneered. "And she doesn't want you to right now?"

His frustration didn't bother Parris. She knew the bully routine too well. "Mr. Capone is keeping track of her schedule."

He barely kept his temper in check. "We'll just see about that."

"And a good day to you, too," Parris murmured as she watched him stride out of the office.

Fifteen minutes later, Parris filed the last of the papers Capone had glanced over earlier. As she stood in the narrow closet, glancing over each paper before placing it in its proper file, Parris suddenly heard Capone's voice.

"And we'll just talk to him and see what he has to say," he said.

Parris wondered what to do. Should she just walk out of the closet and not say a word? Should she stay where she was and hope no one noticed her? Her next thought was that this was the same closet in which she had caught Clair and Danny making love, and she had to quell a nervous giggle that threatened to erupt.

Busy closet.

The office door opened, then closed. Parris held her breath. Just then, Clair walked over and stared in the partially opened door. She gazed at Parris. Then, with a bland expression that looked as if she was selecting dull wallpaper, she turned her back to Parris.

"All right, Mr. Capone. Let's have Danny come in now. After that, we'll have a toast in the outer office for all the old employees who have served you so well these past two years. *If* that suits you, of course."

He chuckled. "I like you, Clair. You have class and style. You even have guts. I like that in a woman."

Parris would bet that the woman in his life didn't have any of those qualities. The poor thing, whoever she was, probably more resembled a doorknob in personality and opinions.

"Hello, Mr. Capone. I'm pleased to meet you." Danny's voice boomed off the office walls. "I'd like to talk to you about some ideas I've got for the club."

"Sit down. I know your brother well. He's been with me a long time," Capone stated. "Tell me about yourself." Al's voice was jocular, but Parris heard that small note of steel beneath. This was Danny's one interview. He'd better get it right.

"I've thought about the operations in the next room," Danny began.

"The numbers?" Capone clarified.

Danny nodded. "I want to expand that operation."

"How?"

"Take over the top floor and add more phone lines. Also have only one exit and entrance."

"And who keeps track of all this?" Capone asked softly.

"A staff that I handpick."

"And what happens to the club?"

"It can continue, but I don't see why you'd want the drain. It doesn't produce that much money."

"Have you followed Clair around?" Capone asked.

"Some." Danny admitted, a smirk in his voice. Parris could just see him telling Mr. Capone about the closet affair. It would be just like the jerk.

"Danny," Clair interjected softly, "helps me with some of my . . . needs."

Capone chuckled low. "I see, girlie. So the grieving widow misses more than her husband's companionship?"

"Yes," Clair answered, sounding shy. "And Danny was good enough to help fill that void on occasion."

Parris wondered what was going to happen next. Was Capone going to give the business to Clair now that she'd admitted her liaison?

"Do you love him?" Capone asked.

"Goodness, no!" Clair chuckled. "Not at all."

"Danny? What about you?"

"Nah. She's just a dame," he said, but his voice wasn't as strong or convincing as Clair's.

"Well," Capone said quietly, his tone changing to one of an authoritative dictator. "It seems to me that the little lady has done one hell of a job and still kept her eyes on the profits. What more could I want?"

"But—" Danny began.

Capone interrupted him. "Our money is made in drugs, booze, prostitution, and gambling. You want to focus on gambling. Clair is handling booze and gambling and is capable of handling prostitution right now. If I decided to expand any of those areas, I have a solid base that she and her husband have built. That's a big plus." A chair creaked as it was pushed back. "So, I thank you for your thoughts, Danny, but I'm betting my money on Clair. Until I say different, she's in charge of operating this club as a part of my team."

Parris was shaking as she stood in the small space and listened to the man's voice. Danny was dead in the water. Clair was on top of the club until Al Capone decided otherwise. Then, if he changed his mind, he could kill both of them and begin again.

Parris wished she could see into the future and make sure Clair was going to be all right.

The outer office door closed and Parris heard Clair's deep sigh. She was apparently still standing close to the closet door.

"Why don't we have that toast now?" Clair said brightly. "And I feel I can really celebrate, thanks to you."

"You'll only be here as long as you do a good job. You understand that, don't you?" Capone's voice was low, his tone quiet.

"Oh, I understand that completely."

"Good. Keep Danny in charge of the gambling end until I find something else for that ambitious young man to do. He might as well service both of us, huh?" A coarse, gruff laugh filled the room. Clair's own earthy sound was incorporated.

It was a good thing Parris was in the closet, where she couldn't reach out and bop Capone in the head!

Then Capone's voice dropped. "One more thing, Clair. If you see that Thomas Elder anywhere, you tell me or one of the boys right away, *capice?*"

"Anything you say, Mr. Capone. But why?"

"Because he's crowding in on my territory and I need to make an example of him. He stepped on the toes of some people in the business, and now they want him out of the picture."

"I see," Clair said slowly. Parris could almost hear Clair's wheels turning. Parris's own heartbeat accelerated until she was sure that the sound filled the closet and echoed into the office.

"I know you know him. I know you been seen with him, maybe even taught him a little, given him some education. But that's over. Danny, he's fine to play around with. He's one of the boys. But this Elder, he's dead. Stay away so your pretty dress doesn't get stained."

"I understand, Mr. Capone." Clair's voice was clear and firm, and an icy chill of fear went zinging down Parris's spine as she realized that Clair would betray Thomas in a heartbeat. Anything to keep her job security.

"Shall we go?" Clair asked.

"Sure, girlie. And by the way, tell your secretary she can come out of the closet now."

With an even gruffer laugh, Capone left the office. Parris's face burned as she realized he'd known she was there all along.

The door widened and Clair stood in the doorway. "So much for being discreet," she stated dryly.

But Parris had only one thing on her mind. "He wants to kill Thomas!"

"Apparently."

"What do we do?"

Clair looked surprised. "Why, nothing. Whatever Thomas's problem is, I'm sure it will blow over. Meanwhile, we'll just make sure that he's not around."

"What did he do that Capone would want him dead?"

Clair shrugged. "Who knows besides Thomas? He wasn't careful, I guess. He's been bootlegging whiskey, maybe he forgot whose whiskey he was bootlegging. He even got some for me, bless his heart."

Relief flooded Parris. Clair wasn't going to turn him in after all. She was just going to ignore the whole thing. Then Parris realized how hot Clair's own seat was. If Capone had wanted to, he could have been angry with Clair—and Parris for overhearing a conversation not meant for outside ears. Heaven only knew what switched on his anger and what tickled his funny bone.

"God, I'm sorry, about being in the closet," Parris whispered. "I didn't realize you were returning to the office so quickly, and I was only doing the filing when—"

"It's all right. Don't worry."

Parris noticed for the first time that Clair was grinning from ear to ear. Her blonde hair even looked electrified—there might have been a hair or two out of place.

"Clair?"

"I'm gonna get him, Parris. The great Al Capone is gonna be in my bed by the end of the week." She sounded so excited, like a child given the promise of a wonderful treat.

Parris stepped out of the closet. "Is that what you want?"

"Of course." Clair looked surprised that Parris would even wonder such a thing. "Doesn't every woman want to bed the great Al Capone? It's bound to be swell!"

"You know, they used to say that, even though Henry the Eighth had six wives and a hundred affairs, he was never a great lover. It was a myth."

Clair shrugged, leading the way out of the office. "It's all in the head, my dear, and my head is ready for Al Capone."

Parris had heard enough to be worried. Clair might have known how to run a gambling casino and restaurant. But was she stable enough to keep her mind on the business *and* an affair? Or be loyal to friends like Thomas? Suddenly, Parris didn't think so. She should have seen the signs these past weeks. Clair would like anyone who was around to help. But if she no longer needed or wanted the help, she would not stand by that person in friendship. She would desert him or her.

Thomas was in big trouble.

For that matter, so was Parris.

Thomas had left Clair's earlier that morning, but hadn't had time to go to his room. He was dressed in the clothes he'd worn the night before. Bebe had freshened them up with a good pressing, but the fabric still looked wilted. One look in the mirror told him that they were barely presentable to drive to his boardinghouse let alone the appointment he and Bebe had that afternoon.

He was running a comb through his hair when Bebe knocked on the bedroom door. They were alone in the house, so she didn't stand on protocol. She reached his side and helped him put on his jacket.

"It's almost time for me to go back to France."

Thomas looked at her in the mirror, his brow creased in a deep frown. "Is it getting that tough around here?"

"Don't worry. It's much harder on Parris."

Thomas reached out and touched her shoulder. "I wasn't talking about Parris. She's one smart lady and can almost take care of herself. Besides, she's not carrying the burden you are."

Bebe's shoulders sagged. She'd been strong for so long. "I really thought I could kill Mr. Capone, Thomas. Until this morning, I honestly *believed* it. But I can't."

"Not even for Charlie?"

Bebe stared up at the man in front of her, her eyes filled with tears. "*Especially* for Charlie. You knew him, Thomas. Growing up, he was your best friend. Do you think he would want me to avenge his death?"

"Charlie isn't here to let me know what he wants, Bebe. He isn't here because a member of Capone's gang decided that one of the most talented writers around—one who won awards from the Writer's Guild, Black Opals, and the Saturday Evening Quill Club—should be killed because he stood up to a bag of worms who wanted protection money. Hell, Bebe, he was even a better writer than Langston Hughes, and he's gone, because he was a good guy! Does that sound right to you?"

"He was my husband, Thomas, and I will always love him with all my heart," Bebe said softly in her sweet French accent. "But I have realized that two wrongs do not make a right. And this is wrong. It is better for me to go home to try to make something of my life than to stay here and feed the revenge in my heart."

Damn. She made sense. But he still couldn't let it go. "Do you really want to return to France?" Thomas asked softly. "You made your name at the Cotton Club and Connie's Inn. Don't you want to stay here and continue with your singing career?

"No. Home is where I need to be." She placed her small hand against his chest. "Home is where you should be, too, Thomas. With a family and a wife who loves you."

An image of Parris flashed in his mind, but he pushed it back immediately. "Not me. I'm not the marrying kind. But don't lose hope that justice won't prevail, honey. Just because Charlie stood up to him and lost doesn't mean everybody has to. I can understand your not wanting to kill Capone, but I'm still going to do everything I can to put him away. I want to make sure he rots in jail. I want him to hear my name every day and know who put him there."

Thomas hated Capone and his kind for Charlie's death, but he also hated his kind because of his sister. He hated her boyfriend, Joey, even more and had vowed to take him down if it was the last thing he did. Unfortunately he hadn't had the chance the other night at the Alley Cat Club. Originally, his newspaper had allowed him to take a year off to find what he was seeking in exchange for an exclusive story, and then, he would return to his job. That year was almost at an end, and although he had lots of information and proof that he mailed to a friend in Philly on a regular basis, he still had a way to go before he felt justified in printing the story. But when Joey had followed his orders to kill Charlie, Thomas's purpose had become twofold, and sometimes all his efforts seemed futile. Maybe they wouldn't be if he got the chance just to put a bullet between Joey's eyes.

He didn't realize he'd spoken aloud until Bebe's voice broke through his reverie. "I am *not* asking permission not to kill. I am telling you not to do it either." Bebe's voice was strong, filled with a conviction that proved she had thought this through and knew her own mind.

"I still think—" He hesitated, unwilling to admit that he really wanted to get Joey more than anything.

"Please, no more thinking. It is all set. You will take me out to the boat in a week from this night. Everything is right and I am ready." She stood on tiptoe and kissed his cheek. "You have been a wonderful friend to both Charlie and me, but it is time I begin a new life. Charlie will always live in my heart, but I must still live in this world. I had better get on with it. I wish you would, too. Give it up, Thomas."

"I'll think about it," he stated doggedly.

He might change his mind about killing Joey, but he couldn't give up working toward anything other than seeing Al Capone and his ilk destroyed. That was the whole point of his story. Besides, if he didn't kill Joey, his sister would still be living with a murderer.

But other problems also cropped up, making him scatter his own logic. Parris. Would she be there to see his success or would she disappear soon? Was he willing to give up the rest of his life with Parris to kill a crummy gangster like Joey? The hatred he felt for the man screamed yes. But his logic cried out, "Are you crazy or just plain stupid?"

"Are you ready?" Bebe asked, bringing Thomas back to the present.

He fidgeted with his tie. "Just about."

"Then let's go meet the man with the boat. I am supposed to pay him for the papers I need to get into France."

"Okay, sweets. Let's go."

They left Clair's house, locking the front door just as the telephone began ringing. "Want to get it?" Thomas asked.

Bebe shrugged. "What for? So some society woman can look down her nose at me while I take a message for Clair to be at a charity luncheon she won't attend? No. We will let it ring."

Thomas walked her to the car and helped her in. They took off for town, each dwelling on private thoughts that needn't be shared.

Parris wanted to cry. Clair and Capone had toasted the bookie staff of what looked like middle-class citizens, celebrating the amount of profit the hard, dedicated workers had achieved. If she hadn't known better, Parris would have sworn they were factory workers whose boss had just received a thumbs-up profit sheet or stock raise. She had to pinch herself to remember they were taking bets across the nation and making profits for an organization that made most of its money off the misery of others through prostitution, gambling, and drugs.

Since Clair and Mr. Capone had once more ensconced themselves in the office, Parris had used one of the bookie telephones and tried to reach either Bebe or Thomas, with no luck.

Damn the man! He had declared his love for her, making her one of the happiest, confused women in the world—then he ran off and wouldn't let her save his gorgeous hide!

And Bebe! Usually so stoic, she had burst into the bedroom and treated Thomas as if they'd been old friends since birth. What was going on? Did he have a girl in every bedroom, or was she imagining things again? She was almost certain they were friends—close friends. But the longer she went without talking to him, the more uncertain she was.

What about Clair? Although she no longer seemed to be interested in Thomas, had she been one of his attractions at one time?

Parris held her head and pressed against her temples. *Stop it!* she told herself. Trying to figure out who was what to whom at this point was ridiculous! Nobody had handed her a scorecard, and she didn't know all the points to add up. Heavens, she didn't even know the rules of the game!

Her mind buzzed incessantly as she listened to the phone ringing on the other end of the line. Still no answer. Where in the world were they?

By midnight, Parris was a nervous wreck. Once, when Clair stepped out of the office and into the bathroom, Parris cornered her.

"Bebe is not answering the phone."

Clair looked surprised. "So what? She's probably in town, doing whatever she does when we're not around."

"Thomas isn't there either. They need to be warned."

"About Capone?"

Parris nodded.

"Don't worry," she said carelessly. "They'll survive. They're the kind who do it best."

"And what kind is that?" Parris asked, barely able to hold onto her temper.

"Oh, you know," Clair said, rubbing a smudge of carmine lipstick off her front tooth. "Ruthless."

"And you're not?"

Clair laughed softly. "Of course, I am! Why do you suppose I know what they're made of, Parris? One recognizes another of her own kind."

"And what am I?"

"Too soft. But very smart." Clair stared hard at her, sending a message that was bone-chillingly cold. "I think you'd better harden up, Parris. No man is worth losing your life over. No man is worth the time of day unless he can do something very special for you."

"What did Sol do for you?"

If Clair was surprised at her question, she didn't show it. "Everything. He gave me position and then opportunity."

"And in return, what did you do?"

Now she looked startled that Parris would ask such a stupid question. "I always took care of him."

"I see," Parris said slowly, wondering how well Clair had taken care of Sol. Well enough to throw him over the edge of reason? Then, suddenly, it didn't matter what her motives were or if she had any motives at all. Nothing mattered except getting to Thomas and warning him of Capone's threat. "I'm leaving early tonight, Clair," she finally stated. "I've got to warn him."

"If Capone finds out, he'll kill you." Clair's voice was calm, her gaze direct.

"I know that. I have to trust you. Can I?"

Clair's stare was as hard as before. Then she relented. Parris saw it in her eyes before she heard the words. "Go ahead. I'll cover for you."

Parris gave the older woman's arm a light squeeze. "Thanks."

Clair's hand went over Parris's, stopping her from running out. "I'll only do this as long as it doesn't look as if I had anything to do with it. But if you're found out, you're on your own."

"And Thomas?"

"I regret it, but he's on his own, too."

"I understand."

Clair sighed. "God, what fools we women are!"

"Don't I know it?" Parris whispered before walking out of the restroom toward the gambling casino.

Danny came running from the back office. "Quick! Sound the alarms! There's a raiding party on the way! We've got three minutes!"

Clair ran out of the restroom and into the casino. Red lights around the ceiling flicked on and off like traffic lights, warning everyone of the impending raid. Some new customers panicked, but most sat calmly and waited for the staff to take charge.

"It's okay, everyone," Clair stated, completely composed. "Please take a seat and watch the show. Meanwhile, nonalcoholic drinks will be served. Please dump all your drinks into the floral centerpieces on your tables. After this business is done, drinks are on the house for the rest of the night."

A round of applause echoed through the room, overshadowing the sound of pullies lifting the gaming tables off the ground and raising them into the ceiling. Now, Parris understood why the ceilings in that room were lower than in the others. Tiles moved aside to allow storage of tables and pulley mechanisms.

Parris watched in astonishment. In a little over a minute, the tables disappeared into the ceiling. Hostesses and waiters opened a closet in the back, rolled out additional small, round tables to circle the dance floor, placed chairs around them, and escorted some of the patrons to sit. Soft drinks were served from large trays laden with filled glasses.

In three minutes, the club was ready and looked as if it were a teen camp for a bunch of goody two shoes. If she hadn't seen it, Parris wouldn't have believed it. Even the audience seemed to get a kick out of it, passing it off as a lark.

When the police entered the front and kitchen doors, several couples were dancing while others stood in gatherings, looking as natural as if this had been going on all evening.

As if by script, several police went from table to table, sipping drinks. A few even looked under the tables. The customers didn't pay the slightest attention. Parris didn't know how it was done, but even the bar in the back room only had sodas on its shelves. Although Parris wasn't sure, she imagined there was a turntable for the shelves.

Four of the police went into the bookie room and office beyond. Clair escorted them. Parris didn't wait around for an invitation. With her small purse in hand and the keys in her jacket pocket, she left through the kitchen when the police guarding it turned away. In two minutes, she was gone from the alley and on the road to Cape May.

At first, she wondered if the police would realize whom they had in the back office and arrest Al Capone. That would give Thomas time to escape. But she knew better. If Capone had ever been detained in Atlantic City or if a club had been the arresting site for a man as famous as he was, that information would have been known in her time. Since Capone wouldn't be arrested, the best thing for her to do was to find Thomas.

She prayed that wouldn't be too hard. She also prayed that Capone hadn't already put word to deed and one of his men hadn't already done the job of killing Thomas.

She wished she hadn't been jolted through time, but her love for Thomas overrode everything.

Whether she stayed in this time period or found a way back to her own, Thomas Elder would live in her heart for the rest of her life.

Damn the man!

Chapter Fourteen

"Thomas Elder, it's after eleven o'clock. Where are you?" Parris muttered as she stood in the sand just beyond Clair's house and scanned the dunes. She hoped—prayed—she would find him before Capone did. But no one was in the house and she wondered what was going on.

Just as she turned, headlights pierced the darkness of the driveway. She stared over her shoulder, hoping Clair and her houseguest hadn't decided to pursue her.

The auto pulled into the garage and Parris walked cautiously back to the house, peeking around the corner.

Thomas stepped out of the driver's seat. Parris heard Bebe climb out of her side. "You will hold the tickets?" she heard Bebe ask.

"Don't worry. I'll handle it," Thomas promised

as he turned and spied Parris. "What are you doing here?"

"Waiting for you," she snapped, not really knowing whether she wanted to kiss him or kill him. "Obviously, I was more worried than you were."

He walked out of the darkness of the garage and stared down at her, his hands reaching for her shoulders. His gaze pierced through her armor. "About what? Are you all right?"

"I'm fine. I risked my neck to try to reach you by phone, but no one answered. After trying for over three hours, I decided to drive here and see if I could find you. Instead, I found an empty house."

"What is it? What's happened?"

She couldn't think of a single way to tell him except straight out. "Al Capone just announced that he wants you dead."

From the shadows behind him, Bebe gasped. Thomas's only show of emotion was his hands' clenching. "Come for a walk along the beach," he said calmly.

Frustration welled. Parris had been worried sick and Thomas was acting as if it were an everyday occurrence to have a price on his head. And while she had worried about Thomas, he had been with Bebe. She felt her aching heart hurt more.

"Bebe, will you be safe here if I leave for a while?" Thomas asked thoughtfully of the woman standing beside him.

"But of course. Besides, we just ensured that my boat will be sailing in a week, yes? I just have to figure out a way to get to it. That should be no problem."

"I'll be back and take you out to the boat myself," Thomas promised. "I've seen it this far, I'll see it the rest of the way. I want to know that you're safe." He grinned devilishly. "Who knows? I may go with you, after all."

"Where?" Parris demanded.

They ignored her.

"Who knows?" Bebe stated sadly. "We may both miss the boat."

Thomas's expression was stern. "You'll be on it if I have to paddle you all the way from here to France."

"What a lovely picture," Parris stated sweetly.

"You are very stubborn, Thomas. So very much like Charlie."

"As far as you're concerned, I've got as much power at the moment as he would have had." He brushed the dark woman's cheek with a kiss. "You take care and be ready to leave one week from tonight. I'll be back to get you then. By that time, Capone's men will be in Chicago and everything will have died down."

"Do you believe that?"

Thomas shrugged. "Who knows?"

Bebe turned and walked back to the house. Thomas watched her, then reached for Parris's hand. He looked down at her for the first time since Bebe had spoken. "You gonna be all right?"

"With what?" she asked warily, not following any of this conversation.

"With staying here and keeping your mouth shut."

"About what?"

He sighed in exasperation. "About me. Don't let them know where I am."

"I won't," she promised, "because I'm going with you."

"No."

"Yes." She took a deep breath. "I left the club to warn you. Just before I left, the club was raided. They'll think I turned the club in and am hiding you."

"Why would they think that?"

"Because Clair is looking out for herself, and if anything goes wrong, she'll look for a scapegoat. If I'm not here and you're not here, they'll have to find someone else to blame."

"You're wrong. That's when the blame automatically goes to the missing parties," he argued stubbornly. "You'd be safer staying here and brazening it out."

"Read my lips, buster," Parris stated, standing toe to toe with him, equally stubborn. "I'm going with you. Wherever you go, I go."

"But what if you disappear? Go back to your own time?"

"First of all, I won't just disappear. Going back, I'm sure, has to be planned. So for now, I'm glue, stuck to you forever. Understand?"

His quick grin disarmed her anger. "Okay, run

in, Miss Bossy. Grab your things and let's go."

She grinned back. "Really?"

He nodded. "Hurry. I'll grab some food while you get your things together." He glanced at his watch. "We should still have another twenty or thirty minutes before they think about checking here."

"Maybe I didn't make myself clear," Parris stated doggedly. "Clair will turn you in. Capone has put out the word that he wants you dead. The police delivered you to the house last night and could get word at any time that your ass is grass." She took a deep breath. "Now do you understand the urgency of getting away from here?"

Thomas bent down and gave her a kiss. "Yes. Get packed. We'll still leave in twenty minutes."

With her shoulders stiff from trying to hold back her tears of frustration, Parris turned to the house, slipped inside, and went directly to her room. Grabbing the voluminous nightgown Clair had given her on her first night in the house, Parris tied the arms together then stuffed the rest of her clothing into the gown. With a wide swipe, she dumped the few cosmetics she owned from the dresser top into the gown. It all took less than three minutes. She hugged the gown to her chest and held the bag containing her wallet in one hand.

With steps as determined as her mind-set, she walked back to the garage. Stealthily, Parris climbed into the backseat of the car and huddled on the floor. If her hunch was correct, Thomas would be there any minute. If she was wrong, she was going to look like a fool.

She hoped she was wrong about Thomas trying to leave without her, but she didn't think so. Either way, Parris was going to ride off into the darkness with Thomas Elder.

A minute hadn't passed before she heard Bebe's soft, low tone. "Be very careful. If you cannot return in time, do not worry. I will go to New York and request help there."

"I'll be back. Meanwhile, take care of her."

"But of course."

"She's stubborn and a little headstrong."

"Just like the man who loves her?" Bebe chuckled.

"Maybe. But it's not seemly in a female."

"Don't be so stupid, *mon cher*. You do not have to survive in this softer body. You do not know the strength we women must have just to survive."

It was Thomas's turn to give a low laugh. "Probably not," he conceded. "But that one would be willing to teach me if we stayed together."

There was a moment of silence; then Thomas spoke again. "If anything happens to me, claim my body and grab my black shoe. It's in the extra pillow in the closet at Mrs. Timmers boardinghouse. The heel is hollow. Then, split the money with Parris, if she's still here."

"Do you expect her to go somewhere else or do you think Capone will catch up with her?"

"No, Capone will leave her alone. In fact, I think Clair will protect her. She wouldn't want Capone to know she made a mistake by having Parris around." Thomas opened the car door and placed his foot on the running board. "I just think she might disappear. That's all."

"Well," Bebe sighed. "If you do not leave here quickly, Capone will see that you disappear, too."

"Right," Thomas said, slipping onto the seat. "Explain to Parris for me and tell her I'll see her next week."

"Do not do anything dangerous, my friend. I don't want to have anything happen to you, too."

Parris didn't know if he answered with a gesture. But the car was fired up and thrown into reverse; then they were out of the driveway.

Parris had never thought those cars had as much speed as the ones in her day, but this thing was eating up the road pretty quickly. What did he think? Was he going this fast because he thought that Parris would dart out of the house and run after him?

Once they reached town, he stopped by his boardinghouse and grabbed a suitcase. Parris was thankful he threw his small suitcase into the front seat instead of in the back, where she was.

"Damn," she heard Thomas mutter 15 or 20 minutes later—just as she was about to rise out of her cramped position.

Then he slammed on the gas. Parris could hear the engine strain, then speed up. She glanced out the rear window, small by her standards, and realized someone was following them. Another car's lights poured through the glass.

Seconds later, a dull thud seemed to pop somewhere in the trunk area. Her heart stopped, then sent a cold chill speeding down her spine. She was sure the thud had been a bullet.

Just as she was about to scream at Thomas to step on the gas, he jerked the wheel to the left, and the car spun in a 90-degree turn. Parris fell over the large hump in the floor, and the breath was knocked from her lungs.

Then the car jerked to the right, and she was catapulted against the side of the car. Another thud sounded on the trunk, followed in rapid succession by three or four more.

"Hurry up, for God's sake!" Parris shrieked, panic swelling her throat.

"What the—" Thomas glanced in the rear-view mirror, arching his neck until he saw her. "Are you crazy?" he shouted back. "You could get killed, you stupid broad!"

"Don't you *dare* call me a broad! And drive faster!"

Both hands on the wheel, he aimed straight down the road to Philadelphia. She only hoped that there were enough police around that the gangsters would stop shooting.

"Stay down!" Thomas shouted.

It was an unnecessary order. Parris was already hugging the floor.

Two, three, four more bullets whizzed into the back of the car.

Another sharp turn.

Another muttered curse. "You damn fool of a woman! I left you at Clair's so you wouldn't be killed!

"And I came with you so you wouldn't be killed!"

"And how are you going to stop that?"

"I don't know!"

The trailing car's tires screeched and headlights jumped eerily in the dark. Suddenly an exploding pop echoed through the air, and then the pursuing car veered into the darkness on the side of the road, its lights disappearing.

Thomas kept going at breakneck speed. Parris stared out the bottom of the side window, then out the back. There wasn't a car in sight.

"What happened?" she asked, afraid of his answer.

Thomas's gaze darted everywhere. "I think they had a blowout."

Parris felt relief. "Are you sure?"

He nodded. "Get up here, in front." It was an order. His mind had switched from outmaneuvering gangsters to Parris.

She climbed over the seat and slipped into the plush leather passenger seat. Automatically, she reached for the shoulder harness, only to realize there was none. "You guys need to install seat belts, shoulder harnesses, and air bags if you're going to drive like this."

"What are those?"

"Safety devices," she explained, glad for a topic that had nothing to do with death and dying or men probably lying in ditches with wounds bleeding. Or Thomas and herself dead from a gangster's bullets.

They drove in silence for another 15 or 20 minutes, each tied to his own thoughts. Parris's hands quit their shaking and she stopped swallowing convulsively. She refused to think about the bullets lodged in the back of the car. She refused to think about anything other than saving Thomas's life long enough to have him help her get back to her own time. A car heading east toward Atlantic City passed them on the highway and Thomas stiffened. So did Parris. Lights disappeared down the road. They both sighed in relief.

"Why didn't you stay behind like you were supposed to?"

"Why did you lie to me and tell me I was going with you?"

"Why don't you just do as you're told?"

"Why didn't you tell me you were going to run without me?"

"Why won't you shut up?"

"What is Bebe to you?"

"What?"

Parris crossed her arms. "If I might die because

I choose to be with you, then I have a right to know what Bebe means to you. At first, I thought you were only friends. Now I'm not so sure."

Thomas sighed, the tension slowly leaving his body. But his eyes continuously darted to the back window. "When I was growing up, my best friend was a kid named Charlie. He lived just below me. His parents were from Jamaica and had come here thinking that this land was paved with gold. They had three kids, and even though they'd found out concrete wasn't gold, they stayed. And they loved each other. Lord, I used to envy Charlie and his family. Love and laughter seemed to be everywhere in their dingy apartment. I never wanted to leave it.

"My dad would get angry when he heard that I was hanging out with those no-account niggers, as he used to call them. I never had the nerve to tell him that they had more than our family ever had. Then, after my dad disappeared, Charlie's family helped my mom, sister, and me survive."

"And you stayed the best of friends?" Parris's voice was low, almost hating to break into his reverie. Funny how difficult situations brought back memories that were sweet, poignant, and sad.

Thomas nodded. "We both wanted to be writers, but Charlie was always better than I. He wanted to write fiction and poetry, and he did it against all the odds." Thomas sighed. "And he won more awards than he had wall space. I was more nonfiction, so I went into the newspaper business, with a desire to someday to write a book."

"And if you live long enough, you'll do it," Parris stated dryly, making a joke so she could continue to keep the danger from the corners of her mind.

He didn't comment on her sense of humor. "Three years ago, Charlie went to Paris, and when he returned six months later, he brought Bebe with him. They set up housekeeping in Harlem and she sang in the clubs, including the Cotton Club. It's one of the best. Just as she was about to go big time, Charlie was gunned down for not giving some punk crook protection money so that Bebe could sing in some of the other clubs. The guy was a close friend of Capone's."

"Dear sweet heaven." Parris voice was a whisper.

Thomas continued, his voice a monotone. "Bebe went into a catatonic state. I picked up the trail of the guy and it led to Sol and the Alley Cat Club. When I told Bebe, she came alive, began planning her revenge. We finally agreed that we would work together. She agreed as long as she could kill Capone for taking away her life. She got a job with Clair. It was so easy it was laughable. I began using some contacts in New York so I could hang out with the rich. I wanted to work my way into the gang and expose them from the inside."

"How are you doing?"

His laugh was harsh. "Right now, I wouldn't say I'm doing too well. Just for the record, neither are you."

"I meant, did you do what you set out to do?"

"Almost. At first, I thought it was Clair's husband Sol I wanted to get. I saw him going downhill right in front of my eyes and I couldn't figure it out. Then I got a tip that he had had nothing to do with Charlie's death and that it was someone else."

"Was Clair in charge of the Alley Cat while Sol was ill?"

"No. Clair told me a guy named Mark was. He worked with her for a while, then left. Clair took over completely about seven months ago."

"And who's the man who killed Charlie?"

"Someone I could cheerfully kill."

Parris was surprised. She'd never heard Thomas say that about anyone. "Why?"

"Because he also lives with my sister."

Suddenly she held the missing piece to the puzzle of Thomas Elder. "Joey?"

He nodded, his expression grim.

"Have they been together long?" she asked cautiously.

"Two-and-a-half years," he stated bitterly. "Long enough."

"Long enough for what?"

"Long enough for her to know what he is."

"Did she say anything when you saw her the other day?"

"Patricia tried to talk me into being nice to that jerk. He's responsible for at least five deaths besides killing Charlie, and she wants me to be nice!"

"Does she know?"

"She knows." His voice was filled with disgust. "She's in love, she says. She also says Joey wants out of the mob, but we all know that won't happen. No one gets out alive."

"Including you?"

"I'm not in."

"I got the impression that that was what this is all about. Al Capone thought you were in, and now he found out you might have done them harm. He's letting you out the only way the business allows."

"What a guy," he said, his voice dripping sarcasm.

They continued driving toward Philadelphia. Parris wondered what would happen next, but she was afraid to guess. The roadsides were dark, making her feel as if machine guns were aimed at them, ready to fire. Her nerves tightened with every passing car. Her ears heard engines where there were none. Her eyes saw figures floating past along the road.

She glanced at Thomas and wondered how he could be so calm. For the first time, she noticed his white-knuckled grip on the steering wheel.

Thomas was not as calm as he pretended. That thought didn't make her feel any more comfortable. One of them ought to know what to do and how this episode was going to turn out!

Before she could ask what he was thinking, he wheeled the car into a side road, turned it around, parked, and turned off the headlights. They had a clear view of the main road.

"What are you expecting to see?" she asked softly.

"Who's behind us."

"But if we keep going fast, they would lose us in Philly, wouldn't they?"

"Maybe."

"And if we stay here, won't they be closer to us than we care to think about?"

"Maybe."

"So why are we doing this?"

He made a sound of impatience. "Do you have to ask so many questions?"

"My life is in jeopardy, too."

"But you don't know the criminal mind," he began explaining, then stopped as he watched a car heading toward Philadelphia approach. "Damn," he muttered. "There they are. They were only three or four minutes behind us."

Parris's eyes strained against the darkness to see the people in the car. "Who?"

"Capone's henchmen."

"Are you sure?"

"Parris," Thomas stated quietly. "Shut up."

She sat stiffly as he started the engine, then

pulled back onto the highway and followed the car 300 or 400 yards in front of them. Deep down, she knew he was right. Questioning every move he made would drive him nuts. It would have driven her nuts, too. But his demand still stung.

Once more, her nerves tightened until her hands felt as if thin piano wires were holding her bones together. Could someone survive prolonged tension due to life-threatening circumstances, she wondered.

The night sky paled on the horizon, and the city lights tinted it a deep blue. They were getting closer to safety, although she wasn't sure what would happen once they reached Philadelphia.

Ironically, she was heading home along the very road that would grow into a major highway and would become a death trap for her family. Unless she could stop it. If wishes were strong enough, they could become reality. . . .

"I'm going home," she vowed aloud.

"When?"

"The next first night of the full moon." After uttering the words, she realized she was right. It *felt* right. "At the exact spot I went in."

"Full moon is next week," he muttered, his foot easing up the gas pedal.

"So be it." For reasons she couldn't explain, she knew she was right. "Come with me."

"I can't." He reached over and took her hand from her lap and placed it on his thigh. "And you don't know that you can either. You've already tried once."

"I hadn't thought it through. Everything needs to be reversed in exact order. It will work. I know it will." She didn't want to tell him that she also felt a pull to the ocean so strong that leaving the shoreline behind was almost an afterthought. "Let's do whatever has to be done so I can get back to Cape May."

Thomas stared in the rearview mirror. "What's the rush?"

She felt his fingers tighten and knew he was just making small talk. Resisting the impulse to throw herself on the floorboard, she turned and looked over her shoulder. Several hundred feet behind them was a car. A big car. Parris squinted. A big black car, just like the car that Al Capone drove.

She groaned.

His hand soothed hers. "Easy, tootsie."

Her bottom lip quivered, and it took everything she had to keep it from showing. "If these are going to be my last moments on earth, then don't let them be spent with that stupid nickname ringing in my ears."

"Gotcha."

"And one more thing," Parris announced shakily. "I just want you to know that I love you with all my heart."

"I love you, too." He grinned, showing his deep dimples. He gave her hand another squeeze, then dropped it and put both his hands on the wheel. "Now, get down."

Once more, Parris did as she was told. This time, however, she was finally ready to meet her destiny.

Whatever in heavens name that was.

Chapter Fifteen

Sandwiched between two gangsters' cars like a piece of thin-sliced baloney, they traveled all the way into downtown Philadelphia. After the first ten minutes of being wedged between them, Thomas realized that they were looking for two people in the car and didn't have a description of the vehicle. Because he was the only one they could see and he was driving safely and carefully, they had brushed him off as another tourist on his way home.

Once they reached the courthouse, Thomas calmly pealed out of the middle, taking a side street and several alleyways. He turned the car around and backtracked, then stepped on the gas.

"You can get up now."

"Thanks," she said dryly, pretending she wasn't

still shaken by the night's events. Parris raised herself from the floorboard and peered out the windows. "But I feel at home here now."

"They're gone. I lost them."

"How did you know they didn't recognize you?"

"I didn't for sure. It wasn't until they didn't pass me or pay any attention to the car that I understood they were just cruising behind us because we happened to be going in the same direction they were."

"Does that mean we're safe now?"

"Not yet," he muttered, traveling up the hill toward three-storied row houses.

The neighborhood was run-down now, but its time would come. Parris knew exactly where they were. Modeled after the brownstones in New York, the houses in this section of town had been renovated in the eighties and had become one of the most prestigious areas in the city.

Carefully monitoring the traffic around him, Thomas slowed, pulled into a street, and then parked just off the corner at the end of the street, the car nose aiming at the intersection.

"Where are we?"

Thomas leaned back, stretching his cramped muscles. "This is my friend Matthew's house. He'll help us."

She curled up in the seat. "Like live?"

"Maybe he can even help you."

"Right," she said, her tone dry and brittle.

Thomas stared at her with eyes sad as well as

heavy from lack of sleep. She reached out and cupped the side of his face. "I'm sorry. You're doing the best you can. I know that."

His gaze darkened as he stared down at her. "Parris, I know this sounds crazy and doesn't make sense at all, but I want you to find your way back to your time." He narrowed his gaze, his eyes searching her face as if memorizing it. "I just don't want to lose you."

Her heart warmed. He wasn't much for saying what was on his mind, let alone what was in his heart. "Thank you."

"Don't you think you might get used to living in this time?"

Parris shook her head, wishing she could lie. "Don't you see? I *have* to try to get back. I don't have a choice." Her hand dropped, touching his. "But you do. Come with me."

"What about *my* family?"

Her fingers tightened in his. "I'm sorry. Of course you need to be with them. I just thought—"

"That since we weren't really a family, I might as well leave them behind—*if* it was possible for both of us to return to your time?"

"*If*," she agreed. "I know it's a lot to expect out of someone. I won't ask again."

"I can't do it, Parris."

"I know." Tears filled her eyes as she realized just how hopeless the situation was. With the way her luck was running, she would not get back. But she still had to try.

Thomas frowned. "Do you have money in your time?"

Parris nodded. "Of course."

"Personally?"

"A little. Most of my parents' estate will go to pay off the bills. I'll still own the two houses and one of their cars. My brother had an insurance policy that was just enough to pay for his burial. He was too young to have amassed a lot of money."

Dim streetlights emphasized the darkness. Parris felt as if they were wrapped in a cocoon of warmth. She leaned against Thomas's strong body and stared out the windshield, wishing the feeling of comfort would last, but knowing it would disappear with the light.

"How old were your parents?" His voice was soft, sweet, and seductive.

She concentrated on the answer instead of the thousands of images that came to mind. "Dad was fifty. Mom was forty-eight. My brother was the baby of the family at twenty-four."

"Would I have liked him?"

"You would have loved him. They all would have loved you." She smiled through a sheen of tears.

His chuckle vibrated against her back. "You feel confident enough to speak for them?"

"Of course."

"And if they hadn't liked me?"

"They probably wouldn't have said so unless you beat me. They respected my opinion enough to let me do what I wanted."

"You make them sound like a swell family."

She grinned. It seemed funny to hear that word. She hadn't heard the expression since the old television reruns from the fifties. "They were."

"Well," he said slowly, his hand rubbing up and down her stomach in a mesmerizing motion. She held her breath. "Whether or not you make it back or you decide to remain, I think I figured out a way for you to become rich."

She turned and looked up at him. "How?"

He bent down and brushed a light kiss on her parted lips. "The stock market."

Parris's eyes lit up. "The crash! It's *perfect* timing! Anything I recognize as still being around in my time will survive the crash and be worth millions!"

"You got it, sister."

"And the stock will split!" she said in wonder. "Good grief, there have to be a million of them over the years!"

"Are you familiar with stocks at all?"

"Some, but I'm no professional." Parris frowned. "But certainly I should know some of the major ones. I had to study them in college."

His mouth nuzzled her neck, stopping when he reached the side of her jaw. "You'll do just fine," he murmured.

Parris sighed. "I know I will. I just want to get started."

"Slow down, toot . . . sweetheart," he amended. "We can't wake Matthew up yet. Give him another hour or so before we tear his usually so-logical thought pattern apart."

"All right," she sighed, relaxing in his embrace. "I guess you don't have newsstands around either."

His mouth touched her nape. "Of course we do. One near here opens in another hour or so."

He gently pushed her forward. "Wait, let's get comfortable."

Turning sideways in the seat, Thomas stretched out his legs and pulled her between them, wrapping his arms around her waist once more. They lay spoon fashion in the seat, Thomas's head resting against the driver's window.

"Are you comfortable?"

"Yes," she said with a contented sigh. "Am I hurting you?"

His chuckle was low. "Not in the way you mean," he admitted in the dark. "And I'm lovin' every minute of it."

She rubbed her head against his chest. "So am I. No one has ever held me like this before."

"It's nice," he said softly.

"It's wonderful," she admitted.

Parris closed her eyes, reveling in the feeling of closeness that wrapped them together. His hands met just below her breasts, his fingers barely grazing their soft undersides.

Thomas took a deep breath. "I love your scent."

"Thank you, kind sir."

He gave a light squeeze. "Now get some sleep. We've only got an hour before daylight."

"I'm too keyed up to sleep," she said. "But don't worry. I'll be still."

His hand covered her left breast. "I can feel your heart beating."

She closed her eyes, loving his touch. His hand fell from her breast, then began unbuttoning her dress, opening it to allow him access to her warm flesh. His fingers were light, teasing as they sought her nipple.

A rush of warmth filtered through her. The darkness enveloped them, making her feel as if they were the only two people left on earth. Parris sighed.

Thomas's mouth pushed aside part of the material and kissed her shoulder.

Parris tilted her head back and his other hand slipped down, gathering the fabric of her skirt until he slipped his hand to the inside of her thigh.

"Thomas," she began breathlessly.

"Shhhh," he said softly, kissing her ear.

His lightly callused fingers slid inside her white cotton panties.

She stiffened. "But. . . ."

"Shhhh," he said again. "Don't argue, just enjoy."

Parris glanced down, realizing that if anyone walked by, he wouldn't know what was going on. Thomas's hand was completely covered by her skirt. She tingled from her head to her toes. She knew it was a reaction to the forbidden— but it was also the danger of being seen that heightened her senses.

His fingers touched her, tantalizing her. Parris moved, slowly, rhythmically.

"Great, honey," he whispered. "Enjoy it."

"Thomas." Her throat closed up.

"Show me," he said in her ear. "Take my hand and show me what you want."

She couldn't. Parris could hardly think, let alone show.

"Come on, baby."

Her muscles tightened, heat working through every part of her body. Her legs moved, aching to feel him inside her.

"It's all right, Parris," he crooned as if reading her mind. "It's all right to enjoy this. I'm here. I'm right here."

"But—" Her voice strangled in her throat. She tried to turn around, but his hold stopped her.

"Shhh. It's all right." His thumb and finger rolled her nipple, causing intense waves of sensation to roll through every nerve.

Thomas was doing this to her. Thomas, who didn't seem to care that this was supposed to be a participatory sport. And by this time, neither did she. Her heart was pounding so loudly she could hear it in her ears.

"Let go. Let go." His whispered orders filtered through, and like magic, she did as she was told.

Her head rolled back, her hands clenching his thighs as if to keep her anchored to earth as she flew over the rainbow with the wind, sun, and heat.

Thomas continued stroking her until she went completely limp, releasing every ounce of her pent-up tension. The warmth of their breath trapped in the car worked like a blanket on her skin, keeping her warm and cozy. And safe.

She closed her eyes. Tilting her head to the side, she listened to his heartbeat and smiled.

"God, you're so beautiful, Parris," he whispered, brushing her lips with a kiss. "So very loving."

Her lashes fluttered; then she stared up at him. "You're the loving one. You didn't have any satisfaction."

"Watching you was satisfaction enough. For now."

"I'm afraid of you, you know," she said, her eyes wide as she stared up at him.

His gaze widened. "I'd never hurt you. Don't you know that?"

She nodded. "I'll hurt so badly when I leave."

"*If* you leave."

"I will, Thomas. If there's a God on earth and He's fair, I'll be able to save my family."

This time, his eyes closed. But just before they did, Parris saw the pain there. She wanted to give him the support, the help, the comfort he'd given her, but she couldn't. She didn't know how.

"Tell me what to do, Thomas," she whispered, twisting around in his arms. "Tell me how to help you. I'll do it, whatever it is."

His mouth covered hers in a kiss that showed his own fear. Tongue battled with tongue, then caressed in apology. His hands dug into her shoulders, pulling her so close she thought she was going to be absorbed into him.

Her hands held his head, wanting him to understand that she knew how he felt and that she needed to give him succor and comfort.

Still he held her tightly. His mouth left hers and she felt bereft. He buried his head in her neck, and for just a moment, Parris thought she heard a sob. But she was mistaken because nothing happened after that.

She stroked his neck and shoulder, then pulled back to look up at him. Dawn was breaking and the private confines of the car were changed into a public arena. Parris didn't care. "I love you so much it hurts."

"I know."

"I love you so much I want to be a part of you."

"I know." He closed his eyes, touching her forehead with his. "I know because I feel the same way."

"What else do the crazy gods have in store for

us," she cried, frustrated with their narrowing choices.

Before he could answer, she pulled back and pressed her fingers to his lips to stop his words. "Hold me, Thomas. Just hold me."

Wrapping his arms around her, he held her to his heart, wishing he could absorb her into his very body, his very breath. Together, they watched dawn approach. Together, they sighed and faced the reality they'd been trying to hide from: They could be killed at any time by some gangster and no one would ever know, and their love would be over in this lifetime.

Thomas sighed. "It's time. Matthew is up."

Finally, after all night, Parris was beginning to get sleepy. She yawned, wishing she had a bed to fall into. With Thomas. "What's Matthew last name? How do you know he's up?"

"Matthew Taggart. His kitchen light just went on."

Parris yawned. "I don't want to move."

Thomas scooted her closer to the passenger side and brought his legs around and his feet to the floor. "You've flat run out of choices. Up and at 'em."

Running a comb through her hair was the best Parris could do before he was out of the car and opening her door. "No more dawdling," he ordered with a smile, but she noticed that his gaze slid up and down the street several times before they made it to Matthew's front door and stepped inside.

Each floor was divided into two apartments, one at the front and one at the rear. A narrow staircase led to the next landing, then the next. One bulb hanging from a long cord was at the beginning steps of each landing. Obviously, lighting hadn't become a science yet. Just a necessity. From what Parris could see, the building was at least maintained fairly well.

Her hand in Thomas's, she followed him up the stairs to the next landing, then toward the front of the building again. Once at the door, Thomas knocked three times; one single knock, then two in rapid secession.

She glanced up at him inquiringly. "It's an old code of ours," Thomas answered her unspoken question.

Then the door opened and light spilled into the dim hallway.

"You son of a bitch! I thought I was dreaming that damn noise!" A big, sleepy-eyed man in a beat-up plaid bathrobe enveloped Thomas in a bear hug. His voice, though softened into a whisper, still seemed to boom through the echoing hallway. "What the hell are you doing back here? Didn't I hear you say you'd never darken Philadelphia's door again?"

"No, you deaf son of a gun. I said my sister's boyfriend told me not to darken Philadelphia's door again." Thomas grinned. "That was just before she hit him over the head with a frying pan and told him he was allowed to do whatever he wanted as long as it didn't include me."

"Yes," Matthew drawled. "And as I recall, Joey took that literally, putting a price on your head."

"It seems your memory might be better than I thought." Thomas grinned ruefully. "So do we stand in the hall all day or are you going to let us in?"

"Come in, come in." Matthew opened the door even wider and stood aside. "Betty Jean and the kids are still asleep, so we'll have to be quiet in the kitchen. I just put on the coffee."

Thomas placed his hand on Parris's back and ushered her in before him. "That's exactly what I need."

"That and a million dollars and your sister's lover killed," Matthew muttered as he led the way through the living room to the small kitchen. Parris thought it was probably a renovated closet. A minuscule table and chairs were stuffed into the center of the floor, leaving little room to maneuver around the refrigerator and sink. Parris had seen other kitchens like this—many in New York City. She just hadn't realized how dated they were until now. Suddenly, 1929 didn't seem that far away from her own time.

Thomas caught her attention. "Matthew, this is Parris. Parris, my best buddy, Matthew. He's the father of three little charmers, husband to Betty Jean the neat-aholic, and best friend to a guy who's not usually allowed to remain long in this town."

Parris shook hands with the big man only because she stuck out her hand. Obviously, shaking a woman's hand wasn't done much in this time. He looked as flustered as she felt.

Parris turned to Thomas. "If your life is in danger here, then why did we come? Why not New York?"

"Because for right now, it's probably the last place they'd look." He smiled. "And because Matthew can help with both problems."

"Both problems?" Matthew picked up on Thomas's words quickly. He placed a coffee cup and saucer in front of Parris. "What both problems?"

Thomas took the steaming cup from in front of Parris and sipped it before offering it back to her. Matthew quickly poured him one, then sat across from them.

"Parris has a problem with time," Thomas said, looking intently at Matthew. "I have a problem with Patricia's boyfriend. I think Joey got to Al Capone about me, and I stole some liquor from the mob, and now they want me dead."

Matthew's cup froze midway to his saucer. "Did they follow you here?"

"Of course not. I wouldn't do that to your family. We drove into town with them this morning, but we lost them." He proceeded to tell Matthew about their time between last night and this morning.

Occasionally, Matthew shook his head or blew a low whistle, but he allowed Thomas to tell his story. Thomas didn't finish until Matt was already pouring a second cup of coffee.

"It's Joey," Matt stated firmly.

"You think so, too?"

"No. I know so. But I'd bet my next drink on your sister's not knowing about it. Joey's a foxy guy, but he's not stupid. He knows that if Patricia knew, she'd leave him. She can tolerate whatever he does for a living, maybe even his killing Charlie, but she wouldn't tolerate anything happening to her family. Love is only strong enough to allow the rules to be bent, not broken."

"I wish I was that sure. I was with her in Atlantic City the other night, and it was like old times until I brought up that jackass."

"What did she say?"

"She said not to make her choose between us. She said she'd choose me and then resent my asking her to."

Matt shook his head again. "She's right, too. She'd be so damn mad, especially if you ever fell in love and she had to watch you have what she wants. What we all want."

"Which is?"

"Love, man. Love given to us by the person we want to give to." Matt smiled. "She needs to make her own choices and pay her own penalties, without big brother looking over her shoulder and telling her what she's doing wrong. I thought you knew that. She loves him. She lives with him. It's her choice."

"I thought I had choices, too." Thomas reached

over and held Parris's hand in her lap. "But I was wrong."

"How?"

"I didn't realize that, whether or not we want someone to love us, we still love them."

Matt chuckled. "How true, how true. And it means that they can put that rope through your nose and lead you anywhere." He gave a broad sweep of his arm, encompassing the cramped kitchen and beyond. "And *that* kind of thinking can lead you straight to one of those houses you'd never thought you'd get near: a brownstone. You find yourself and your little mimeographs living on top of each other while you work day and night, studying and working to keep that brownstone in your life. And it's all right."

"You love it," Thomas corrected.

"I love them," Matt corrected again. "*It* is only a piece of property that will live on far longer than I will." He raised one bushy brow toward Parris's lap, where their hands were entwined. "And you? Are you ready to find what you never thought you'd seek?"

"I found it." Thomas grinned. "That's part of the other problem."

Matt's glance bounced to Parris, then back to his friend. "The one with time?"

Parris suddenly felt uptight. But there was nothing to lose, and perhaps, just perhaps, Matt might have something to contribute. "I met Thomas in the Atlantic Ocean," she began.

Haltingly, with great attention to detail, she continued with her story. Matt's expressions changed from incredulousness to disbelief to shock.

When she finished, a tall, thin woman moved from the kitchen doorway to stand behind Matt. She crossed her arms over his chest and looked down at her guests. Parris would have thought Matt's wife was plain—until she looked into the kindest, sweetest eyes she'd ever seen.

"That's quite a story." Her comment was stated in an even voice, but there didn't seem to be malice in her words.

"I believe her." Thomas's words were thrown out like a gauntlet.

"So do I." Betty Jean's voice was soft but firm as she stared Thomas right in the eye. "No one could make all that up and convince you of her earnestness unless there was a whole boxful of evidence that her story hadn't touched on in this telling."

"She's right," Matt said, his hands covering his wife's. "Thomas, you've never been one to suffer fools. In fact, your quick temper with other people trying to pull the wool over your eyes is almost legendary."

Parris felt Thomas relax his defenses, and in turn, she allowed hers to ease, too.

"Show them your watch, Parris."

"I don't have it. You do."

He looked startled. "Why would I have it?"

"Because I kept it in your dresser drawer."

"It's not there now," he announced with conviction. "It hasn't been there for a long time." He frowned. "Not since the police searched my room for a lead on the boat's explosion. Or so they say."

Betty Jean's eyes got wide. "Did they take anything else you know about?"

"No. Just her watch." His voice was filled with disgust. "I bet they weren't the police after all. I think they were the mob, looking for something, anything that could help them pin me down."

"Think it was Joey or someone from Capone?"

"I can't tell."

Matthew frowned. "It might be a part of your sister's problem. What if Joey wanted to make sure that Patricia hadn't been sending false or maybe secret information to you about their lives so he had your room searched?" Matt said shrewdly. "I'd react the same way he did. In fact, I'd make sure you were dead, and by someone else's hand."

Betty Jean's eyes never left Parris. "Sorry, guys, but that's old news. You sorry simpletons are the past. I want to know about the future."

All eyes turned to Parris. "What do you want to know?"

"What's it like?"

"Does the world become one unified country?"

"Can you really travel to Mars?"

Parris laughed, answering the last question first. "We've traveled to the moon several times.

We've sent satellites to other planets and they've sent back marvelous pictures. But we don't live on the moon or anywhere else, for that matter."

They began popping questions as quickly as they got an answer. Two more large pots of coffee were drained. Bacon and eggs with a mound of white toast were devoured as Parris tried to explain the various theories on cholesterol and fat in the American diet. Gas stoves led to a discussion of the newest appliances. An auto's backfiring made Matt question the transportation of the future. And later, when three sleepy children entered the cramped kitchen, Matthew and Betty Jean began asked about toys, childhood illnesses, and college.

The next time Parris looked at the clock, it was almost noon. With eyes that could hardly stay open, she excused herself and found the bathroom. When she returned, she heard their low-toned conversation before she reached the door.

"And if she's not lying, then we've got some rough times ahead." It was Matt's voice, edged with the telltale rise of skepticism.

"It's so hard to believe." That was Betty Jean.

"I know," Thomas stated. "But I believe her. As crazy as it sounds, I believe her completely. What's really funny is that Clair called me a week or so ago and told me that she thought Parris was clairvoyant and didn't know it. But Clair recognized several things Parris said as being true or having come true very soon after she'd said them."

"Like what?"

"Well, Parris said something about George Burns being almost a hundred and his wife Gracie being his partner. If she's really talking about the comedian, I saw him a couple of weeks ago at the vaudeville theater. His *new* partner is a young woman named"—he paused for effect—"Gracie."

Parris walked to the door. "Does all this postmortem mean you believe me?" She wasn't going to mention she had her identification as proof in her purse in the car. That would set off a whole other series of questions and she was too tired. She hoped Thomas didn't mention it either.

It was unanimous. "Yes." Even the children, not knowing what was being discussed, chimed in.

"Great," Parris said with a tired grin. "Then, is it all right if I take a nap? I'm wiped out."

Betty Jean walked to her, placed an arm around her shoulders, and led her to the children's room at the back of the apartment. "Thoughtless clods," she called over her shoulder. "Come on. This may not be the most comfortable room in the house, but it certainly will be private compared to the rest."

Parris gave the other woman a light hug. "Thanks," she said. "I'm too tired to care about anything other than closing my eyes."

Two unmade beds and a crib with its side down filled the small room.

"Take your pick," Betty Jean stated, reaching for the sturdy drawers. "I'll grab some clothes for the girls and a few extra diapers for little Matthew and get out of here."

Parris loved the baby boy, who was crawling around on the floor, occasionally banging on a pot with a wooden spoon. He had the most endearing grin she'd ever seen. "A little guy like that could make a woman want more children."

Betty Jean laughed. "The problem is that those little guys grow up to be bossy big guys, just like their daddies."

"Ummm," Parris said as she lay down on the first bed, hearing nothing but the incessant buzzing of time in her ears.

Chapter Sixteen

They had been sitting at the kitchen table for the past two days. Matt had a large pad of paper in front of him and a pencil in his hand, taking notes while Thomas prompted Parris's memory with questions. Lots and lots of questions.

Betty Jean bustled in and out, berating them for bombarding Parris with questions. Everyone would smile, then return to what they had been doing: extracting information. Sometimes, Parris would have to repeat herself two or three times before Matt had her words in a legible state on his pad. His inability to understand some of the things that she took for granted pointed out just how ignorant she was. She knew those things existed, she just didn't know how to explain them or how they worked. Things like boom boxes with compact disks, panty hose, microwaves, spas, and polyester. Parris had never realized until that moment how wonderful the invention of the tape recorder was.

The day before Matt had picked up a newspaper that listed all the stocks traded on the exchange. Since then, the three of them had gone through the list with a fine eye, and Parris had picked every stock she'd ever heard of. By the time evening came and the children were finished eating and put to bed, Parris was finished thinking.

"Enough," Betty Jean stated angrily the second night. "You've put her through the wringer again and again. Get out of here and leave her alone for a while."

It was an order given in a voice the men wouldn't brook. Parris leaned wearily in her straight-back chair and gave a smile of thanks to her newfound friend. Both men stood and stretched.

Thomas leaned down and gave Parris a tender kiss on her cheek. "We haven't been very nice to you, have we?" His blue eyes were so filled with remorse that she felt sorry for him.

Her smile softened her answer. "No."

"Could I tempt you to go out with me?"

"Now?"

Thomas nuzzled her ear, warming her skin with his breath. Her weariness seemed to dissipate as her muscles became less cramped. His hands curved to her shoulders, and she moved fluidly under his ministrations.

"Just you and me. And dinner. And then a hot bath."

She closed her eyes and listened to his low voice weave a spell. "And then?"

"And then, me. I get to hold you in my arms all night."

She frowned. "What about—"

He kissed her frown away. "We'll be fine. Philadelphia is a big city to get lost in."

Smiling, she opened her eyes and stared up at him, feeling the softness of his gaze melt her very insides. "When do we leave?"

"In fifteen minutes."

"In an hour," Betty Jean said from the sink. "Parris finally has time to take a nap before you start her on another whirlwind."

A smile pricked Parris's cheeks as Thomas gave a snort and said, "I'm not doing anything that would harm her, Miss Nosey."

Placing a hand over Thomas's, Parris squeezed it. "Betty's right. Give me an hour."

Leaving the two of them, Parris headed to the bedroom. The children were already asleep, one in the crib and the two toddlers in one bed.

She lay down on the single bed and closed her eyes, reveling in the quiet that surrounded her. But her mind was awash with too many questions. She didn't know how much information they could act on. After all, if they had any hope of realizing a strong financial return, they would need a lot of money to buy stock in the companies she'd remembered. Where were Matt and Thomas going to get the money?

She didn't know anything anymore.

Before, when she was hoping to convince Thomas of her time traveling, she was certain who she was and where she wanted to go. She was also certain that she could get back. Occasionally, a negative thought would enter her mind, but she'd always ignored it.

Now that everyone believed her, she wasn't sure she believed herself. As odd as it was, she thought that maybe she was crazy and the rest of them didn't know it. While they'd been talking she had wanted to shout, *"Don't pin your hopes on me. I don't know where the hell I'm going, let alone have the ability to lead you there!"* But she hadn't.

What if she couldn't get back? What if she tried one more time only to drown? For what? A crack—a very slim crack—at saving her parents and brother. And what would happen if she fell into another time and another place? One that had nothing to do with either this time and Thomas or her time and her family? What then?

The door opened quietly. Parris kept her eyes closed as she lay there, waiting for some sound to tell her who it was and what he wanted.

The springs sagged as Thomas sat down on the side of the bed. She knew it was Thomas; she could tell by his scent, which she loved.

His fingers brushed a curl away from the side of her face. With slow deliberation, she opened her eyes and stared at him. The dim hallway light barely spilled into the room, outlining his lean form.

"I just wanted to be near you," he whispered softly. "Go back to sleep."

"I can't sleep."

His hand soothed her cheek, a small smile played around his full mouth. He was so tender and so endearing, it saddened her.

"What's the matter?" His voice was low.

Tears filmed her eyes. "I'm so scared I'm shaking."

His blue-eyed gaze widened. "Of me?"

A lump formed in her throat. Of all the things she was scared of, he was the main one. But she couldn't admit that. It would prove how very much she loved him, how much she was willing to do for him. She'd already told him she loved him. She didn't have to tell him how deep and devoted that love was. She felt vulnerable enough.

Instead, Parris shook her head.

His fingers grazed her cheek, then lightly outlined her ear. "Talk to me, Parris. Don't shut me out."

"What if I can't get back?" Her voice was a whisper. "Everything I know will be gone. Everything I believe will be false." A tear spilled from her lashes and ran down the side of her cheek. "Everyone I love will still be dead."

"I won't let you go. I won't." His whisper was defiant. "You're not going back."

"I have to try."

"What would it take to make you change your mind and stay? Isn't it enough that I'm here? That I love you more than life itself?"

His gaze was open. Gone were his usual walls of defense. Even the self-confidence he usually exuded had evaporated. Instead, she saw his vulnerability and need for her, which he never showed—nor did she.

Her hands covered his dress shirt so she could feel his heartbeat. He breathed deeply and her hands moved. Thomas was a man. Living, alive, and so very much loved. Her heart swelled and she tried not to shed another tear. They were both too tired to cope with their overburdened emotions as it was.

"I love you with everything in me. But we don't stand a snowball's chance in hell of making it work for us," she answered softly.

His hands covered hers. "You don't know that. We only know what *won't* work." His fingers tightened. "It won't work for you to try to go back to your time. You've already tried it once, and I almost lost you. What makes you think you could do it again and succeed?"

"I wonder the same thing," she said softly, her voice barely above a choked whisper. "But I have to try. Don't you see?"

His hands clasped hers. "No! I don't see! You're going to fail and both of us will wind up losers!"

Thomas's mouth closed over hers, bruising in its intensity. When he pulled away, she still lay compliantly, her eyes closed. Tears trickled down her cheeks, and her heart felt as if it had broken in two.

"Listen to me," he ordered in a gruff whisper. "You're staying here and I don't want any arguments. No more trying to return to your home, no more swimming into the middle of the ocean. Do you understand? Start thinking along those lines now, and by the time we go back to help Bebe get to France, you'll know I'm right."

She couldn't argue. She couldn't even drum up a good reason to fight him. Instead, she did the only thing that made sense to her exhausted mind. "All right," she agreed. "I'll think about it."

Relief filled his eyes. Thomas smiled, but it was a smile of wariness, not triumph. He didn't quite trust her. "I'm leaving now. I'm sending a cab for you in about an hour. You just get in and do whatever he says. I'll be waiting for you."

He began to rise, but she caught his shirt. "Where are you going?"

"To get a hotel room for my sweetie. You need a good night's sleep that isn't interrupted by the patter of little feet."

Her grin was sleepy. "You mean you're sacrificing your wonderful spot on the couch to give me the advantage of sleeping in a bed I'm not taking away from a child?"

He looked slightly sheepish, but not bowed by her sarcasm. "Something like that. Are you game?"

"You bet," she whispered in agreement. "Just don't forget the bubble bath, heated towels, and champagne. Oh, and strawberries and cream for playtime."

Thomas kissed the tip of her nose. "What a delightful idea. But strawberries aren't in season."

"In season?" she asked. "Don't you have greenhouses?"

"Not enough to have strawberries on the market." He looked at her again. "Why? Can you get them year-round in your time? What fresh foods can you get that aren't seasonal?"

Placing a finger over his mouth, Parris halted his questions. "Enough. I'll talk about it later. Much later."

Instead of answering, Thomas leaned down and gave her a hug, holding her long and breathing in her scent. He needed this woman in his life so badly, and the thought of badgering her into leaving scared the hell out of him. "Sorry," he finally muttered into her neck. "It was just habit."

Her arms came around and held him close. Her fingers ran through his thick, dark hair. "Apology accepted. Now, tell Betty Jean to wake me in an hour, okay?"

"Right. But don't change or clean up. Just come the way you are."

"May I brush my teeth?" she teased.

"No."

One more light kiss on her parted mouth and then he forced himself to pull away. "Damn, but I want you."

Parris smiled, her eyes finally closing. "See you in an hour."

Then she fell asleep.

Two hours later, a taxi pulled up in front of a posh hotel. The cabbie turned to her with a smile. "He said to knock three times on the door of Room 716, then enter."

A lighthearted giggle filled Parris. "Room 716," she repeated just before stepping out of the cab. "I'm sorry, but I don't have any money for a tip."

His grin was as wide as the open door. "That's just fine, miss. I already got my tip."

The interior of the hotel was beautifully decorated in mauve, green, and gray, with potted plants gracing the area around every pillar. Marble floors were covered with Oriental rugs that Parris would have bet her next paycheck were real. Everyone was wearing his finest, men in suits and women in hats and gloves. Parris was certain their gems were real and originals—nothing paste and replicated. Costume jewelry hadn't become popular or the making of it hadn't become an art form yet. But just wearing jewels in public was different from her own time. Parris had forgotten how formal and trusting the world had once been.

Quickly, she walked to the bank of elevators. A bellboy waited patiently for the needle above the door to announce the elevator was on the first floor. Parris had to grin. The young man was wearing a uniform with a small box cap on his head, held in place by a black chin strap. She'd seen pictures of bellboys dressed like that, but encountering it in real life was a shock.

Once in front of the room door, she took a deep breath and told herself to calm down. She was coming here to rest and to see Thomas away from prying curiosity and little ears. It was only a big deal if she made it so.

Three sharp knocks seemed to reverberate through the hallway, more a declaration than an announcement that she had arrived. She jumped at the sound. Nothing happened; no one called out, the door remained closed. She twisted the knob, found the door unlocked, and entered. In her day, the door would have automatically locked out anyone in the outside hall.

The sitting area was small and filled with brocaded fabrics and overstuffed furniture, not in the style of the soft lines of art deco, but of the frilly curves of the Victorian era. To one side was a door to the bedroom.

"Thomas?" she called as she walked through the bedroom door and looked around. This room was three times larger than the outer room. And its decor was much simpler, thank goodness.

Running water echoed off ceramic shower walls and into the bedroom, sounding louder than it was. The door was partially ajar, and when she reached it, Parris stuck her head in.

"Thomas?"

He reclined in a bathtub overflowing with bubbles, a tall glass filled with a burgundy liquid in his hand. "Come on in. The water's fine."

Parris leaned against the doorjamb, a smile tugging at her mouth. "I see you've made yourself at home."

"And so will you." He raised a brow and gave her a look sexy enough to melt the Arctic Circle. "Are you going to stand there and let these bubbles die before you enjoy them?"

She saw his knee peek out from an island of suds. "Are you sure there's room?"

"You'll never know till you try." It was a challenge.

Parris reached for the buttons at her throat. "I'll be right there."

Stripping quickly, she tossed her clothes on a chair by the bed, then walked into the bathroom and stepped into the wide, deep tub and sat opposite him. She had felt Thomas's appreciative eyes follow her every move, and instead of feeling self-conscious, she felt more confident.

Thomas handed her a glass of wine he'd just poured from the bottle sitting on a stool at the side of the tub.

Parris sipped, then leaned back and let the dark, sweet wine spice her tongue before she swallowed. "Mmmm."

He took her foot and placed it on his thigh. His hand circled her instep, and he began massaging it. Magical touch—magical and wondrous. She moaned again.

"I haven't seen you this way since the last time we made love." Low and teasing, his voice sent sensations down her spine.

"What way?"

"So receptive to my touch, so ready and pliable to whatever I might want to do."

She opened her eyes and stared across the bubbles at him. "If this is your idea of foreplay, I want more."

His brow creased. "What's foreplay?"

"The warming of Parris to the idea of making love *before* the making-love-to-Parris mode kicks in."

"Is all this on record in the science books?"

Parris nodded, closed her eyes, and rested her head against the back of the tub. "Don't forget the other foot."

"Yes, ma'am." His voice was docile enough, but when he changed feet, his fingers bit into her toes for just a second, reminding her who was in charge.

She grinned, sipped her wine, and kept her eyes closed.

When his hands wandered up to soothe her ankle, she purred. It felt like heaven. It felt so sensuous. It felt so very . . . sexy. With painfully slow progress, his fingers traced up her calf and thigh, stroking and soothing as they traveled.

Moment after moment passed while he teased her with his touch. Her muscles turned to molten lead. Tension sang through her body. The room was so quiet she could hear the bubbles softly popping.

His hand reached his ultimate destination and Parris's breath caught in her throat.

"Don't stiffen up," Thomas whispered in a coarse, gravely voice. "Just relax. This is for you."

Parris opened her eyes and stared across at him.

He smiled and melted her heart. "Close your eyes. Pretend I'm not here."

"That's a little hard to do," she whispered, unable to voice more than a few words.

He parted her legs more, and his fingers pierced her so sweetly she wanted to cry with the need he had aroused.

With movements that blended yet commanded the warm water swirling around them, he manipulated her responses so that she had no will of her own. Everything centered in the warm water surrounding them. Her limbs were jelly. Thomas's hand was her nucleus. His fingers weaved a spell, capturing her in its magic.

She couldn't move, yet she wanted to squirm into his arms. She was afraid to lose contact with his hand, but she wanted more. Her lashes fluttered.

"Shhh," Thomas whispered in a low, sexy tone.

His other hand moved up her leg, stroking as he touched her, setting her afire. Then he teased her breast, his fingers light as air making her nipple pout in expectation.

Her breath caught in her throat. Wired invisibly to him, she waited, her body tuned so finely to every nuance, to every slight movement.

Slowly, tantalizingly, he moved his fingers. Brightly, so brightly it blinded her even though her eyes were closed, Parris experienced the most intense orgasm she had ever known. Her body stiffened, her breath stopped, her heartbeat reverberated like a jungle drum. Then she reached the heights of the clouds and was cushioned by the warm, fine feeling that electrically flowed from him to her, through her.

He soothed her long after she returned to earth, stroking her skin, helping her to keep the euphoria of his touch.

She opened her eyes and looked at him. He smiled so sweetly a lump formed in her throat. "It's my turn."

His head shook slowly. "No. It's time for you to finish your wine, dry off and slip into bed."

"But—"

"Later will be time enough. Right now, we both need rest."

Her lethargic smile matched his. "Later," she promised.

He lifted her glass and placed it at her lips, allowing her to sip without expending energy to hold it. She sipped several times, liking the taste of what normally would have been a heavy wine. "It's wonderful. Better than Chablis or Chardonnay."

For just a moment, he frowned in puzzlement. "Don't you have Chianti in your time?"

She nodded. "But it's not as popular anymore. The lighter the better."

"No matter what it is, the better the taste, the better the wine."

Setting the glass on the side of the tub, Thomas continued to stroke her muscles. Parris didn't move. She couldn't. Soon all the bubbles would be popped and gone and she'd be sitting in chilled water.

Thomas moved and the water waved back and forth. Parris stirred.

"Stay there," he ordered. "I'll be right back."

She dozed.

"Parris, stand up," Thomas commanded, his voice in her ear. "It's time for bed."

Groaning, she tried to push his words away. She was so tired. Everything had caught up with her and she was loath to move. She didn't need to go to bed. She was comfortable right where she was.

But holding her under the arms, Thomas pulled her up. She protested, but was too tired to do more than that.

Within seconds, a large fluffy towel was wrapped around her shoulders, and she was being helped out of the tub and led toward the bedroom.

The fluffy duvet was pulled halfway down the double bed. Pristine sheets were shoved aside and pillows fluffed. The bed looked like a cloud. Just as Parris dove for the mattress, Thomas slipped the towel from her body, allowing her the luxury of sleeping nude on sheets that were of such fine percale that they felt like silk.

"Later, dude," she mumbled into the pillow.

She fell asleep in the middle of Thomas's answering chuckle. The smile on her lips was in anticipation of waking in his arms, making love to him, smiling into his eyes.

Not a bad combination under any circumstances.

Chapter Seventeen

Parris popped a piece of crusty bread into her mouth, then sipped on a demitasse. Late-morning sunshine poured through the window. After savoring the espresso, she resumed talking. "And then Dad made me hand over ten dollars every week until the ten-speed bike was paid off. It wasn't until I graduated from high school that I found out he'd put all that money back into my savings, and it had been collecting interest since I was fourteen."

Thomas's gaze was laced with envy. "He sounds like one swell guy," he said huskily.

She nodded for emphasis. "He was. The best. Many of my friends had trouble relating with their fathers when they were growing up. But I didn't. He was busy, and sometimes we had to make appointments to be with him, but he never canceled on us. Neither did Mom."

His brows raised. "Your mom wasn't home?"

"Thomas," she explained with a drawl. "*Leave it to Beaver's* mom died in the fifties, thank goodness."

"There you go, talking in riddles again."

She had the grace to look sheepish. "Sorry. That's a television program that showed the mother as being a perfect housewife, but a dimwit who couldn't make a decision about raising her children without checking with her husband. It was a co-dependency type of thing." One look at his puzzled expression told her that there was no explaining how almost everyone had turned to self-help books that advised on everything from how to clear one's conscience to how to perform one's own face-lift with muscle contractions.

"Is this one of those times when you say, 'You had to be there?' "

"Right."

"In that case, can we talk about your family some more? What was your brother like?"

Parris gave a silent sigh of relief. A change of subject was fine with her. Besides, she'd never known anyone more eager than Thomas to know what a family was like.

"Jed was a pest until I grew up. Then we talked about once a week, sometimes in the middle of the night. He'd get all wound up over something and decide he needed to tell me. I decided that

I could afford to stay up for fifteen or twenty minutes and listen."

"Sounds like a one-way relationship." Thomas bit into a roll, his white teeth tearing the bread neatly.

Parris felt that lump that always formed in her throat whenever she thought of her brother. To her, Jed would always be alive in her heart. Always. "Whenever I needed him, he was there."

Thomas reached out and touched her thigh. "You miss him most of all."

She swallowed hard. "Yes."

His hand dropped away. Embarrassed, Parris stared out the window at the city silhouettes. She couldn't explain the terrible weight of death that she'd carried with her from her time to this time. It wasn't quite as heavy, but it was still there, like a shadow on the sun.

Thomas's question burst into her reverie. "Where did your mother live when she was growing up?"

Parris flashed a quick smile. "Down by Chadds Ford," she answered, naming an area that had become a suburb of Philadelphia. "Her parents were born and raised in downtown Philadelphia, then moved when they bought a little farm there."

"And your dad?"

"He was from Pittsburgh. He didn't move here until after college."

He offered her a bite of his roll. She accepted. After she finished, Thomas stood and took the tray off the bed, placing it on the side table. He was naked and the sun gleamed on his skin as if he were made of bronze. Parris didn't think she'd ever seen anyone as beautiful as Thomas. He wore no adornment other than a fine layer of dark hair that covered his lean, hard body. Unabashed at his nakedness, he strode back to bed, fluffed the pillows, and rested his back against the headboard. Then he patted the bed. "Come here," he coaxed. "I want to hold you for a little while longer."

She didn't have to think twice. Sliding next to him, Parris felt as if she'd found her home. His arms circled her, ensuring that she was as close and as comfortable as she could be. One lightly callused hand rubbed up and down her arm. The other rested on her abdomen and thigh as casually as if they were used to being so intimate every hour of every day.

"Now," he said after depositing a light kiss on the top of her head. "Tell me what you want to be when you grow up."

It only took an hour to explain the intricacies of being a CPA.

It took another two hours to make love leisurely with just the right amount of loving to satisfy them both.

It was much later that afternoon when they drove slowly through Parris's grandmother's childhood neighborhood. It had been a shock to Parris's system to realize that her mother hadn't even been born yet, and that her grandmother would be a child of ten or so. It didn't seem possible.

They drove up one street and down the other, watching neighbors sitting on steep concrete steps leading up to building fronts.

Men in sturdy work clothes and stout dark shoes, metal lunch pails in hand, walked home from trolley stops. Kids of various ages played marbles and ball on the sidewalk. Old women tended to blossoming flowers growing in wooden boxes on the ledges of kitchen windows. These could have been scenes from a period movie, showing Philadelphia in the summer of 1929. But this was real—too real.

Just in front and to the left of them a young red-haired girl with pigtails sat on a stoop, a rag doll curled on her lap.

"Pull over," Parris said excitedly.

"Why?"

"Just do it," she ordered, her hand already on the door handle.

Thomas did as he was told, pulling almost even to the steps where the little girl was. Parris stepped from the car, her purse clenched tightly in her hand. Her heartbeat pounded against her ribs.

With slow, deliberate steps she walked up to the steep stairs, then sat down on the step just below the little girl.

Parris smiled. "Is your name Dorothy?"

The little girl's eyes widened. She nodded. "Who are you?"

"My name is Parris."

"Like in France?"

Parris nodded, unwilling to explain the difference in the spelling to a child. Besides, the child would grow up and know the spelling. This child was her mother's mother. Her grandmother.

"Do you live around here?" the girl asked, clutching her doll's hand.

"No, but I have relatives who live here," Parris explained. "I wonder if I could ask you to do me a favor."

"Mama says I'm not allowed to leave the step. Papa's on his way home."

"That's fine. What I'm asking you to do is very simple, Dorothy. It has to do with something I need you to remember and pass on to your little girl when you grow up."

The little girl pulled on a braid. "What's that?"

"Just tell your daughter that she will have a wonderful life, but that on May fourteenth, 1993, she is not to travel. Not for any reason. And her family is not to travel on that day either."

The little redheaded girl laughed. "You're funnin' me, aren't you?"

Parris didn't smile. "No, honey, I'm not. Someday, you'll grow up and have a family of your own. You'll have two wonderful daughters. And one of them, Marguerite, will marry a man named Joseph. She'll have two children, a boy and a girl. The girl will become a CPA, the boy an actor. You will all make loving memories with each other. You'll spend alternate holidays with each of your children. But no matter what happens in their lives or in yours, you must remember to tell them not to travel on May fourteenth, 1993. Ever." Parris stared deeply into the little girl's eyes as if she could brand the date into her mind. "Never."

Dorothy shrugged, then looked down at her doll. "If you say so."

"I do," Parris said firmly. She gazed at the bowed head of the child who would look so different by the time Parris grew up. The beginning of her grandmother's expressions were there, but they were so brand-new it was hard to truly believe this was her ancestor.

"Just a moment," Parris said, running back to the car. Thomas's pad sat on the backseat and she grabbed it, then a pencil.

"What are you doing?"

"Writing a letter to my grandmother," she muttered, scribbling as quickly as she could. Once done, she folded the paper like a business letter and went back to the little girl. Thomas followed and handed her an envelope holding the hotel emblem on the corner. She gave him a thankful look and sealed her letter inside.

Dorothy's big, solemn eyes followed her every move. Parris held the letter out to her. "I want you to take this and put it somewhere safe. When you're older, please open it and read it carefully."

"What's it say?" the child asked. "How old? I'll be twelve years old in two years. Is twelve old enough?"

Parris smiled. Twelve must have felt so much older than being almost ten. "It's a letter that says everything I've just told you. And maybe you should be a little older than that when you open it," she said softly. "Maybe when you're twenty-one or so."

Dorothy frowned. "That's *old*," she said.

Parris laughed. "It certainly is," she agreed. "But it's not as bad as it sounds."

"Really?" Dorothy tilted her head and gazed earnestly at Parris. "Mom says that sometimes she feels as old as Noah's Ark. Do you think she really means that?"

Emotion too complicated to sort through welled inside Parris, almost overpowering her speech. She swallowed the lump in her throat. "Maybe she feels that way, Dorothy, but she doesn't look that old, does she?"

Dorothy shook her head. Then her eyes grazed over Parris's shoulder. "There's my papa!" she exclaimed, her expression turning to sheer delight. "He's taking us to the circus tonight!"

Parris glanced over her shoulder. A man of perhaps 30 years or so was strolling toward them, his lunch pail keeping rhythm with his debonair step. A tweed cap sat jauntily on the back of his head, allowing dark curls to spill onto his forehead. A wide grin framed startlingly white teeth.

"Dorothy!" he called.

The young girl jumped up and ran toward her father.

Parris moved to the sidewalk and, with a trembling smile, she watched her strapping great-grandfather give her girlish grandmother a hug. It was amazing to watch him as he was. All she'd ever seen was a rather formal picture of him taken when he was in his mid-fifties. He looked so formidable and stoic in that photo—nothing like the young man walking toward her.

Dorothy, one hand in his, clutched Parris's envelope and her doll's hand in the other. She grinned as she skipped by his side, her braids bobbing up and down.

Parris walked toward the car waiting at the curb. Thomas sat waiting behind the wheel, watching everything quietly.

"Dorothy, don't forget what I told you," Parris called, stepping to the door and opening it.

Dorothy stopped in her rush up the steep stairs. "I won't," she called, waving. Within a second, Parris was forgotten.

Parris's great-grandfather peered at her quizzically, his smooth brow furrowing. "Who is that lady, Dorothy?" Parris heard him ask his daughter.

"Her name's Parris, like France, Papa," Dorothy explained, more intent on her jumping up the stairs than in her father's question.

Thomas pulled the car away from the curb and the rest of the conversation was lost. Parris twisted in her seat and stared through the small back window, wanting to see the scene as long as she could.

The child held out the envelope Parris had given her and she saw her great-grandfather take it. Then Thomas turned the corner.

"Do you think it worked?" Thomas asked.

Turning around in her seat, she sighed. "I'm not sure but I hope so. She gave the envelope to her father."

"Your great-grandfather."

"Yes." She stared down at her hands, feeling so many different emotions she could hardly keep track. She should have been thrilled to meet her long-past relatives in their younger days. They were so alive and real, and she would never be able to think of them in the same way again. Her great-grandfather would never fit into the role she'd placed him in because of one stern-looking photograph hanging in her grandmother's hallway.

And her grandmother had always said that times were different when she was growing up. She'd told stories about her parents' old neighborhood. She had smiled when she'd explained how her parents had coddled her, keeping childhood a part of her life much longer than the children of Parris's day had. She'd told stories of her youth during her infrequent visits to Parris's parents' home. Such a shame that others didn't have that idyllic childhood, she would say as she concocted one of the desserts she was famous for.

Every year during the holidays, she would leave her home, an apartment near downtown Philadelphia, and enter her daughter's realm. But she'd never been comfortable there. She wanted her own world, her own things, her own space, she used to laughingly say, quoting the slang of the day. And the day after Christmas, she'd return to her own home, happy and satisfied with her own life.

Although they loved her, Parris and Jed never seemed to find time to visit. They called her dutifully once or twice a month, but their lives were so hectic, they explained. She always said she understood. And Parris was sure she did. But somehow, Parris knew she'd lost out on a very rich experience. Her grandmother was always a modern woman. But, it wasn't until her death that she found out her grandmother had been living with a man for her last three years! Her own parents had known and never said a word.

That interlude in time had shown how much Parris *didn't* know and how much she needed to learn. If she had time, she would do it right, learn about the lives and times of her family and their friends. Maybe even learn what made her the person she was.

"Where are we going now?" Parris asked, wanting to turn around and return to the house where her grandmother was a child. She wanted it so badly.

"We have to say good-bye to Matthew, then head back to Cape May."

That got her attention. She hadn't expected him to say that. "What?"

Thomas turned another corner, his gaze continually striking off the rearview mirror. "We've got to go back."

"Isn't that a little crazy?" she asked, confused. "Capone is looking for you and you want to go back there?"

"I'm going back to finish arrangements to get Bebe out of here."

"Bebe can take a plane and get out of here. She doesn't need you."

"Bebe is here illegally. She can't get out legally unless she goes through bureaucratic red tape. Besides, she's not safe here either."

He didn't say who else wasn't safe. He didn't have to. Obviously, he meant Parris and himself.

"Let me get this straight," she said slowly. "For days we've been on the run from the mob, dodging them to the point of not being able to stroll down the street without looking over our shoulders. We're up to our eyeballs in problems, with nowhere to go, and you want us to head back to Cape May so we can help Bebe leave the country illegally, compounding any problem we might have."

"Right."

"You're an ass, Thomas Elder."

"Coming from you, that's a compliment," he stated dryly. "You're the one who told me about paradox, remember? Something about not changing the past so that the future won't explode."

"I was speaking figuratively. But changing whether or not my parents die isn't changing the course of the world. They won't have more children, won't be a part of the major scope of things."

"So you think you can decide—be judge and jury—as to what can be changed and what can't?"

"That's right." Her tone rang with conviction. "If I couldn't change anything, I wouldn't have given Matthew and you any information about the future for fear you would upset the balance, which you could do much more easily than I can by bringing my parents back."

He grinned. "You've got a point, tootsie. As usual."

She nodded in a queenly fashion. "Thank you, but I would have taken this chance no matter what the point or if there was no point at all. I'll do anything I can if I think it will help keep my family alive." Her determined streak showed. "Besides, I'm also the one who told you Capone was after us. And I was the one who tried to save your butt. Instead, you selectively ignore my warnings."

"I haven't ignored them, Parris," he said wearily. "I'm just trying to do the best I can. I promised Bebe I would help her, and I will. But just because I'm going back doesn't mean you have to go back, too. You can stay with Matthew and

Betty Jean. I'll come back for you later."

"Oh, no, you don't! I'm going with you, no matter where you go. I'm not taking the chance of you not only making stupid decisions, but also making decisions that could threaten your life."

He shot her a grin. "What's the matter? Do you think you might become attached to me? Careful, tootsie. Those words smell of commitment."

"Those words *are* commitment," she corrected. "And I'm crazy for going along with any scheme of yours."

He reached for her hand, and she reluctantly allowed him to draw it to his pleated pant leg. "You love me and you know it. You might as well admit it."

For a fleeting moment, Parris wondered if all men were so frustrating, but then she decided she already knew the answer. Of course they were. "I do, and I did admit it. And it's because I feel this way that I don't want you to get yourself shot or killed. I can't understand why you want to flirt with death when we both know Bebe can catch that boat on her own."

"I *don't* know that," he maintained stubbornly. "I was led to believe I could get whiskey from a fisherman, but it turned out that the jerk was angling to kill me. I can't trust that Bebe will be on that boat until I get her there."

"Okay, okay." Parris sighed. "What do we do? This car is like a neon sign to Capone's men.

How can we get away with going back into Cape May and not being seen?"

"When it comes to hiding from Capone, there is no we, Parris," Thomas stated firmly.

"Please understand that there won't be any you either, if I'm not with you." Her smile was sweet while her eyes bore into him like stilettos.

Thomas was smart enough to know when he was licked. "Let me think about it, all right? I don't want you to worry your pretty little head with details," he said.

"Don't patronize me," Parris cut in, her nerves snapping one at a time. "You can't think as quickly as I can, so don't try."

"Talk about patronizing!"

"You're such a male chauvinist," Parris continued as if he had never spoken. "Without my input, buster, we wouldn't be alive to have gotten this far."

"Without you, tootsie, I would be traveling lighter, faster, and without explanation every time I turned around."

That hurt. "Without me, you'd be buried in cement up to your neck while eighteen-wheelers made a mud pie of your face."

Thomas turned the corner to Matt's street, then slid into the parking place, still empty from yesterday. He palmed the keys and turned to her. His gaze blazed with anger. Parris watched as that anger was slowly doused. "Another one of those absurd expressions I've never heard."

Then, just as wonderfully, she saw his love for her gleaming in his eyes. "Without you in my time and life, I'd be so damn lonely." His admission was like a warm balm to both of them.

She touched his mouth, not wanting him to speak the words aloud because doing so would acknowledge what she was leaving behind when she tried to return to her own time. *If* she could return to her own time.

"Thomas, I have no choice. I must try. There is no other way to help my family."

He kissed the tip of her finger. "You just did, by telling your grandmother about the accident."

"Maybe, maybe not," she said. "I can't guarantee the letter won't be lost or that she'll tell them or they'll listen to her."

"So you're going to try to return anyway."

"Yes."

"Parris," he began, only this time he was the one who hesitated. "I argued with you when we first met because I thought you were insane. Then I argued because I enjoyed our sparring. Now I'm arguing with you because I love you so damn much I don't want to live without you." He bent even closer and she smelled his special scent, which seemed to burn into her senses and ignite them. "Stay with me, Parris. Stay with me."

She closed her eyes to keep the tears from falling. It didn't help. His wonderfully deep voice washed his words into her soul, and she prayed that she would be able to withstand the great temptation of giving in.

"Oh, Thomas," she whispered, outlining the contours of his jaw. "If there was ever a reason to stay, it would be you. It would definitely be you."

His mouth claimed hers, his kiss telling her better than words could say of his love and of how lost he would be without her.

She clung to him tightly, kissed him just as gently, missed him almost as much as if she'd already left him.

He pulled away, touching her forehead with his as he caught his breath. "If there's a God in heaven, you'll stay with me," he murmured hoarsely. "It's where you belong. Where you were meant to be."

Were all her efforts futile? Was she risking death in exchange for a life with Thomas? And if she ever did get back to her time period, what were the chances that things would be the same as when she left? *Unlikely*, said a voice inside her head. There was no reason to believe she could return before her family's accident. Hell, she hadn't even been able to return at all, let alone figure out how to get there early!

She was fighting windmills, and suddenly she knew it.

"I'll stay," she finally said. "I'll stay because I can't imagine being without you."

He closed his eyes. "Thank you, sweet Jesus." His words were said for both of them.

The decision was made. The blessing was bestowed. Parris felt both relieved and guilty.

But Thomas's arms around her made everything okay.

For now.

Chapter Eighteen

Saying good-bye to Thomas's friends wasn't easy. Parris had emotionally adopted the warm and loving family, especially the children. And Betty Jean had mothered her throughout the days they'd been cramped together in the small, crowded apartment.

But as Thomas drove away and Parris waved, she realized that time, just as Einstein maintained, was really relative.

She might have known Matt's family for a short time, but she felt as if she'd known them forever. And Matt and Betty Jean would most likely be dead by 1980. But their children would live well into the 1990s.

The thought of Matt and Betty Jean hurt. On the heels of that idea was the next: Thomas would be gone, too. And Bebe. Clair. Of course, Al Capone.

And if she didn't leave this time, as she had promised Thomas, she would be gone, too. But she would have spent her life with Thomas and his friends, not alone without a family.

"A penny for your thoughts," Thomas said, taking her hand and placing it on his thigh as he drove down the road, one hand on the steering wheel.

She refused to tell him how wonderful that small act made her feel. Instead, she ignored it, pretending it was normal instead of extraordinary. "If I stay, I'll never live to see my own time."

"Probably," Thomas conceded. "But if we elude Capone, we'll live a full life in this time, tootsie."

"Parris." Her correction was automatic.

"Parris." His answer was automatic, too. He squeezed her hand, reminding her of their own deepened relationship.

She sighed in contentment. "And we'll be together."

He tightened his hold on her hand. "Together." He grinned endearingly, giving her a peek of his dimple. "Is that a marriage proposal?"

"Saying the word together hardly amounts to a marriage proposal," she scoffed, but her heartbeat quickly accelerated.

"Oh," he said, pretending confusion. "And here I thought you were asking for my hand."

"*I* was asking for *your* hand?"

He nodded, but there was a definite twinkle in

his eye. "And I was going to tell you that things were going so fast that I needed time to think."

"Do you really?" she asked, but her own smile was barely in check.

He nodded again. "But being a decisive and logical man, I've thought it over and I agree. We ought to be married."

She widened her eyes innocently in question. "To anyone in particular or do we each go out and find someone on the street?"

He groaned. "If I wasn't driving this car, I'd haul you onto my lap and spank you good."

"Sounds kinda kinky to me," she mused. "I didn't know *you* enjoyed that type of thing."

"Parris," he warned.

"On the other hand," she said blithely, "who knows what goes on in the privacy of the bedroom between two consenting adults—"

"Parris." His voice lowered an octave.

"—as long as one of them isn't me? I'm not into violence."

He gave a choked sound as the car veered to the right, stopping on the edge of the road on the outskirts of Philadelphia.

Turning, he grabbed her shoulders and pulled her toward him. "Tease or don't tease, I don't care. All I want is a straight-arrow answer from you," he growled in a low voice. "Are you going to marry me or not?"

"Are you asking?" she said softly.

His fingers tensed. "Yes!"

Parris smiled sweetly. "I accept."

His fingers bit into her shoulders, then loosened their grip as her answer sank in. "You will." It was a statement, even though he was really asking for confirmation.

She covered his hands with hers. "I will."

His blue-eyed gaze narrowed in determination. "When?"

Parris shrugged. "Whenever."

His fingers tightened again. "Name it. When?"

Her eyes glowed with a mischievous glint that told him just how happy she was. "As soon as possible. Whenever you want. Now. Right this minute."

His lips crashed down on hers, claiming her with a kiss that bordered on violent branding. Then he softened his grip, his mouth no longer hard and demanding. Parris reached up and touched the sides of his strong face, her fingertips soothing him as much as herself.

When Thomas pulled away, his eyes were closed as if in pain. "Damn, I don't know how this happened, but I don't think I could live without you, Parris."

It was an admission that came from deep inside his heart. One that left him much too vulnerable. It was very frightening and even more exhilarating. She was afraid of holding that much power over him and needed to share it.

"I know," she said softly. "Even though I talked about it, when it came down to the wire, I wouldn't have been able to leave you, darling. I don't know what I would do without you near me." She smiled so she wouldn't cry. "Even when you're at your worst."

His gaze was electric as he stared at her. "It's a good thing you realized this before you jumped into the ocean again, lady. I would have had to jump in after you. Then we both would have sunk. I can't swim."

Parris stared at him blankly. "You what?"

"I can't swim." He said the words simply, but they had the magnitude of a bomb.

"I *found* you in the ocean."

"Me and a piece of wood buoyant enough to float," he stated dryly.

"But you swam out to me!"

"I *ran* out to you," Thomas corrected, twining a piece of hair around his finger. "The sand forms a shelf for a long way. The tide had almost brought you back to me when I spotted you."

"Did you know where the shelf ended?"

"No."

His answer said it all. Her heart swelled with the love he'd demonstrated in the most unique way. It had been a gift that she hadn't understood at the time. "Oh, Thomas," she sighed, unable to put her own emotions into words.

"Let's get Bebe on her way home so we can put this behind us and get our own lives on track." His voice was firm. His hoarseness gave away his secret, however. He was still too moved to act as if nothing had been discovered.

She pressed her lips to his in a light, swift kiss. "Let's get going."

The late-afternoon sun had already disappeared behind them as they drove toward Cape May. Once they were there, Parris had no idea what they would do, but she trusted Thomas enough to know he had a plan. He would watch out for them, she was sure. He knew far more about the place—and the time—than she did.

Silence pervaded the car, with only the loud sound of the engine filling the void. Lulled by the quiet, Parris curled her legs under her and cuddled next to Thomas.

"Put your head on my lap," he said softly, and she followed his order, closing her eyes as she felt his hand glide down the side of her arm to rest protectively on her waist.

Within seconds, she was asleep.

When Parris awoke, Thomas was turning off the Atlantic City road, heading toward Cape May.

She pushed her hair back and squinted out the windshield. "It's raining."

"It just started, honey."

She looked at Thomas. His expression was grim, his face drawn, his fingers, white at the knuckles, wrapped around the steering wheel. "I've caught up on my sleep. Let me drive."

"I'll be fine. We've only a little while to go."

"Yes, but—" she began, worried that he was feeling badly. She searched the back window to see if they were being followed, but there was no sign of a car anywhere. No headlights.

No men in black or white suits trying to get to them.

"Thomas, is something wrong? Did something happen while I was asleep?"

He stared at the road as if signs were appearing. "No. Nothing happened."

No, nothing had happened. But slowly Parris recognized the problem. He'd been living on the edge for so long. So very long. And then she came into his life and complicated even the simplest of things. His life had been turned upside down and inside out. And he was returning to a life-threatening situation.

Thomas jerked the steering wheel and slid on the highway. Parris grabbed for the dashboard, bracing herself as he turned the car around. His foot slammed on the gas, and they shot down the road, retracing their drive of just moments ago.

Parris righted herself. "Okay, I give up. You've decided to head back to Philly for some reason. Would you care to tell your fellow traveler why?"

"I've got a stop to make in Atlantic City," he stated tersely.

"Where?"

"At my sister's hotel."

"Your life is in danger and you're visiting your *sister*?" she asked incredulously.

"It's *because* my life is in danger that I'm doing it. She's my family," he stated grimly. "Whatever else—she's my family."

Her heart wanted to break with the thought of him being hurt, either physically or emotionally. But she also knew that he had to do this. Somehow in his past, his sister had intertwined steadfastly with his sense of responsibility. Because Patricia had chosen to live in sin, he felt all kinds of guilt. Because she had chosen to love one of the gangsters Thomas had vowed to ruin, he had to fight to make her see the error of her ways with everything he had in his mental arsenal.

He wouldn't give up and allow his sister and himself peace of mind until he did.

Tension creased every line on his face. Parris kept her silence, knowing there was nothing she could say that would make him change his mind. Once again, she was just along for the ride.

"Damn it."

Thomas glanced at her. "What's wrong?"

"I'm tired of being taken from one place to another without ever choosing our destination."

"What does that mean? Is it another riddle from the future?" His voice sounded exasperated.

Parris watched the lights of Atlantic City glow through the darkness as they turned off the highway to a smaller, two-lane road and coasted toward the lights of the Steel Pier. Once there, Thomas passed it by and went two blocks down to the Elegante Hotel.

He parked across from the hotel's porte cochere, turned off the ignition, and stared at the entrance. "Stay here," he finally ordered in a weary voice. "If something happens, take off and find Bebe. She'll take you with her."

A film of perspiration covered her face. Panic aimed at her heart. "You're not going anywhere without me."

He sighed heavily and reached for the door handle. "I said stay here."

"And I said you're not going without me." Her voice was equally sure.

"Parris," he said, then gave another sigh. "Okay, you're one stubborn woman, and I'm too damn tired to tell you what to do. You don't listen anyway."

She smiled tightly. "Thank you."

After one searing look, Thomas stepped out of the car and headed toward the hotel entrance. It was up to Parris to keep up with him.

He stopped at the front desk, asked directions, gave a cursory glance around the lobby, dismissed the people there as if they were of no consequence, and punched the elevator button.

Parris barely kept up with him. Obviously, the man wasn't afraid of Capone's thugs spying or setting him free in the spirit world. Either that, or he was too angry to be sensible.

Parris decided it was the latter. As she was about to tell him so, the elevator arrived and they stepped on. A so-called elevator boy—who was probably 60 years old or more—obeyed Thomas's terse answer when he asked for the floor number.

"You should have been more careful," Parris stated in a low voice as the elevator creaked and groaned its way to the third floor.

No answer.

"This isn't wise."

Again no answer. She would have been more pleased if even the elevator boy had said something, anything, rather than give her an odd look.

The elevator jerked to a stop, and the boy opened the cage door, then the main door. His gaze never left her body as she and Thomas stepped into the hallway.

Two doors away from the elevator shaft, Thomas stopped and gave a heavy rap to the frame.

When the door opened, Patricia seemed as surprised as Parris was. The statuesque redhead stood barefoot in a formal, royal-blue silk dress. Her hair was piled in curls on top of her head. She looked tired, but not at all hostile, as Parris would have thought. In fact, Parris was surprised Patricia was there. She'd honestly believed that his sister would be at the club, or at least out painting the town with her boyfriend. From the looks of it, she had been been out, but had called it an early night.

Patricia's face changed from surprise to concern. "Are you feeling all right, Thomas?" she asked.

"Is he here?" Thomas's tone was flat.

She nodded before answering aloud. "Yes."

"I need to talk to you."

One eyebrow arched. "I gather that. It must be important, or you wouldn't bother coming when Joey was here." She stepped away from the door and opened it wider. "Come in."

Parris followed awkwardly. She wasn't sure what to do or whether to explain her presence. Instead, she remained silent, acting as Thomas's shadow.

Patricia took a seat on the red velvet chair that faced the Victorian sofa and stared at her brother. Patricia seemed to ignore Parris, who was separated from her by a small rosewood table.

Thomas sat on the edge of the couch cushion. "Where is he?"

"Downstairs. He'll be back in five minutes."

He leaned forward. "Patricia, leave him. He's killed more men than you could have nightmares about. He killed Charlie and someday he might even kill you."

"He hasn't killed anyone and he won't." Her voice was as sure as her brother's. "Just because he's in the mob, you think the worst of him."

"I *know* the worst. You're stupid and stubborn if you think I'm lying."

Patricia's expression didn't give her tension away—her hands did as they twisted in her lap. "You don't have any proof he killed Charlie, do you? So without it, don't expect me to believe it. Anyway, according to you, no one is good enough for me."

Thomas reached for her hand and held tight. "I'm begging, Patricia. I'm begging you to leave him. He's red with other people's blood. You'll find someone else. You're young and beautiful. You can have anybody."

Patricia's eyes widened; the same startling blue color that glinted in Thomas's was even more prominent in hers. "I know I can. And I've chosen Joey. You just don't agree with my choice."

"Listen to me!" Thomas yelled. "He's wrong for you! Joey is a murderer and a hood who'll never change. I don't want you to wind up in a dump somewhere."

"He's never hurt anyone. Besides, he loves me."

Thomas leaned back and watched her through narrowed eyes. "Joey's got a hit man after me, Patricia. He wants me dead."

"My God, I can't believe you'd lie to me to get your way," she muttered, standing.

"I'm not lying! If you can't see what a scum he is, what can I do to show you the facts? Do I have to show up dead? Do you? Charlie already has!"

Finally, Thomas got through to his sister, although it wasn't the response he expected.

"Listen to me!" she yelled back. "You've interfered in my life ever since I can remember. I love you, but you're not responsible for me. You're not my father, my mother, or my conscience!" She stopped for a moment, catching her breath.

She took a deep breath and began again. "I'm staying here until tomorrow. Then I'm leaving—with Joey—for Hollywood. I will write you or maybe even call you. At Christmas. On your birthday. Maybe even Thanksgiving. I will *not* mention Joey to you and you will not ask me about him. We'll continue that way until I think you're adult enough to understand me or until you don't deserve my phone calls. Then I'll either ask you to visit or never call you again." Her eyes still blazed with ice-blue anger. "Do you finally understand?"

Parris suddenly understood the connection between redheads and legendary tempers. It wasn't that Patricia looked any more angry than her brother. It was that every red hair on her head resembled fire, her blue-eyed gaze a match, and her words the flame. She was awe-inspiring.

But Parris's heart went out to Thomas, who finally understood. "You don't mean that."

"I do."

A key rattled in the door and Joey walked in. He stood with his back to the closed door and palmed his keys in his tuxedo pocket. If *GQ* magazine had existed in this era, Joey would have been on the cover. He was handsome and well dressed and had a certain panache. "Well, well, well."

"Joey," Patricia warned.

His eyes flew to her, giving her an intimate glance before looking at Thomas again. "Right."

Dismissing Parris, he walked to Patricia, leaned over, and nuzzled her cheek. But he cautiously watched Thomas as he did so.

Thomas stood up, every movement fraught with stiffness. "Please remember what I said."

Patricia stood up and faced him, looking more like an Irish fairy queen than a gun moll. Her chin tilted up, and her eyes sparked a stubborn fire. "And please remember what I said, brother. Thanksgiving isn't that far away."

He and Joey stared at each other. A smile played around Joey's mouth. He wasn't sure what the visit was about, but it was apparent that Thomas hadn't won.

"Call off your thugs, Joey. I'm not ready to die any more than Charlie was."

Joey didn't bat an eyelash. "I don't know what you're talking about."

"Yes, you do. You killed my friend, Charlie, but you don't care. You just don't give a damn about anything."

"I love your sister," Joey answered smoothly.

"Like an asp loved Cleopatra?"

Joey didn't answer. His smirk said everything.

Then, with measured steps, Thomas turned and walked toward the door. In the tense silence, Parris followed.

He opened the door and stepped aside to allow Parris to exit first. She stepped into the hallway just ahead of Thomas, and just behind him was Joey.

With his hand on the knob, Joey closed the

door very quietly. Thomas, stone-faced sober, waited more patiently than she'd ever seen him before. Parris felt as if she was a spectator in a 1940s grade-B movie. She wanted to laugh—almost. However, Joey was real. So was Thomas. So was she for that matter. And they were all just as capable of dying.

The gangster's expression was stoic. "I'm taking good care of her."

Thomas stared back, his expression just as deadly. "You're treating her like a whore, and you know it."

Joey jerked toward Thomas, then contained himself. "I'll explain this just once to you because you're her older brother and all," he said in a low whisper. "But I'll never say it again."

Both men stood almost toe to toe, eye to eye. Joey spoke in a tone that hardly carried to Parris, let alone down the hall. "If I marry your sister now, the mob will have a hold on me. If I wait until I can make a clean break, then it won't matter and they'll never be able to hurt her to get to me. So, I'm waiting."

"For how long?"

"As long as it takes. Maybe a day. Maybe a year."

Thomas snorted. "You're lying. You're in the mob. Those things don't change. And what about Charlie, did you give him any time?"

"Look, I'm gonna tell you for the last time I don't know any Charlie and I didn't kill him. As for your sister, all I'm saying is that I'm gonna marry her someday and it might take a long time for her to get in touch with you once we make the break. I just want you to know that, if we disappear, you shouldn't be alarmed. We're gonna be safe."

Thomas continued to stare into Joey's eyes. Long moments passed, and Parris held her breath as she waited for him to take the next step.

"And what about my life?" Thomas asked. "I've gotten kinda attached to living."

"It's not me. Honest. It's Al Capone. You trespassed on some of his men's bootlegging territory. They complained to him and he put out the word." He smiled. "Capone takes care of his own. You know that."

"Now why is it that my instincts tell me you're lying through your teeth again?"

"It's true. I love your sister. Killing you wouldn't get me high marks in her book. I wouldn't take the chance of losing her."

Parris believed him. But then, what in heaven's name did she know about all this?

"I got your word?" Thomas finally asked gruffly.

"My word. My life," Joey confirmed, equally gruff.

"Good enough." Thomas didn't add how close Joey had come to losing his life.

Without another word, silent messages of threats and promises, intimidations and warnings seemed to flow between them before Parris could smell a tentative peace between the two.

Joey opened the door and stepped back in, pretending that Thomas and Parris weren't in the hallway.

"Joey?"

"I'm here, honey. I just wanted to check out the lobby," he answered before the thick door closed.

"Well, I'll be damned," Parris finally breathed. "The man's in love and wants his soon-to-be brother-in-law's blessing."

Thomas took her arm and hustled her toward the elevator. "Don't cuss."

"That's it? That's all you have to say?"

"That's it."

The elevator ride down was silent except for the attendant's wheezing as he moved the switches and handle. Parris couldn't help the grin that kept tickling her mouth. But she couldn't do anything until they reached the door.

Once outside, Parris lifted her head and howled laughingly at the moon.

It wasn't until then that she realized how changed a life could be in such a short time. A full month had gone by since she'd entered Thomas's life and times.

The moon was almost full again.

Chapter Nineteen

After stopping at Thomas's boardinghouse to pick up his left shoe, which he threw in the back of the car, Thomas headed for Clair's house. But when they came to it, Thomas drove past it at a steady clip and continued for another quarter mile. Once out of sight of the driveway, he pulled onto the shoulder and killed the engine. The wind played with the dry sand, allowing a light layer to swirl around the car.

"Did we really have to stop for you to get your shoe?" Parris asked as she took off her own shoes and stepped from the Bentley.

"Absolutely. Let's just call it insurance. Are you ready?" he asked and she nodded. "It won't be as bad as you think. It's only a couple of long city blocks."

They began the walk back to Clair's house.

"This is dangerous, you know. Capone's car is there. He's still visiting."

"That's exactly why no one will think to look for us there."

"You're just doing this to thumb your nose at him." Parris's words were met with silence. "Either that or you've taken stupid pills."

He sighed heavily. "Probably. But it's still a sound plan."

"Do you think Clair's going to go along with this?" she asked, wishing she had shed her hose, too. Sand was trapped between the fine silk and her skin.

"She might not be crazy about the idea, but she'll do it."

"Sleeping in the attic above Capone's room sounds like sheer folly to me. Stupid folly."

"I didn't say we'd stay above the jackass. I said we'd stay in her attic. If he's below us, I'd be too tempted to throw a beam at him."

"How about sneaking into my old room?"

"Nope," he said after a few seconds' thought. "If we spent the night in any room, it should be Bebe's, so no one will have call to look in there."

Sand was building inside her hose. The breeze continued pushing the fabric of her dress between her legs. If they walked much farther, her knees would be rubbed raw.

"Are we having fun yet?" she asked.

Thomas laughed. Outright laughed.

It was a wonderful sound that swept around her, wrapping her in a feeling of happiness. Her world was a mass of confusion, but she had made Thomas laugh. In the record book in the sky, that had to count for something.

The house suddenly appeared. Like a anachronism, it squatted in the sand, looking as if it belonged in the foothills of Pennsylvania instead of perched on the shifting sands in Cape May. It also was dark. Sometime in the last 15 minutes, the lights had been turned off.

Thomas's hand shot out and clamped on her arm, stopping her. "Shh."

Her eyes probed the darkness around the house. Then she saw him. Leaning against the dark form of a car in the driveway was a man straight out of all the gangster movies she'd ever seen. He wore a dark suit that blended with the shadowed car and the pearl-gray darkness of the full moon. Only the triangle of white shirt exposed by his jacket gave him away. One leg was cocked against the running board, a machine gun was propped on his knee.

"Does life imitate the movies or do the movies imitate life?" she said softly.

Thomas's hand clamped down on her mouth. "If he hears a sound, he'll shoot first, then see what he hit. So be quiet!" he whispered in her ear.

Parris nodded to show she understood.

So that any noise they might make wouldn't be readily noticed, they stayed downwind, making a wide arc in front of the guard. The side of the house was quiet. Motioning Parris to stay where she was, Thomas followed the side of the house to the back patio wall and cautiously peered over. From his stance, Parris knew there was another man standing guard there.

Now what? she wondered. A new full moon rode in a partially clouded sky. They couldn't hide beside the house forever. If one of those goons wanted to circle the building, he'd find them for sure. She glanced around. An upturned rowboat squatted halfway between the wall and the ocean. They might be able to hide in there if they had enough time to slip under it.

Thomas grabbed her hand. "Follow me," he ordered, ducking down and walking swiftly along the outside patio wall. By the time they'd gone halfway around and stopped at the gate, Parris was breathing heavily. She felt as if the world could hear her.

Still, she waited. Thomas peered through the wrought-iron gate to the patio. She crouched down behind him, telling herself to calm down.

Suddenly, he pulled her arm. "Now!" he hissed and ran across the opening, dragging her along with him.

She stumbled at the entrance, then fell into the sand on the other side of the gate.

It took a minute or so to catch their breath enough to continue. Parris was torn between nervous laughter and tears. She felt so silly slinking around Clair's house in the middle of the night. What she should do was go inside and say, "Look, I want to sleep in my bed and then I'll leave in the morning. You guys just go about your business."

But it wouldn't work. So, there they were, imitating cat burglars.

When they reached the other side of the house, Parris was relieved. She didn't want to admit she was out of condition, but her legs told her differently. They shook from the effort to keep them bent while running in the sand.

Thomas loosened his grip on her and edged to a standing position. Her fingers tingled, and for the first time, she realized how hard he'd been holding her hand. He was as scared as she was.

With a light touch, he raised the window. He stepped in, then helped her over the sill. She held her breath, listening to the sounds in the house.

Clair's room was on the right. Sexy, melodic moans in rhythmic cadence reverberated from her room. Once more Thomas took Parris's hand as they tiptoed down the hallway. Since Clair and her guest were busy, slipping into Bebe's room wasn't hard.

"Thomas!" Bebe whispered, then got out of bed. "I knew you to be a damn fool. I just didn't believe you were also very stupid! How did you get in?"

"Through the hall window." Thomas sat down on the edge of the double bed and rubbed his face and neck wearily. "Can you hide us until tomorrow night?"

Parris sat in a white wicker rocker in the corner of the room. Her eyes refused to close, but her body screamed for sleep.

"I'll try, Thomas. Stay in this room. No one comes in during the day."

He gave an exhausted smile. "Thanks. In less than twenty-four hours this will all be over."

Reaching into the closet, Bebe pulled out a dress. With a single movement, she slid the straps of her gown off her shoulders and let the garment slide to the floor in a sensuous whoosh. Parris sat mesmerized, watching the woman with skin the color of molasses standing naked in the moonlight. Perfectly formed, she looked more like a mannequin than a living person. With decisive movements, she pulled a maid's uniform over her head and fastened the buttons on the shirtwaist.

Parris dragged her eyes away and was caught by Thomas's knowing gaze. His grin was a bond. His gaze said *Isn't she beautifully formed? But she's not you, and don't go thinking that a perfect body is what I want, because it's not. There's more to it than that.*

Parris gave him an answering smile and his eyes lit with appreciation and love.

Bebe went to Thomas's side. "Do not snore, my friend, or there will be a long slumber for us all. After they leave for the club, I will try to bring in something to eat. Today is Mr. Capone's last day. He goes in the morning."

"Why is he still here?" Thomas asked.

"Because Clair decided to bed him, and he cannot refuse that which is free for a hotel room and a new girl who might be more frightened or less uninhibited." Her voice held scorn for the two in the other room.

"Has he bothered you?"

"No. One of his men has been a pest, but his attentions didn't last long. Capone decided he liked my cooking too much to let the fool ruin a good thing." She walked to the door. "Get some sleep. You both look as if you haven't slept in days." Then she walked out the door and closed it behind her.

Thomas fell back against the bed and held his arms out to her. "Come on, Parris."

Parris left the rocker and went to lie next to him. Curling into his side, she let her hand stray to his chest, her fingers playing with shirt buttons. "What now, O, Mighty Leader?"

Thomas pulled her even closer. "Now, we wait until nine tonight. Then we take Bebe out to the middle of the ocean and put her on a cabin cruiser. From there, she'll be taken to a larger boat, one that's already passed through customs. In six days, she'll reach France."

"What about us?"

"We'll come back, ditch the boat, pick up Sol's car, and head out west. They'll never find us."

"What about your career as a journalist?"

"It's all over now, tootsie. I'll turn in my story, which is almost all written. Then I'll get my money for completing it, and we'll be ready to go."

"Then what will you do?"

"I'll have to think up another career. Maybe writing fiction under a pen name instead of nonfiction. As long as I continue writing for newspapers and magazines, you'd be in jeopardy, too." His arm tightened. "I won't have that."

"And you won't resent me for stopping you from doing what you most want to do?"

Without releasing her, he rolled to his side. He lifted her chin and stared into her eyes. "What I want to do most, Parris, is live my life with you. If it means going to the other side of the earth, I will."

His eyes were so brilliant she closed her eyes and swallowed hard. A moment later, she opened them again and stared back up at him. He was more dear to her than life itself. "I love you, Thomas. I love you with all my heart."

That devilish sparkle lit his blue eyes again. "I'm glad you appreciate me, woman," he growled. "Because for the next sixty years or so, I want a passel full of gratitude from you."

Her fingers flipped his shirt button through its hole. "Should I start now?"

Thomas cocked his head, listening to Clair's moans still filtering down the hallway. If Clair was busy, so was Capone. "Now," he decided, rolling on top of her.

But Parris pushed him back. "Oh, no, big boy," she laughed huskily. "Now it's your turn for a special brand of torture called The Parris."

And torture him she did. She knew because he kept muffling his own cries. It was over an hour later when they fell asleep in each other's arms.

Just as Parris awakened to Thomas's kiss, the bedroom door opened and Clair walked in looking every bit as calm and controlled as ever. With careful precision, she closed the door and took several steps into the room.

"What in heaven's name are you doing here?" she whispered to Thomas, who was fully dressed and bending over Parris.

Parris wondered what he was doing, too, especially since he was dressed. He smelled of salt air. New salt air. But she decided not to press the issue. Instead, she made sure the sheet was pulled up over her breasts and tucked under her arm. Then she rolled so it wrapped around her. Standing, she reached for her clothing on the floor. Her nerves tightened with every silent moment as she waited for Thomas to speak.

Thomas calmly raised a brow in question. "Should I tell you the truth or do you want to guess?"

"The truth!" she hissed.

"I stole a rowboat to take Bebe out for a ride. After I've done that, Parris and I will leave again. No one will ever know."

382

Clair came closer, bending over Thomas as if she were a swooping bird. "Are you *crazy?* Capone has your name at the top of a hit list and you want to take Bebe *boating?*"

"Bebe's not coming back, Clair. I hope you can do without her."

Clair's eyes widened. "You're taking Bebe away from me?"

Thomas nodded. Yes. And I won't return either," He grinned boyishly. "Are you gonna miss me?"

"You bet your sweet rear end I'm gonna miss you. Especially after you tell me what's going on."

"How much time do we have?"

"It'll be an hour before Al wakes up. He always takes a nap after nighttime . . . activity."

Thomas's smile grew even wider. "Confess, Clair. Was he worth all you've been through?"

Clair didn't ask what he meant by *been through.* Neither did Parris.

A small smile flirted with the corners of her mouth. "Yes," she said simply. "There's something about power that makes me warm all over. He's got it. Sol used to have it." Her eyes grew dreamy. "It was worth it." Suddenly she focused on Thomas again. "But he's one hell of a lousy lover."

Thomas chuckled low. "There's always a price, Clair. If that's the least of it, you'll do great."

Clair had to grin back, then suddenly her expression sobered. "I'm giving you twenty-four hours to get done whatever it is, as long as you leave Capone's men alone. If you're still around by then, I'll tell him you're here."

"Fair enough." Thomas stood. "Have a good life, Clair."

"Good luck," the older woman said before turning her back on them and leaving the room.

Thomas sat back down on the bed. "Whew."

Parris finally found her voice and cleared it. After having worked and lived with Clair, she still didn't know if she could trust her. "Do you think she'll keep her word?"

Thomas looked worried. "For about an hour or until she rethinks the situation and comes up with another answer." He stood. "Come on, tootsie. We're getting out of here. Get dressed as quickly as you can. I've got the boat waiting."

"I thought we weren't leaving until nine o'clock tonight," she whispered back as she slipped into her clothing.

"I lied. It was safer for everyone if I was the only one who knew when the boat was arriving. I just told Bebe."

As Parris sat on the wet sand, she drifted into a light sleep, her head propped against the side of the rowboat.

Her parents were looking for her on the beach. Her father kept calling her name. Her mother was crying. Jed was running as fast as he could along the shoreline, his gaze searching the waves for her.

They couldn't see her standing by the house, waving at them. "Mom! Dad! Jed! I'm right here!"

Still they kept searching.

Parris tried to walk to them. She honestly did. But there was an invisible wall between them. She *knew* it was there. Her only hope was that her parents could see through it and know she was all right.

She tried yelling to get their attention, her throat straining to scream loud enough to get through the wall. Her heart hammering heavily, Parris pounded on the wall.

Jed kept running and her mom and dad kept searching the sea. If only she could break down the barrier and be with them. Banging her fists piteously against the inpenetrable wall, she continued to shout. Tears flowed. . . .

Thomas touched her shoulder. "Are you all right?"

She awoke with a start from her dream and gave him a smile of reassurance. "Yes."

His look confirmed that he doubted her, but he turned back to the matter at hand. "Then try to relax. We've got another ten minutes or so before she'll be here."

Parris shifted her behind on the sand, grateful she had worn her jeans and sneakers.

They were a half a mile from the house waiting for Bebe beside a small rowboat on the shoreline.

The wind had grown from light breezes to stiff gusts. Clouds scudded across the sky. But Parris wasn't worried. She'd been in storms before and, God willing, she'd be in one again. She didn't want to die. She didn't! And she didn't want her life to depend on the whim of a woman who could or might want to snuff it out.

"Insane." The word popped from her lips, startling her.

"No," Thomas said as he plopped down next to her. "Just late."

"What?"

"Bebe," he explained, his eyes searching the dark area toward Clair's house. "Time is running out. If she doesn't come in the next five minutes, we won't make it."

"When she gets here, I'm going with you."

"You're staying on shore until I return. That was the deal."

They'd been through this before. But she'd be with him on that boat if it was the last thing she did. The man she loved didn't know how to swim, and she would take no chance on losing him by accident. There were a thousand other ways they could die.

A big gust of wind slammed sand into Parris's face, and she quickly turned away, coughing.

"Damn!" Thomas pulled her against his chest, trying to shield her from the harshness of the fickle weather.

She wanted to cry. They were playing roulette with their lives. Was it really possible to escape the mob? She knew that, in her day, it was often impossible. But this era was half fact, half fiction. Pulp magazines glamorized the Twenties just as they did the cowboys from the Old West. Neither was true, but what else was false?

Thomas's arms tightened around her; then he pushed her away. "Here she comes. Come on. We've got to hurry."

Bebe ran down the beach, not seeing them until she had almost reached the boat. "Capone knows something is up. I think one of his men is following me!"

Thomas was already shoving the boat into the water, and whitecaps flipped inside. "Get in the boat!"

Parris grabbed Bebe's arm and waded into the water. She shoved the woman into the boat. With panic bubbling in her mind, she ordered Bebe to the rear seat. With more energy than expertise, Parris helped Thomas push the boat over the first waves and into deeper water.

"Get in!" he shouted, and she wasted no time rolling inside the wet boat.

Thomas climbed in the other side, scrunched down on the middle seat, and wrapped his hands around the oar handles. Giving a heave, he began to row.

Parris sat next to him. "Let me help!"

"No!" he shouted back. "I'll need your help later, when I'm tired."

Suddenly the water calmed and Thomas stepped up the rhythm of his strokes. Thomas had said they were to meet a powerboat in the first lane of ocean traffic, about a half mile offshore. Parris kept her eyes peeled for the other boat. She wondered how long they would have to wait before it found them. Right that moment, she felt they resembled the proverbial needle in a very watery haystack.

Half an hour passed. Weren't they halfway to England yet?

"There!" Bebe shouted.

Parris squinted into the horizon, but she couldn't spot a thing.

Thunder rolled over the water like a giant tidal wave of sound. As soon as the thunder stopped, the rain began.

What started as sprinkles turned into sheets of rain that moved sideways across the water and pelted them with what felt like thousands of tiny needles.

"There it is!" Bebe cried.

Dim lights bobbed and blinked, dipping and sawing in the water. Thomas laughed loudly, and Parris and Bebe joined in. He began rowing with renewed determination. The ordeal was almost over.

The exchange took less than five minutes. Bebe's small bag was looped on a rope and pulled onto the deck of the large boat with a hook. Next, Bebe gave Thomas and Parris a hug and climbed the ladder. Once aboard, she waved down at them. It was hard to see in the rain, but Parris was sure she was crying.

Suddenly, two more heads appeared at the rail. Stunned, Parris barely believed her eyes. Patricia and her gangster boyfriend stood in the pouring rain, frantically waving for Thomas's attention. Parris tugged on his arm, then pointed up to the railing.

The boat pulled away, its engines revving slowly as it began picking up speed.

Patricia cupped her hands and shouted, "I love you, Thomas. Stay well!"

"Where—" he shouted, but it was too late. Instead, he waved, knowing she could see only a little better than hear, but at least she knew that he'd seen and understood her.

Thomas's tears streamed down his face. Parris squeezed his arm and he smiled.

Thunder rolled again.

The large boat revved its engine into a full throttle.

Parris watched the larger boat slowly recede. It wasn't until it was 100 feet away that Thomas picked up an oar and teased. "Now you can help me row, tootsie. I think I'm tuckered out."

Emotionally, she was, too. Wearily, she sat next to him and began tugging on the oar. It took a few minutes before they settled into a rhythm together.

She vowed to herself that once they were back on shore and dry she would sit down and sort through all the emotions that were jumbled together so piteously in the pit of her stomach. Maybe then, all this would make sense. For one thing, she most definitely was going to get out of Thomas once and for all the reason his left shoe was so important to him. But despite all the puzzling questions, she was lucky she was still with Thomas. Bebe had no one.

The rain slackened and Parris almost felt a brightening of her spirits. They'd done it. Now they could get on with life. Find a place to settle down, raise children, and dream the American dream. Together.

Dawn was breaking. But when she looked up to find the shoreline, hoping she could see it, it still wasn't visible. Another boat was. At first, she thought it was a fishing trawler, but it was going too fast and heading directly for them.

"Thomas!"

He'd already seen it. Holding his oar above water, he squinted against the rain. The boat continued looming down on them.

Parris's heart crashed somewhere around her toes. Instinct told her to flee, but there was nowhere to go. A bullet whizzed by her hand and lodged in the side of the rowboat.

"It's Capone's men!" she shrieked. Every nightmare she'd ever had in the past month was coming alive.

The men's faces at the helm of the boat were as dangerous-looking as the boat bearing down on them. Eight or nine men crowded the bow of the boat, watching them. Danny and his henchmen were three of the faces she recognized.

Lightning streaked across the sky, eerily illuminating the sea. Another bullet zinged by her ear. Then another. And another. The larger boat was practically on top of them. Parris looked around, frantically seeking escape. A small whirlpool was forming on the side of the rowboat. Whitecapped waves were cresting everywhere. There was nothing else to do.

"Jump clear!" she yelled.

"No!"

"Damn it, jump!"

"I can't swim!"

"Either way we're dead! Jump!"

The bow of the large boat slammed into the side of their puny rowboat just as Thomas reached out and grabbed Parris's hand. The sound of splintering wood rent the air as they were unceremoniously dumped into the icy ocean.

"Shit!" Thomas yelled.

"No," Parris cried in anger and frustration as Thomas's hand began slipping from hers. With the little strength she had, she clasped his fingers tighter and prayed for God to intervene.

Another bullet snapped into the water.

The palm of her free hand stung as saltwater touched a cut. The last thing she saw was a big black cloud scudding across the sky to expose the full moon laughing down at them. . . .

Epilogue

Maxine Merchant's Nationally Syndicated Column

> *Big plans for Christmas are being formed at Thomas and Parris Elder's estate in the Pennsylvania mountains. Their open house this year boasts some of the elite from across the continent. Rumor has it that Parris is presenting her Chrismas gift early to her author hubby in the form of an announcement. Do I hear the patter of little feet?*
>
> *Matt Jr., son of high-powered financier Matthew Taggart, who was a family friend and financial adviser, is flying in from Philadelphia next weekend in his private jet, bringing an impressive entourage of family*

and close friends with him. The Taggart family made their money in shrewd stock investments after the Crash of 1929.

Another celeb guest is Betsy Santuil, the celebrated jazz singer whose French-born mother, Bebe, was the toast of Europe in the early Forties. Also included in the guest list are some of the VIPs from Thomas and Parris's favorite charity for Alzheimer's disease.

On hand to help welcome their esteemed guests are Parris's parents, Mr. and Mrs. Joseph Harrison, and her handsome brother, Jed Harrison, the up-and-coming star of Payment in Kind. *It was his brother-in-law who offered him the part. Since Thomas wrote the screenplay, the talented writer got to say who would star. Critics are predicting an Oscar for Jed's performance.*

Thomas, in case you don't remember, is the creator and writer of the campy detective stories that take place in the Roaring Twenties, now adapted into the sizzling new television series Tootsie's. *There hasn't been a series to compete with its popularity since* I Love Lucy. *When asked where he got the name for the detective agency, Thomas smiled and said his sweet wife and financial manager was the inspiration.*

Wouldn't you just love to know the inside story on that one, readers?